CRATER COUNTY:

A LEGAL THRILLER OF NEW MEXICO

by JONATHAN MILLER

Patty

Enjoy
the
book!

J C Miller

rattlesnake

Gallon

Published by
Cool Titles
12121 Wilshire Blvd., Suite 1201
Los Angeles, CA 90025
www.cooltitles.com

The Library of Congress Cataloging-in-Publication Data Applied For

Jonathan Miller—
Crater County: A Legal Thriller of New Mexico

p.   cm
ISBN 0-9673920-4-7
1. Mystery   2. American Southwest   3. Legal Thriller   I. Title
2004

1 3 5 7 9 10 8 6 4 2

Cover design by Amy Turner, Simplified Design Studio
Book editing and design by Lisa Wysocky, White Horse Enterprises, Inc.
Marketing by J.D. Haas: jdrocks@jdhe.com

For interviews or information regarding special discounts for bulk purchases,
please contact us at njohnson@jrllp.com

ABOUT THE AUTHOR

Jonathan Miller is an author and an attorney practicing criminal law in Albuquerque. He is a graduate of the Albuqerque Academy, Cornell University, the University of Colorado Law School, and the American Film Institute; and has taken writing courses at the University of New Mexico and UCLA-Extension. He hopes to use the proceeds of this book to pay off his student loans before he dies.

Also by Jonathan Miller:

Rattlesnake Lawyer
Amarillo in August

Jonathan Miller dedicates this book to his family.

Cool Titles and Jonathan Miller
proudly support the Ingram Cancer Center

IN THE DISTRICT COURT
14th JUDICIAL DISTRICT
COUNTY OF CRATER

STATE OF NEW MEXICO, PLAINTIFF

vs.

JEREMY JONES, DEFENDANT

COUNT I

FOR THE MURDER OF SARAH SANCHEZ,
A NATURAL PERSON

ARREST

A faint screeching sound echoed through the distant canyon walls. Sirens? All the way out here? Luna Cruz couldn't quite identify the noise over the beat of her pounding heart.

"How the hell did I get so out of shape?" she asked herself silently, too winded to get the words out. Luna biked past a wooden cross on the side of the dirt road. Three red roses lay at its rickety base. Another drunk driver strikes again, she thought. She pedaled a hundred more yards then reluctantly stopped her bike. For a moment, only a moment, she swore. She coasted to the dirt driveway of an old mobile home, the only vestige of civilization out here in this stretch of the New Mexico High Desert. She'd long since exhausted her one bottle of water for the ride.

Luna's left foot hit the dirt as she came to a halt. She felt relief from the endless oppression of the sand hills and rock mesas that had stolen the air out of her lungs for the last few miles. At thirty, she was in better shape than anyone else in Crater County, but that was little consolation to either her legs or her lungs right now. She cursed her bike as if it were its fault.

With a glance, she recognized where she'd stopped—"Shark's High Desert Tattoo," an old mobile home that hadn't been mobile for quite some time. The windows were boarded up and a weather-beaten mural showed a ferocious sea creature that challenged her to "Get your mark from the Shark!"

Luna glanced down at her exposed skin. She wore her usual black bike shorts and sports bra on rides, so there was a lot of skin to choose from. She had once promised herself the Olympic rings around her belly button when she made the triathlon team, but that certainly wasn't going to happen, not anymore.

She took a good look over at Shark's, now that the oxygen had finally made it up past her neck. Shark's looked abandoned, but two old cars sat in the dirt parking lot. The place had always given her the creeps when she had biked past here as a child. It still did. No, she definitely wasn't going to go inside and ask for water, and definitely wouldn't swipe a drink from the garden hose.

She took off her helmet for a second and wiped the sweat out of her long brown hair. Luna hadn't known the desert could get so humid, but storm clouds were appearing over the horizon with the last of the summer monsoons.

Then she heard something clearly this time. Definitely police sirens way in the distance, but definitely coming her way. More police sirens than she'd ever heard in her life.

The wind picked up and she coughed when the dust hit her throat. She covered her mouth with her hand. She didn't want whatever was inside Shark's to hear her.

The sirens grew closer as more dust blew into her lungs. She had forgotten about the dusty desert winds while she'd been up in Boulder, Colorado. Boulder had those *Chinook* winds of course, but they were nothing like this.

Luna checked her pulse again. Still way too high for a pace this slow, wind or no wind. She totally abandoned the prospect of water with the realization that she'd better get moving if she wanted to hit Hell's Hills, her goal for the afternoon, before sunset. The entrance was barely half a mile from here. How fast had she been able to do a half-mile back in the old days?

"We made it this far. . . ." she said to her bike. The bike clearly did not want to move.

"Follow the yellow SAND road," she sang softly to the bike. If she hadn't devoted so much time to training, she probably could have been a decent singer. She giggled. The sand out here was a dirty yellow, all right. Somehow her amusement made her bike inch forward.

She pedaled furiously away from Shark's, even though she headed straight into the wind. She hit the dirt road turn-off to the hills, right as the first sheriff deputy's marked car arrived at the parking lot. The vehicle turned off its sirens and waited for rein-forcements. Luna wanted to stop and turn and check out the one bit of excitement in the entire county, but conquering the Hills seemed like the only way to salvage the day.

"Follow, follow, follow, follow, follow the yellow SAND road."

She pedaled harder and she soon didn't have any breath left to sing.

"Did you hear something?" Jeremy asked Shark. Shark didn't reply. The inside of his trailer had terrible acoustics with all its nee-dles and ink absorbing every decibel of sound. The small space was deliberately designed to put people ill at ease. It looked more like a cluttered medieval torture gallery than the yuppie tattoo joints over in Albuquerque. The boarded up windows kept every particle of light from getting in.

Shark had a small plastic model of a dinosaur that was supposed to look like the monster from the Alien movies. "At Shark's, no one can hear you scream," declared a cardboard sign behind the mon-ster.

Shark, all seven feet of him, had been a biker in one of the out-law gangs. He wasn't exactly known for his bedside manner. When you looked in his eyes, you did see the soul of a tortured artist, although with his art the word "tortured" had all kinds of other implications.

As for Jeremy, he was way too cool for Crater County. He could pass for an Aryan Elvis on his good days. If he'd grown up any-where else, he'd be a superstar already, but when he'd come back home to Crater with a dishonorable discharge and a drug problem, a life of petty crime and probation was the best he could muster.

Today was not one of Jeremy's good days. He was strung out, but it was more than that. Normally, his voice was the smooth bari-tone of a radio talk show host and he wouldn't have sounded out of place giving the weather report in the depths of hell. Now he sound-ed like a teenager with his voice changing.

"I just asked if you heard anything?" he asked again. He defi-nitely wanted to get his ink done quickly, before whatever was outside interrupted. Shark didn't respond as he came over with the tattoo gun and looked at the earlier examples of his work that graced Jeremy's muscular frame. He was an artist indeed. Shark's first ink on Jeremy had been the Crater High School Comets logo on his left shoulder when he was seventeen. After that, Jeremy's illustrated history detailed his Marine Corp stints in the Far East, then his eighteen long and lonely months in the penitentiary of New Mexico's north facility.

A serpent now emerged from the crater on Jeremy's left shoulder, extending all the way to the right shoulder, with detours at his heart and neck and a long stay at his belly button. Aryan Elvis could pass for a Japanese Yakuza gangster from the neck down.

Jeremy squirmed a third time. "Something's out there. Hurry your ass up."

Shark said nothing. After twenty years on top of his late, lamented Harley, he wouldn't have heard the sirens anyway. He lifted the tattoo gun and looked into Jeremy's ice blue eyes.

Jeremy indicated a gap between the thumb and forefinger of his right hand. There were two small tattooed crosses there already, nearly an inch high. There was barely room for the third.

"I still don't get why you're doing this," Shark said, readying the needle. "But as you know, my favorite color is green."

"I bet it is." Jeremy smiled at the private joke between them. "Just my way of getting in touch with my feelings," he said.

Shark didn't bother to ask for more detail. The customer was always right. He did it quickly—a downward stroke, then a quick stroke to the side. Perfect. He drew a little bit of blood.

Jeremy didn't flinch on the downward prick, but the side-to-side got to him. He had a tear in his eye, despite himself. It wasn't just from the tattoo, of course. That one little prick had penetrated all of his defenses. He now cried from both eyes. Even the serpent's eyes grew redder.

Shark laughed hysterically as Jeremy bawled. Suddenly, he stopped laughing. Even his old damaged ears could hear the sirens now. . . .

Luna kept glancing behind her. The dirt roads outside of Shark's had never held so much traffic before. Every car was filled with cops—state troopers, SWAT teams, plainclothes guys—every car except one. A black car, a Saturn maybe, was stuck in the middle of the police convoy. Gigantic tumbleweeds formed a gauntlet on both sides of the road, preventing any escape.

Squad cars whizzed by the black car, honking their horns furiously. Once the cop cars hit the turn off for Shark's, the black car finally had the road to itself and began accelerating.

Luna noticed some dust coming from one of the dirt roads up from town. She couldn't help but smile. There was something very familiar about that particular dust storm, as well as the car and the driver at the eye of it.

She forced herself to turn away. "Focus," she said to her bike. "Focus, baby focus." She had now reached the entrance to Hell's Hills Moto-Cross Park. The park had been built into the sandy hills that had formed against an old granite mesa that was a hundred or so feet high. The rocky cliffs towering over the hills reminded her of the Roadrunner cartoons. There were real roadrunners out in the mesas, but here the coyotes didn't always lose.

The park had been built back when Crater County had kids, and those kids had money for bikes and parents who cared enough to take them biking. There were still a few abandoned bikes on the trails, but the kids and their parents were long gone.

Since the park had closed, no one came here anymore. The last evidence of humanity was the infamous "Yazzie Car Wreck," a tangled burnt hulk of a pick-up truck, halfway up the "advanced course."

The dirt road entrance was padlocked shut and the little entrance gatehouse had crumbled from neglect. Luna slipped her bike underneath an opening in the barbed wire and walked the bike to the start of what she called "The Road to the Wreck." This dirt road certainly didn't lead to any emerald city.

She hoped that the bike could make it. It was a ten-year-old mountain bike, and she could feel it between her legs, trying to turn itself around to avoid the next half-mile.

"You're not going anywhere," she told it, "except to the top."

She set her watch to zero, erasing the forty-seven minutes and fourteen-point-six seconds from before. This was going to be the real workout for the day.

Luna glanced eastward in the direction of Shark's once more. Seven state police cars had pulled into the parking lot and the black uniformed troopers were getting out, guns drawn. So much for focus.

Then she noticed the only car headed eastbound toward Shark's. Sure enough, it had been the cause of the dust storm coming in from town. It was Nico's old Corvette, all right. She could see the red even from here. Nico had put a police siren up on top, just in case anyone forgot that he was one of the good guys. He must have taken the back roads, just so he could kick up some dust and show up those stuck-up state troopers from the district office.

Nico . . . now was not the time to think about Nico. Still, she couldn't help but take one last glance back toward the Corvette.

It was perhaps the only vehicle that she liked in the world, the only car that didn't make her claustrophobic and carsick when she was inside it. What did that say about Nico, when the best thing she could say was that being with him didn't make her nauseous?

"Go Nico!" she said out loud. She felt a tiny tingle when she spoke his name.

Oh my God!

The Corvette was headed right at the black car on the narrowest part of the road.

Near miss!

The black car swerved away with seconds to spare, taking out a few weeds along with it. Never slowing, it took out a few more weeds then accelerated away from the almost-accident.

The Corvette screeched to a stop and began to make a U-turn to follow the black car. It had barely turned back an inch before it resumed its course toward Shark's.

Nico must have something important to do to keep going east. Even as one of the good guys, he never would have let some asshole get away with something like that.

Luna looked at the setting sun, then at her stopwatch. She would find out about all of this soon enough. She clicked on her stopwatch. She was on the clock now, with her last chance at redemption. Although she wanted to turn around, she focused, baby, focused, on the "Road to the Wreck" and the twisted metal milestone. *"Follow, follow,"* she hummed to herself.

Marlow drove the black car very, very quickly away from the near miss with the Corvette. He almost hadn't swerved back, but it wasn't time, not yet. This would have to be perfect.

Marlow was naked. At thirty-five, he was still in pretty good shape, despite everything that had happened in the past few weeks. A suit, complete with shirt and tie, hung from a hanger in the back, along with his underwear.

In the front passenger seat, he had a few Navajo trinkets that Yazzie had given him—a dream-catcher and a turquoise fetish necklace. There might be some new kid from Acoma who made a better clay pot, or some old lady from Taos Pueblo who worked more magic with silver, but all around, no one in New Mexico could touch the Yazzie family in their artwork.

Well that certainly wasn't true now, not anymore. Marlow fiddled with the necklace one more time. There was an unopened bottle of Jack Daniels in the seat, and a bottle of Sheep Springs Mineral Water with a funky label of a sheep drinking from a desert spring next to it.

He sipped the water. He'd wait for the Jack until he'd made it to the top and there were no cops around. What was it with all the cops out today? He looked around one last time, just to be sure. Neither the cops nor the Corvette had turned to follow him. They were all in Shark's parking lot, getting ready. Something big was definitely going down.

He passed the main turn-off into Hell's Hills Park. A minute later, he came to another dirt road turn-off.

Old Summit Trail Road, Private Road, No Trespassing!

The rusted padlock had been put out of its misery with a shotgun. Now that the kids had all left for better opportunities elsewhere, the sheriff had never bothered to replace the lock. Marlow hurried out and opened the gate. After he drove through, he didn't close it behind him. Why bother?

Old Summit Trail Road was much more of a trail than a road, barely wide enough to fit his car. A few dirt switchbacks quickly planted him on top of the mesa. Mesa meant "table" in Spanish, and it indeed felt like he was on top of a giant rocky table top out here in the desert. Then it was about a hundred yard straight shot to the edge, a straight shot out of here.

He looked at the setting sun. It was hazy and dusty out here. Visibility was limited, almost as if there was indeed an invisible Crater wall blocking him from seeing too far. He still had a few minutes left if he really wanted to do this, really wanted to do this right. He turned off the ignition. He wanted silence for a second.

He tried to imagine the mesa back when the tribes had come here for their ceremonies, but he couldn't get into the moment. There were so many beer bottles and used condoms in the rocks that whatever ancient magic had been here had long since left for a better location. There had been some ancient myth about this place, something about lost lovers jumping off the cliff in some Native version of Romeo and Juliet, but even Yazzie hadn't been able to remember the story anymore.

Marlow stiffened as he heard the sirens get louder, and then suddenly stopped. No, the sirens were definitely for someone else. He turned on the ignition.

Nico and Van Leit got out of the Corvette in Shark's parking lot. The uniforms were already in position, guns drawn. They did have an official Crater County Sheriff's Department squad car—an old Crown Victoria—back at the justice center, but the Corvette was just so much more fun. Van Leit smiled and signaled to the uniforms that it was time. As Crater County sheriff, he was nominally in charge of the moment.

Nico let Van Leit have his moment of glory. Van Leit lived for this stuff, or at least he pretended to. He was forty-five and had been a cop in some capacity for his entire adult life. His brown plaid suit, sandy brown toupee, and sandy brown mustache blended in well with the desert. He was a big man who had played junior hockey way up north. A few small Michigan colleges had recruited him, but he hadn't been quite quick enough, and had played too dirty in all senses of both words.

Van Leit bent down into the car and took a quick swig from the small bottle of whiskey he kept with him. Nico shook his head.

Nico never blended in. He kept his sunglasses on even though the sun was almost over the ridge to the west. He wore a shiny gray suit and a black t-shirt, with a discreet gold chain around his neck. He had shaved his head and refused to wear a hat on a windy late afternoon like this. The ladies loved the trademark "Nico Look."

In the ten years they'd worked together, Van Leit and Nico had developed a good back and forth. They often completed each other's sentences as if each could read the other's thoughts. Then again, it wasn't like those thoughts were particularly profound.

"Don't you wish your little girlfriend was here?" Van Leit asked, for the tenth time today.

"She's not my girlfriend," Nico replied for the tenth time. "Not for twelve years."

"After today, that most definitely will change," Van Leit said with the same smile.

"Change is good," Nico responded. "Change is good."

Van Leit signaled to the troopers as if he were a film director. "Let's roll . . . action." The troopers shook their heads. They were cops, not actors.

Nico smiled back at Van Leit. They both were ready for their close-ups. Nico suddenly felt nervous as he walked toward the front door. He was suddenly very glad that the camera crews weren't here after all.

Inside Shark's, Jeremy wiped his eyes. He didn't want them to see him like this, but now that it was all finished, he could finally relax. He looked at the third cross tattooed on his hand with a great deal of satisfaction and prayed to it as if it offered some kind of salvation from those outside.

Shark looked toward the gun hidden behind the counter. Too far away. Then he took another quick look at his wall safe behind the "Scream" sign. As long as the little alien didn't squeal, the newfound wealth inside would be safe.

"It's all good," Jeremy said. His voice was the devil's DJ. "Now's when things *really* get interesting. Do we have someone on line one?"

"Open up! It's the sheriff!"

Shark lacked Jeremy's newfound faith. He stopped in his tracks. He had first done time years ago in New York on insider trading, the second time on computer hacking and copyright infringement. In the joint, the former accountant and digital artist had told everyone it had been involuntary manslaughter on the first and voluntary manslaughter on the second. One look at this giant with the body of a basketball "power forward," everyone had easily believed whatever he said. By the end of his tenth year in the Federal Pen in La Tuna, Texas, his millionth tattoo and his billionth 500 pound bench press, (not to mention countless prison rapes), he couldn't even remember what he had done anymore, and had been accepted into the gangs when he got out.

Still, with three strikes, he'd lose the little he had re-built for himself over the last twenty years of freedom, once the authorities found his guns, his drugs, his porn and especially his money. If he could hear the cops, there must be a lot of them out there—a *helluva* lot of them out there.

He took one last nervous look at the hidden wall safe then looked at Jeremy and shrugged.

Jeremy wiped the last of the tears from his eyes, and gave a silent amen to the little cathedral that now graced the space between his thumb and the rest of his hand.

"It's open!" he yelled, as if inviting them in for tea. "Come in and make yourselves comfortable."

Two troopers burst in. They pointed their very big guns right at Jeremy.

Jeremy kept his hands over his head, even though he hadn't been asked. He smiled.

Nico and Van Leit stared at each other. This was almost too easy. Nico backed off one step. He'd let Van Leit have the moment. "Age before beauty," he said to his partner.

Van Leit grabbed Jeremy roughly, threw him down, and cuffed him. "You little puke! You better have a good lawyer."

"I've got the best."

Nico picked up his cell phone and dialed Diana's number. "We got him."

Nico looked down at Jeremy's hand and spied the fresh tattoo of the third cross. Despite his best efforts, he threw up.

"You're a sick fuck!" he said to Jeremy.

Jeremy just smiled, as if he'd been waiting for this moment his entire life.

In the sparse "Channel 8 Albuquerque" lobby, a sign read "The Land of Enchantment's Most Enchanting Newscast!"

To Diana Crater, news was never enchanting. She thanked Nico over her cell, then turned it off and put it in her purse. She looked for her watch and frowned. She knew where she had left it, but she could hardly go back for it now.

She glanced at the wall. It was five-fifty-seven. Perfect timing.

She shouted out to the receptionist, "Tell the anchor we got him."

Diana had drunk three cups of coffee, spilling just a tiny bit on her white blouse, but she was indeed ready for her close-up at last and had even bought her latest arraignment outfit at Dillard's in the Cottonwood Mall in anticipation of the arrest. She had saved thirty percent for opening a credit card account, and that would be the extent of her enchantment for the day.

Channel 8 had talked to her after Yazzie too, along with the rest of the civilized world, but now she was going to slam a real live serial killer, all by herself.

At thirty-one, Diana had become Crater County's district attorney by default. She'd been lucky to be a native of Crater, the great-granddaughter of the town's namesake, and a niece of the late, great Judge Crater.

As of last year, she was also the last of the Craters, "Like being the 'Last of the Mohicans,' but with a better wardrobe and better hair care products," she often joked to her friends in town. Her hair was short, but fashionably spiked in a manner that was just a little too stylish for a small town girl.

She didn't have an opponent for DA. In fact, when she declared for the job, she was the only lawyer who lived in the county. Running the office was only her second job out of UNM law school and New Mexico State undergrad. She'd spent less than a year in the DWI division up in the First Judicial District, the courts in Santa Fe, Espanola and Los Alamos. Most of her peers were still in the tiny Santa Fe magistrate court, way out on Galisteo Road, pleading Ag DWI seconds down to DWI first, no jail time, praying that they could get one of the slots at the felony division or a good government job at the Attorney General's office.

Diana hoped that they could see her now. She knew she looked good in white, although she couldn't help but laugh at the irony of it. She hadn't felt this good since she was "Miss Crater County" in the Miss New Mexico Pageant. She'd been unopposed for that too, but that had been twelve years and forty pounds ago.

Despite all her success, Diana often thought that it had all been downhill since her senior year in high school.

"Thanks, Stephanie Park Live," The receptionist said with a giggle into the phone.

Diana looked at her. "'Live' is her last name?"

The receptionist smiled. "Our anchor woman once introduced herself at a party as 'Stephanie Park Live.' We never let her live it down."

Diana couldn't help but laugh. She could relate. Her first week on the job, she had been so excited she had told her gynecologist in Albuquerque that "Crater County District Attorney Diana Crater" was here to see him.

A male make-up artist hurried forward, "You're that district attorney, right?"

Diana nodded.

"You look real young," he said. "Where are you from again?"

"Crater County." Diana anticipated the man's next question. "We're not the Meteor Crater in Arizona. Or Crater Lake up in Oregon. Or even Craters of the Moon in Idaho. It's different. We were named after a family, not after a real crater."

She waited a beat and added the old joke that residents always said to outsiders. "There's no crater in Crater County, it's just a state of mind."

The man said nothing as he applied some more make-up and way too much hair spray, considering that it had already been gelled.

"They need you right now," he said, when he was done. "You're going to be the lead story."

Her phone rang again. It was Nico again. He told her about the three cross tattoos.

"That's sick," she said, genuinely disturbed. She then realized that this whole thing wasn't really about her after all.

It took a moment, but she made it be about Diana again. Perhaps it was better that the Channel 8 news van couldn't be bothered with making the hour and half drive out to Crater County. There would be no close-ups on the flashing lights and cops. There would be only her.

Why wasn't she happy?

Because three people she knew were dead, that's why.

Inside the studio, Diana took a last glimpse in the mirror just as the anchor said "I'm Stephanie Park Live from Albuquerque. We go immediately to our lead story. Live from the newsroom, here's Crater County District Attorney, Diana Crater."

Diana didn't hear the anchor's first question. It didn't really matter.

"I'm happy to say that we have Jeremy Jones in custody right now. He's the prime suspect in three homicides."

She didn't hear the second question either before responding. "When a man brutally kills three people—his girlfriend, his girl friend's mother, and her new boyfriend—people like Jeremy Jones just don't belong in civilized society."

Pictures of an old woman, a young man, and then a pretty young woman flashed on the screen. Then an old picture of Jeremy came up. He looked more like a bleached James Dean in this photo. A James Dean with amphetamine eyes.

"I will do my best to see that Jeremy Jones gets a fair trial." She took a dramatic pause. "We are going for the death penalty on all three counts."

It didn't really matter what the third question was. "And I've just learned that after each murder, um . . . each alleged murder, Jeremy Jones got a tattoo of a small cross. This man is sick."

Stephanie Park Live gasped. Her graphics person immediately began preparing a "Three Crosses Murder" graphic.

Diana smiled. She might have made a few more statements in the next ninety seconds, but she really didn't remember. Before she could catch her breath, the man had taken the mike off of her and wiped off her make-up. Stephanie Park Live had already moved on to the previous lead story, the latest bombing in the Middle East.

On her way out, the make-up man gave her a thumbs-up. "Congratulations. I hope you get that sick bastard."

"Don't worry, we will."

It had only been a minute, maybe two max, but it had definitely been worth the hours on the interstate.

Diana adjusted a small American flag lapel. She hit her pager. She had to call Luna. "Luna my love," Diana typed in, using the nickname from their high school days that she'd stolen from Luna's mom. "Get your bony ass over to the justice center."

Luna didn't hear the page over the thumping of her heartbeat. Only twenty seconds up and her lungs had decided to take yet another vacation. Still a hundred yards till the Yazzie wreck. She forced her eyes on the remains of the old pick-up that had flown down from the top of the mesa. There'd been yellow tape around the wreck, but it had long since dissolved into the dust, and everything that hadn't been evidence had long been salvaged for parts by the coyotes.

"Just make it to the top," Luna said to her bike, not moving her lips to take away valuable oxygen. "Then it's all worth it."

There was no way she could make it to the top, but something made her pedal faster. "At least make it to the wreck," she said to the bike. "Just make it to the wreck. Focus, baby, focus."

Marlow revved the engine just for fun. On top of the mesa, he could hear the echoes cascade off the granite and limestone cliffs throughout the entire county.

He took his foot off the gas for a moment to listen. After the echoes died down, he heard the last sirens from down at Shark's. It was quiet down there. The wind stopped. It was six-oh-two and the sun was nearly down.

He revved the engines again. This was it.

He looked at the big bottle of Jack Daniels, started to open it, and then thought better of it. Yazzie hadn't been drunk anyway; it had been a bi-polar condition that had never been diagnosed, right?

He closed his eyes and recited the Navajo prayer Yazzie had taught him.

He opened his eyes. "Harrison Yazzie, *y'in sha' yay*," he said. He hoped that he had said something close to "My name is Harrison Yazzie," but despite his years of study, his Dine (pronounced "Din-ay") language was still a work in progress.

Still, at that moment he wasn't a thirty-five-year-old white lawyer from Los Angeles, he was a fifty-year-old Navajo potter from Nageezi, New Mexico who had driven his loving wife and adorable children off this very cliff for reasons that no one had ever discerned.

Unlike Yazzie, he had his reasons, and unlike Yazzie, he hoped he didn't survive the fall.

Suddenly, the sirens began again from down below at Shark's. The convoy had snared its prey and was heading home in triumph.

Marlow rolled up his windows to drown out the distraction. No, nothing is going to stop me now. He put the car into gear and drove the Saturn straight toward the edge.

Luna didn't know whether it was her lungs or her legs that gave out just before she hit the wreck. She blamed her bike, of course. She just knew that it couldn't go another inch. Luna pulled off the trail and walked the bike up to the burnt-out metal frame.

She looked up toward the summit of the trail, did a mental diagnosis of both her bike and her body's condition and shook her head. The summit definitely wasn't going to happen today.

Luna looked at the wreck. No one had ever laid a wooden cross out here for the dead Indian family, or if they did, it was long gone. Probably just as well. That couple were famous artists, right? She couldn't remember, but there was something artistic about a twisted wreck all alone in the middle of the desert.

"I should dump you right here where you belong," she said to her bike.

She took another deep breath as she remembered when she was the star of the Crater High Cross Country Team and could make it to the top without even breaking a sweat.

"We can still make it," she said to the bike.

It was going to get dark soon anyway so she had to turn around, right? Suddenly, she heard the revving of a car's engine. All the way out here?

She saw some dust coming from the other side of the mesa. At first, she thought it was connected to the sirens, then realized it was coming from the wrong direction. The revving motor grew louder and louder.

Marlow put his foot all the way down. The black Saturn had no acceleration, especially not on the sand of the mesa, but after a few awkward yards, the car surprised him. The car was as sick of life as he was and wanted to end it. He locked his arms on the steering wheel as he got closer to the edge.

Luna's pager rang again. She heard it this time. She looked at the summit one last time.

"Maybe next time," she said to the bike. "I'm letting you off easy."

She now had a real excuse. There was a written message from Diana. She keyed in the response "OK" and hit send.

But she wasn't okay. She was too tired to move in any direction, even downhill. She still needed to catch her breath here for a few more moments.

Marlow had now hit full speed on top. It would be only a few seconds of mesa, a few more of free fall, then it would all be over.

He tried to write his own obituary. What would they say about him? He'd make the papers here, of course, and maybe even in Albuquerque. But would they care back home in L.A.?

"Lawyer loses case after two years, then drives over cliff, just like client," he said to himself. That wasn't a headline, not in L.A.

It didn't matter. He wasn't going to be around to read it anyway.

Van Leit and Nico shoved Jeremy into a squad car, the last of the convoy. Nico certainly didn't have room in the Corvette.

Jeremy's tears were long gone now. He was a bad ass once again. He was the serpent. He wore his handcuffs with pride. "I want to ride in the Corvette," he said. "I call shotgun."

"I bet you do," said Nico.

"I get one phone call," Jeremy said. "Guess who I'm calling?"

Nico said nothing as he reluctantly handed Jeremy the phone.

"Seriously," said Jeremy. "Guess!"

Luna's legs and arms cramped up even more. Between them, they didn't even have the energy to turn the bike around. She now heard the roar of the car on top of the plateau. She looked over at the wreck. Luna didn't have to be an automobile expert to know where the laws of physics would send another car coming over the top.

Her bike still wouldn't move. Another betrayal. Maybe God was punishing her for ending up here, for being too wimpy at the Olympic trials and too stupid to get a job out there in the real world. If that's what His will was, so be it. She didn't have the energy to argue with her body or her bike right now. She had lost again.

Marlow could just barely see the edge of the mesa, then clear New Mexico desert sky and the very last rays of the setting sun. The Saturn raced closer to the point of no return. . . .

Suddenly, his phone rang.

He ignored the first ring . . . he tried to stay in the moment.

It rang again. Maybe this was redemption.

He took one last look over at the edge of the cliff, just a few dozen yards ahead.

It would be so easy . . . it would all be over.

With the third ring, he slammed on the brakes.

Down below, Luna heard the screech of the brakes against the dirt. She felt a dusty wind fall down on her, then a small stone bounced against the twisted metal of the wreck.

She looked up just as the black Saturn stopped at the edge of the plateau.

Marlow took the call right at the edge of the mesa. He listened for a moment then said, "I'll be right over."

He stared down at the strange reflection below. At first he thought it was some glistening angel, or something out of a Navajo vision, then he realized that it was a human being in a bike outfit with reflective gear that glimmered in the sunset. Yazzie would have called it some kind of sign. Yazzie was a smart man, but he saw signs and symbols in everything that happened. But a sign or symbol of what?

The biker looked back up at him. They were about fifty yards away. The sun finally set. They turned around and went their separate ways.

Luna's muscles were still tight as she turned around. By the time she passed the wooden cross at the side of the dirt road, the winds had already blown away the three red roses. Probably just as well, she thought.

BOOKING

Once she hit the paved roads, Luna's bike and legs both decided to work again. Still on her bike, Luna coasted past the freeway exits, then kept going past her house on the way to the justice center in beautiful downtown Crater. It had been downhill all the way, and the wind was at her back. It took her half the time and nearly none of the effort the outward trip had taken.

She thought about changing her clothes, but she was late already. She'd promised Diana she'd wait by the phone and didn't want to get caught in yet another lie. Things were delicate enough already, when you'd been on the job for only a week. Working for an old friend made it difficult to know how much you could get away with.

Law was supposed to be the "day job" to pay the bills for her training. "You'll always need a back-up," her mother, Ruth, had always said to her. "You can't do triathlons forever and the world will always need lawyers, even distracted ones."

Luna had actually bounced her deposit check to the University of Colorado Law School, but Ruth had paid the admission fee, just to make sure her daughter went. Luna had nearly busted out of Boulder while doing the training, but had always managed to squeak by. She had studied Federal Rules of Evidence by listening to taped class notes as she jogged up Boulder's mountain, the Flatirons, and had mastered the Bankruptcy Code (mastered enough for a 71) while biking up and down the Peak-to-Peak Highway.

The sign at the entrance to town said, "Welcome home to Crater."

Welcome home, all right. Crater's not a town, it's a state of mind. She repeated the old joke to herself for the millionth time. The only state of mind in the state of New Mexico that would hire her—so much for her mother's admonition that the world would always need lawyers.

"You had your chance and you blew it," Ross Peters at Metro had said back when she'd quit to train for the Olympic trials full time. It hadn't been that big of a transition from work to training. She'd already become notorious for her late mornings and even earlier afternoons. She wondered if the real reason Ross hated her was because he was an injured vet who walked with a limp and was jealous of the way she seemed to hurdle over the cubicles on her way to court.

Ross hadn't quite said, "You'll never work in this state again," but he might as well have. In the entire state, only Diana would have her. Then again, no one else would have Diana. The guy she had replaced had left to take a job as a janitor at an adult bookstore, according to Nico.

Luna always felt like she passed through invisible crater walls when she made it into the town. There wasn't much to it. There was the Crosswinds truck stop by the freeway, with a handful of fast food restaurants catering to travelers.

She never went inside the Crosswinds, not even for gas, because it was so expensive. No local ever did. It was a gigantic modern monstrosity that was in Crater, but not *of* Crater. There once had been an oil refinery next to it. The abandoned refining machinery was still lit up to deter vandalism. In the eerie green light, the towers of the refinery were indeed the closest things to an emerald city out here.

They all lived and worked down here, half a mile away in "Old Town." There were a few ranching supply stores, a market, a bank, one decent restaurant (The Rustler) and one saloon, the 66 Stars. The only profitable business in town was the liquor store, Nez's Native Spirits.

There still was a middle school, but the big building that had once held Crater High had been converted into a rehab center. An old billboard in front still said "Go Comets!!!" Next to the old

Crater High, there was the small medical clinic that had once been her dad's. It now housed two nurses and the traveling osteopath every Tuesday and Wednesday.

She pulled into the Crater County Justice Center in the heart of Old Town Crater. Even though the adobe building housed the sheriff's office, the DA and the courthouse, the justice center was barely the size of her favorite Mexican restaurant in Boulder. A few State cars had kept their flashing lights on, probably just for show by now.

The red Corvette was already there. She had even lost her virginity in it at seventeen. Other than a new coat of paint, it hadn't changed much over the years. And, except for the hair, neither had Nico.

Welcome home to Crater. It was a state of mind all right.

Marlow got into his clothes as he drove. He almost felt like an addict coming off a high as he broke character, shook it all off, tried not to think about it anymore. His brain hadn't totally shifted to self-preservation however. Marlow grabbed the underwear as he made it down Old Summit Trail Road. Next, the pants. He had to coast a bit for that. Finally the shirt, then the tie. With every article of clothing, he left the mesa top behind. His hair was still long enough to be tied into a ponytail. He almost grabbed the knife in his car to hack it off right there.

Jeremy again. Jeremy Freaking Jones. How many times had he represented Jeremy in the last year alone, in between his hearings on Harrison Yazzie? Two years ago he had taken the Yazzie case out here because no other private lawyer on the contract list would take such a loser, especially not at the usual contract rate. It seemed like a way to get into the public defender department's good graces, an "in" to either Albuquerque or Santa Fe, and then one more year before he could finally go back to L.A.

The first Yazzie trial was a hung jury and the second was a mistrial. Moral victories, he had told himself, considering that the rest of the state wanted to hang the man in a fit of anti-Navajo hysteria. Unfortunately, after the third trial and the subsequent execution,

Yazzie wasn't around any more to put down as a reference.

Marlow adjusted the mirror and played with the ponytail one last time as he passed the "Welcome Home to Crater" sign. He took a deep breath and stopped the car for a good five minutes. The trembling in his body finally stopped, the adrenaline had evaporated into the high altitude air.

He tried to clear his mind a little more before he faced reality. Marlow thought back to the summer he was eighteen, right before USC. His dad had known two people who swore they could get him into the industry. He did the cold reading at the Paramount lot at eleven A.M. He was supposed to be a vampire for a drama. The audition ran long. He then had to hightail it over the Valley for Warner's for the one P.M., where he was supposed to be the gay honor student for a sitcom. Or was it the other way around? After a sig alert on the 101 and an hour of mainlining carbon monoxide, he couldn't remember. He was mixing up monologues and cursing his dad by the time he passed the exit for the Hollywood Bowl.

He didn't get either part, of course.

There was still some residual trembling. For some reason he thought of that vision—that mysterious woman in the desert. Yazzie was probably right. It did probably mean something.

The trembling stopped for good. He was ready. He would choose life, at least for the rest of the afternoon. . . .

Moments later, he made it into the justice center parking lot. He heard a thump.

Shit.

Marlow worried about his tires and hurried out to find a small bottle of cheap Wild Stallion whisky in a paper bag. Luckily, his tires hadn't been punctured. He looked up at the lot. The red and blue lights kept revolving. There was something shiny that reflected off the red and then the blue.

It couldn't be; was that the angel from the desert?

The lights turned around again and Luna saw the black Saturn. Oh my God. Was that the same car?

She shook her head and hurried toward the door. She and

Marlow arrived simultaneously. They stared for a second, as the blue light came around, then the red.

It couldn't be him, she thought. This guy looked like a million bucks. Where the hell's this guy been all her life? His suit was a real Armani, or a very good duplicate. He was handsome, although slightly bookish with his glasses. He stood up straight, hardly the type of guy who drove off cliffs for an afternoon's entertainment. She even forgave the ponytail.

Marlow couldn't take his eyes off of her either. She was still in the black sports bra and spandex bike shorts, with their reflective strips glittering. She may have found flaw after flaw in her own body, but even with his glasses, he sure couldn't see any.

He was struck speechless for a moment.

So was she.

Marlow was a gentleman. He held the door open for her.

"My name is Luna Cruz," she said.

"Are you a relative of the victim?" he asked, even though he knew the answer. "I'm uhh . . . sorry for your loss, uhh . . . Luna."

"I'm the assistant district attorney," she said. "I'm going to nail this little scum to the wall. And you?"

"Sam Marlow," he said. "I'm defending this little scum."

They both laughed nervously. There was something they were supposed to say to each other, some quip that would make this awkward moment seem less awkward, but neither could think of it. Their desperation of an hour ago was like a distant memory.

They stared at each other for another long second, until they finally made it through to the sheriff's office in the back.

Jeremy was the center of attention, even seated. He was the Heavyweight Champion of the world and Nico and Van Leit were the corner men. Jeremy looked up at Marlow. "Where the hell were you?"

Jeremy's words shoved Marlow back into character, his tough lawyer character. "I'm sorry," he said. "Traffic was a bitch."

Jeremy smiled. Luna couldn't help but smile as well.

Marlow suddenly seemed taller when he stood next to Jeremy, as if he was one of those comic book villains who took energy from those around him. Nico and Van Leit moved to another part of the room to get away from the aura.

"Why the hell are you even thinking of talking to him without me present?" Marlow asked.

"We just thought we'd give him a chance to save his life here," Van Leit smirked. "Looks like he done blew his chance when you arrived."

Marlow could smell the alcohol on Van Leit's breath. He didn't know what pissed him off more about the sheriff right now, that he was a drunk or that he was probably the litterbug who had thrown his bottle into the parking lot.

Marlow let it ride. He had to concentrate on the case. He turned toward Luna. "Save his life? So if he confesses right now, you can personally guarantee that he won't get the death penalty?"

Jeremy was about to protest, but Marlow silenced him with a hand on his shoulder. There was a long beat.

"I said, if he confesses right now," Marlow said. "Can you personally guarantee that he won't get the death penalty?"

Nico and Van Leit said nothing. They turned to Luna. She gulped. "Hey, I just work here," she said. "You know I can't make a promise like that."

Nico tried to fall on the grenade for Luna. "Maybe she can throw out the death penalty for the first murder—Felicia's mother, Sarah Sanchez."

Van Leit thought this was funny as well. "We can throw out the death penalty for the murder of Felicia's boyfriend. What was his name?"

"Thayer Brown," said Nico.

"Yeah, he doesn't have to die for the murder of Thayer Brown," said Van Leit.

They both looked over at Luna expectantly. She played along. "But unfortunately, for the murder of Felicia herself, I'm afraid that Diana is going to insist on the death penalty. They were friends, you know. Sorry."

She faked a giggle.

Jeremy looked over at Luna. He laughed right back at her, a

very fake laugh. He nodded at Marlow.

"Then my client has nothing to say to you," said Marlow. "We're invoking the 'ain't saying shit' clause of the Federal and State constitutions."

"You and your clauses," said Van Leit, almost on the edge of slurring his words. "How about my favorite, the Santa Clause?"

"What's Santa Clause gonna bring for your buddy Mr. Yazzie?" Nico asked. "Oh wait, I guess he's not bringing anything to Mr. Yazzie anymore for being naughty.'"

Van Leit laughed "Remember Joey Begay?" he asked. Begay was another Navajo who had committed suicide, even though Marlow had successfully defended him.

Nico smirked. "Why be Yazzie?"

"When you can Begay?" Van Leit piped in, repeating a popular refrain regarding Navajo names in these parts.

Marlow was silent for a moment. That hurt. He had loved all of his Dine clients, and had believed their occasionally outrageous stories of abuse at the hands of Van Leit and Nico.

Jeremy laughed, breaking through Marlow's reverie. He was the devil's DJ, all right. "I ain't Yazzie. How many trials did it take you boys to nail him? And didn't they have to bring in some real cops, and bring in the real lawyers from the Attorney General's office, then move the whole thing to Tucumcari, where there isn't a single damn Indian, before you got your little lethal injection?"

He now looked over at Luna. "A little history lesson here. You boys have arrested me *how* many times there, Nico?"

Nico said nothing.

"See me and Nico, we go back to Crater High football days. Go Comets! Then we worked at the mines that summer after school. Back when they were still running. Used to smoke joints together after our shifts. Remember those days, Nico?"

Nico still said nothing.

Jeremy turned toward Luna. "In between tokes, he used to say how much he totally wanted to take you and—"

Jeremy was hardly a subtle mime with his pelvic thrusts. Angered, Marlow couldn't help but attempt to defend Luna's honor, even though Jeremy was his client. "That's enough, Jeremy." He turned toward Luna. "We're done here."

Luna stared at Jeremy in rage, even after he'd stopped thrusting. She cursed under her breath, but kept her composure. Prosecutors aren't supposed to have feelings, right?

But Jeremy wasn't done. "Since my man Marlow took over my case, how many times have you convicted me, Nico? How many times? How many times has my man Marlow walked my tattooed white ass out of this here jail into the clear blue New Mexico sky? How many times?"

Jeremy hugged Marlow. "This here's my man!"

Jeremy didn't even look at Nico. He gestured at the detention center guard who was waiting outside the glass door. "I'm ready."

The guard came inside and took him away without another word. It felt like every ounce of oxygen had gone with them.

"Jeremy Jones has left the building," Marlow couldn't help but say.

Everyone took a deep breath as the oxygen slowly returned. Luna stared at Van Leit, Nico and Marlow. She could tell that these three didn't like each other much, and now Marlow suddenly seemed to shrink before her eyes, almost as if he had just lost his bodyguard.

"I assume your boy doesn't want to testify at the grand jury?" Luna asked him.

"My boy? Well, yeah . . . that's a pretty safe assumption."

"I can't really tell you anything until Diana gets back," she said.

There was a long beat. Van Leit got up. "Hey Nico, we got to let them do lawyer stuff for a minute."

Nico didn't want to get up. He pantomimed a "call me," glance at Luna before Van Leit pulled him out of the room.

Luna nodded back.

Marlow stared at her for a moment. There was something about her. No, she wasn't the best lawyer in the world, but damn, he could see a fire in those tight abs of hers that had the potential to make her become it. What did he call it—love at second sight?

He knew he had to say something to make the moment last.

"How the hell did you end up out here?"

"I'm from here," she said.

He couldn't believe that. This goddess was a Crater High Lady Comet?

"I've been gone for about twelve years," she said as if that were some type of explanation. "I lived in Boulder, went to school, then law school, took a brief job over in Metro in Albuquerque, than back up to Boulder while I did my training."

She didn't talk any more about training. It tended to intimidate most men. Marlow didn't press the point.

"Glad to be back?"

"What do you think?"

"Has Crater changed at all?"

She thought for a second. "It's gotten smaller."

Marlow was going to ask her about what Jeremy had said, but thought better of it. Her and Nico . . . ouch!

He wanted to throw up at the thought of this perfect woman with that jerk cop. He tried to think about the canons of ethics when it came to dating opposing counsel.

As she walked out the door, she took his breath along with him. This woman was indeed the angel from the desert. No, she wasn't quite there as an attorney yet, but she had the potential to be the perfect woman *and* the perfect lawyer. He could be the one to teach her, right?

And that was a butt worth getting disbarred for.

TARGET LETTER

Luna was now the permanent guest at her mother's guesthouse. The complex had been through a few additions since Luna had left. By her sophomore year at CU undergrad, her mother had been master of the stock market and had made an avalanche of improvements to spice up the ranch for the resale market. Unfortunately, once the mines closed and the town cleared out, it was doubtful that any corporate exec would turn this into his "work-from-home mansion," and that corporate exec certainly wouldn't house a visiting vice president over in the quaint little guest house.

Luna liked her little structure, even though she treated it like a college kid home for the weekend. She had piles of clothes and papers everywhere. Outside, it looked like a nice little satellite of the long southwestern ranch home that she couldn't help but call the Mothership. With all the bells and whistles, the glass greenhouses and satellite dishes, the ranch really did look like a spin-off of "Star Trek, the Santa Fe Generation."

Luna started Monday with a ride, but way shorter than usual. She still had cramps from the Hills. Neither she nor the bike recovered like they used to. Afterwards, she ran the forty yards over to the Mothership for her mother's coffee. She had given up coffee while she had been training but, now that she was back in town, it was a good way to gear up for the day.

Luna didn't mind living in the satellite. There was no place at the Mothership for her anyway. Her mom had converted Luna's old bedroom into an office to house all of her computer equipment. Every other room was filled with books and relics from her mother's journeys.

Living forty yards from the Mothership was enough to pretend that she didn't really live at home, but just stopped in from a near-by galaxy for an extended visit.

She visited every morning, of course, just in time for breakfast. Her mother's kitchen was gigantic and almost felt like a greenhouse with its glass windows facing the mountain view to the south. Ruth's coffee was always exotic—usually a gift from one of her Internet pen pals. Today was Afghanistan, a Tora Bora blend.

At fifty-five, Ruth Goldstein y Cruz could still pass for forty, and was even thinner than Luna. Luna always thanked her genes whenever she saw her mother. Ruth had jogged every day of her life, but after a bad double-knee replacement surgery, she now walked with a cane, and could no longer drive. Flying was damned near impossible. Her medical malpractice lawsuit against the doctor was still on appeal and her legal malpractice suit against the lawyer had just been filed.

Ruth had grown up in a rich North Shore suburb of Chicago and had fulfilled every Jewish mother's dream of marrying a doctor, the late Dr. Cruz, whom she had met at Northwestern University up in Evanston. Ruth had told her mother that this Hispanic doctor from New Mexico was definitely going places.

Unfortunately, Crater was the last of the places he'd go. Little had she known that Cruz's residency at UNM and the clinic in Crater was it. She would never get her house in Lake Forest. There was a very small lake in Crater, but certainly no forest.

Ruth still did consulting work for her various causes over the Internet, but with her knee she couldn't get out as often. She had her groceries sent out from Wild Oats in Santa Fe once a week and ordered her clothes off the Internet. Ruth still dressed for breakfast as if one of her Internet friends from England were going to come all the way over and join them for tea.

Ruth read about Jeremy's case in the statewide edition of the *Albuquerque Journal* and couldn't help but point out that it was Diana's picture on the cover and not Luna's.

"You've always been so much smarter than she, Luna dear," Ruth said.

"Don't I know it, Mom."

Ruth routinely clipped out parts of the paper and pointed out various opportunities to Luna. There was a new aerospace company that was expanding in Albuquerque. "A law degree is always a stepping stone."

"I'm dyslexic mom, and I failed math," she said. She often felt that her mom was still mad at her for getting waitlisted at both Stanford and Northwestern. She was right.

"There's still time to make something of your life, dear," Ruth said.

Luna looked at her watch. Well, there wasn't time today. "Got to run, Mom," she said. "Don't worry, I'll change at work."

She gave her mom a hug. Her mom didn't let go until she'd held her for an extra second.

"Luna, my love," she said, "you did have a raw deal by just missing your one chance at Olympic glory, but you have to make the best of this hand you were dealt. Look at me. I'm even more stuck here than you, but I make the best of it. People won't take you seriously if you don't take yourself seriously and I don't think you're taking yourself seriously if you're riding around town in spandex so tight I can practically see your—"

Luna escaped her mother's grasp and hurried out the door before Ruth could finish.

Marlow prepared a little bonfire in the big stone grill that came with his small rental house. His house was a little adobe place that he rented month to month since the Yazzie case began. He never signed a lease because he always wanted the flexibility to leave at a moment's notice. That moment had not come in the past two years.

He had never bothered to tend to his backyard. The grass had long since died, but it did have a nice stone grill. He took every flammable trinket he had gotten from Yazzie, all the stuff he had bought at that big gallery on Route 66 in Gallup, even the fry bread, and put it in the grill.

He recited his Yazzie monologue one last time for old time's sake. "Harrison Yazzie, *Y'anin-in-shay.* I grew up in Nageezi. . . ."

He kept a dream-catcher and a few old good luck charms. Marlow still held onto a few superstitions and it was probably best not to tempt the gods too much.

He poured some lighter fluid then lit a match. Within seconds it was over. Some turquoise beads were still down there. He covered them with ashes.

Washing his hands in the bathroom, he couldn't help but look at the mirror and the reflection of "the Shrine." The Shrine was a bulletin board holding every single rejection letter he'd ever received—from the Harvard Westlake High School in Los Angeles, onto Harvard itself, then countless law schools and law firms. The moisture in the bathroom had crumpled many of the older letters.

There was an NBA card for former MVP Alan Iverson, giving a growling look at the camera with his tattoos and cornrows. "What's the difference between you and Alan Iverson?" Marlow often asked himself as he tried to out-angry Iverson's expression. "He was smart enough to get into Georgetown."

The Shrine was incomplete, of course. Many more of America's finest institutions had interviewed him and then never bothered to spend the few cents to reject him. He never got letters from all the soap operas or commercials, much less the student films he had tried out for in his years after USC when he tried to make it as an actor, before relenting to parental pressure and going to law school.

"How can you defend murderers?" someone always asked him when he went to Albuquerque for his dose of civilization and continuing legal education.

Marlow wanted to show them the Shrine and all the wilting letters. "What the hell else can I do? When something better comes along, I'm out of here."

He turned off the faucet. Before he could get too worked up, he went outside to the living room and opened his old files on Jeremy Jones. He had represented Jeremy on five prior cases, all felonies, all of which had been dropped to misdemeanors, or dropped totally.

Then he went through the survey. That had started when he did legal aid clinic at UNM (his safety school), when an African American client had told him, "You don't know shit about shit. How can you defend me, you rich white motherfucker?"

Once he could talk intelligently about the difference between East Coast and West Coast rap, his client had opened up to him, and when he quoted the late Tupac Shakur in a closing argument, his client told him he was the best lawyer ever.

Since then, he made every client take a survey—favorite songs, favorite foods, right down to favorite colors. Jeremy's was black. He would have to change his wardrobe and start listening to Elvis.

He pinched his gut. He'd let himself get a little soft from the fry bread during the Yazzie years. Jeremy liked the Big Bad Rustler steak at the Rustler—very, very bloody and smothered with green chile. Marlow did have a solo flex machine and he'd have to pump some serious iron to get into Jeremy's league.

He did have a psych profile on Jeremy from the first mayhem case. Jeremy was a borderline psychopath with anger management issues off the chart. He was extremely intelligent and, had he been at any school other than Crater, his learning disabilities and bi-polar act would have been caught early. Jeremy probably would have been a better lawyer than Marlow. A little anger would be all right, he thought. Maybe it was time to start sticking up for himself. He could learn a lot from Jeremy Freaking Jones.

He reluctantly put away his glasses and got out his old contacts. Through sheer force of will, he convinced his eyes to accept them, and actually hold onto them for a change.

"Mind over matter," he said.

Now time for the big change. He took a knife out of his drawer and stared at it. It had been Yazzie's knife. The old man had given it to him right before he'd been sent away and realized that he wasn't allowed to take a weapon with him. Marlow could see himself in the shiny blade. For a brief moment, he thought he saw Yazzie.

"*Ya ta hey*" he said to the reflection. "*Ha gone neh*, Harrison Yazzie."

Harrison Yazzie was now officially gone.

He took the knife and hacked off his ponytail. Jeremy Jones was now his new neighbor.

Luna felt the weight of the stares as she pedaled through town with her bare midriff and sports bra. "Do I really look like that much of a slut?" she asked her bike. The bike indicated that she should probably wear a sweatshirt and sweat pants from now on.

She made it to work at the Justice Center at nine-oh-seven. It was an unusually hot and humid morning and she sweated even more than usual. In Boulder, she claimed that she "glowed" rather than sweated, but perhaps it was the stress, because she was damp all over by the time she'd arrived and locked up her bike.

Shit. It wasn't like she was that late. Diana usually didn't get in until nine-thirty anyway. Diana's Lexus was in the "reserved for" space, Van Leit's pick-up and Nico's Corvette parked right next to it. Shit again.

Inside the Justice Center, it looked like they hadn't changed their clothes, with Van Leit in his brown plaid jacket, Nico in that hip black blazer and T-shirt, and Diana in her bright power suit.

Luna realized that she was mistaken, they had all changed clothes. Van Leit's jacket was one shade browner with horizontal stripes rather than vertical. Nico's blazer was the same, but he now wore a white T-shirt instead of a black one. Diana's suit was blue rather than white.

The men loaded stack after stack of boxes out of the lobby and into what had once been Luna's office. Diana didn't have to say anything to Luna. She just pointed to the stacks of boxes.

"I thought I had until nine-thirty," Luna called out sheepishly.

"Luna, put some clothes on!" Diana called. They were nearly the same age, but Diana now acted so much older some of the time. Luna's theory was that Diana was still the high school prom queen, who now only pretended to be an adult.

She sure was good at pretending. "There are grown-ups here," Diana said sternly. "And please take a shower. You reek!"

As she hurried out the door, Luna felt very aware that they stared at her in her biking shorts, even Diana. Luna made it back to the female officers' locker room. There had never been a female officer out here in Crater County, so a shiny new locker room had awaited her when she finally took the minimum wage job.

Maybe it was the stares she got today, but Luna felt compelled to lock the door behind her. She wanted a quick shower, but once the warm water hit her, she didn't want to leave. She shaved everything below her waist, had since going off to CU. She thought the extra weight of hair would slow her down. She had tempted fate during the trials and look what happened.

She looked down at her body. In the mornings, right after a ride, she was still perfect. Even if the donuts and Doritos for the day, and blue corn chicken enchiladas for lunch, seemingly made her gain ten pounds before her five o'clock ride . . . but mornings she could pretend that she was an Olympian.

"Need any help washing anything?" Nico pounded on the door.

She was almost sorry that the door was bolted shut. She hurriedly toweled off. "In a minute."

"You better hurry," Nico said. "Or you won't make it to the end of your second week."

Marlow stood in front of Sarah Sanchez's small adobe house and stared at the yellow crime scene tape and wooden boards surrounding it.

"She saved me from pornography," he couldn't help but think. Sarah had worked part time at the local convenience store that was the town's only source for magazines and movies. She'd always worn a big cross. On his first weekend in town, he had tried to buy a *Playboy* and she had asked him for identification.

"Identification for a *Playboy*?" he'd asked in disbelief.

"I can't sell it to you without ID." She was serious.

He feared that the woman would tell the entire town that the new lawyer was a perv, so he never bought a magazine, never rented a movie with a harsher rating than PG-13 when she was there. Even when she wasn't, he feared that the other clerks would tell her.

Now that she was gone, he had the urge to rent *Bikini Bandits 7*, but couldn't. Somehow Sarah would still know.

And now he was representing her killer, excuse me, her *alleged* killer.

"Sorry, Sarah."

• • • • •

Luna definitely did not enjoy finding her office converted into a storage closet, with her expected to remain inside. Another deputy, Shatrock, had joined Nico and Van Leit and the room could barely contain them all, even standing.

Shatrock was a real cowboy with a handlebar mustache and wore the sheriff's uniform, ten-gallon hat and all. Nico and Van Leit gave him a wide berth and Luna soon realized why. Shatrock smelled of horse shit.

"We send him out whenever there's a dead animal in the middle of the highway and somebody's got to clean it up," Nico had often joked, usually well within Shatrock's field of hearing.

The two plainclothes detectives immediately changed their demeanor as Luna entered the room. Jesus, are they sucking in their guts and flexing? Luna thought to herself. At least Van Leit doesn't reek of cheap Wild Stallion whisky for a change. And Nico, he doesn't need to try so hard. He still looks perfect. That shaved head definitely gave him a more urban look out here for the boonies. Shatrock had too much gut to suck in, so he didn't even try. After a few more mumbles, he finished his statement to Diana. He stared at her silently, waiting for a response.

Diana took a few more notes in her girlish hand. She had actually learned how to take shorthand in high school, and often joked that she was probably better suited to being a receptionist rather than head DA of an entire county. She was probably right.

"Thank you, Deputy," she said at last.

Shatrock stood there.

"You can go," Diana said, after a long moment.

Diana closed her eyes for a moment, as if she could still see the victim right in front of her. She took another breath and tried to regain her composure. As difficult as that was, she knew this wasn't like when she was third runner-up for Miss New Mexico. She wasn't going to break down in front of these assholes, especially not in front of Luna. She would always be the sophomore and Luna would always be the freshman.

"You okay, Di?" Luna asked.

"Yeah, sure," she said. She pointed to the boxes. "I knew these people. It's getting to me. . . ."

"We all knew them," said Van Leit. "That's why I want to get this little puke Jeremy."

Shatrock left. Nico and Van Leit muttered some joke to each other.

"Did I miss anything?" Luna asked.

"Not really," said Nico, still laughing. "Shatrock came late to the first two murders, but was the primary on the third. We don't ever let him do any real investigating where there's a human being involved."

"That's where the varsity comes in," said Van Leit.

"Crater's Finest," said Nico.

They looked at each other and responded in unison. "We solve no crime . . . without overtime."

"Let's get on with it," said Diana at last.

Van Leit had a suitably sheepish look as a way of apology. Luna took a look at him. His eyes were a little red, but he had sobered up for the morning. He pointed toward a large box on the floor as if it held some secret that would lift the situation. He strained as he picked it up and lifted it onto Luna's desk. The box was on top of Luna's files for a traffic case. She was about to protest, but stifled herself.

"Here are my files on the first case," he said. "Sarah Sanchez. Felicia's mother."

He pointed at some pictures. The first was Sarah Sanchez in life.

"She looks like my mother," both Luna and Diana said simultaneously.

"She looks like everybody's mother." Van Leit was now all business. "First I went to Felicia's house on a domestic violence call. She said she was worried that Jeremy was going to do something to her mom. There'd been a struggle. So I took some evidence, some blood, then hurried over to Sarah's house."

He showed them the house on a small map. They knew where it was. "Victim is sixty years old, Caucasian mostly, but part

Hispanic, part Native American. Three gunshots to the left temple."

He took out a second glossy photograph. Sarah Sanchez looked like she was praying—her hands were clasped right by her heart. She was on the floor by her bed. She leaned toward the bed and her head touched a pillow that lay against the headboard. There were three distinct bloodstains on the white pillow.

Luna didn't even look at the picture. She hadn't seen a gory movie since high school with Nico, and she'd buried her head in her hands the entire time, much to Nico's regret. She pretended to use her X-ray vision to focus on the traffic case buried under the box.

"Failure to use turn signals," she said to herself. That's what she wished to God she was prosecuting right now. "Failure to use turn signals."

Van Leit dug deeper into the box. He showed some diagrams and exhibits from the state crime lab in Santa Fe. He explained them the best he could.

Diana nodded with the name of each expert. There was a Lee Yazzie on ballistics, no relation to the Yazzie of the last case, and a Dr. Goldfarb from the coroner's office, who had done the autopsy. Their signatures on the blood splatter report were like seeing Gucci on a handbag to Diana. Diana nodded. She tried to project confidence, but didn't entirely succeed. Time to change the subject.

"Did you know Felicia's mother at all, Luna?" she asked.

"No," Luna replied. "I think she was friends with my mom." Her mom didn't have any friends within five hundred miles, but it seemed like the right thing to say.

Van Leit lifted another box. "And for the icing on the cake, we got an eyewitness, Katy Baca, the waitress over at the 66 Stars that saw Sarah Sanchez yell at 'Weird Jeremy' and tell him to stop messing with her daughter because her daughter 'had done moved on.'"

He paused for dramatic effect, but lost the moment and had to look down at the witness's statement.

"Jeremy said 'I'm gonna kill you, bitch,' to Sarah right as Ol' Katy Baca was bringing a beer. Then he looked right at Sarah Sanchez and said 'I hope you got that, because I mean that and I never lie.'"

He pointed to some more scientific stuff. "We've got bloodstains, positive match to Jeremy. First at Felicia's house where they'd had the fight earlier in the day, next on Sarah Sanchez's dresser. He must have cut himself on the window breaking in, then bled on the dresser."

Diana nodded again, but looked over at the DNA experts just to double-check Van Leit's conclusions. Bingo. "Good work, Van."

Van Leit smiled. He winked over Luna and almost bowed. Luna couldn't help but stare at that sandy toupee, worried that it would fall into the evidence pile.

"Don't worry, Di," said Van Leit. "We got this little puke dead to freaking rights on the Sarah Sanchez case."

"Okay," she said. "We got one down. Two to go."

Marlow didn't quite make it to the Crosswinds truck stop to see where Thayer Brown had died. He ate at the McDonald's across from the truck stop. The sun had just risen over the top of the old oilrigs and Marlow changed his seat because of the bright light.

Jeremy ate here a lot and now Marlow would have to follow suit, if this would really work. No locals ever ate at the truck stop itself—its cafeteria was criminally overpriced, as were all the grades of gas. Since the Crosswinds was owned by a national chain, none of the locals worked there either, which was a point of major contention over in Old Town Crater. The corporation housed a rotating crew of out-of-towners in some tacky mobile homes out back by the abandoned oil tanks.

For locals, there was an invisible line by the first gas pump. No local ever crossed over to the other side. Even eating at McDonald's was pushing it. He opened the Styrofoam box. Nine times out of ten, the eggs in his Big Breakfast were good and runny. Today they were burnt to a greasy crisp.

Marlow liked watching the passers-by and plotting their stories. The place was only a handful of locals, and the rest were the travelers who didn't want to pay the cafeteria's high prices. It was packed today because of the highway road crew taking a break after working the night shift.

There was a car load filled with Hispanic gang kids, on the way to L.A. for a gang summit. Ever since the movie *Stand and Deliver,* where a caring young teacher taught kids advanced math, Marlow always had a secret fear of the *cholos* getting in his face and doing differential equations.

Thank God! He saw two women in UCLA sweatshirts. They looked a little too mature for freshmen. Graduate students, maybe. By the sound of their accents, they were from New Jersey or Philadelphia, and heading back to Westwood for the fall quarter. Damn, it had been a long time.

The grease of the eggs bored a hole through his gut. He looked around. There were three very large men waiting to go to the bathroom. Apparently the eggs hadn't agreed with them either. He had defended two of them on drunk driving and one on disorderly conduct. Marlow suddenly felt very claustrophobic. It wasn't just his gut. The pain now spread through his entire body and had morphed into a full-fledged panic attack.

"I've got to get out of Crater!" he said to himself, but somehow managed to pull it together before the UCLA students could see.

"You look like the only normal person here," one of them said as she walked up next to him. She was Asian and drop-dead gorgeous. "Do you mind if we join you?"

"I'm not that normal," he said with a smile.

"We'll take our chances," she said. "My name is Remy."

"My name's Jeannie," said the other one. She was an exotic beauty of an indeterminate mixture of races. She went up to exchange her order. They had given her an Egg McMuffin instead of a sausage biscuit with egg. She claimed to the counter boy quite loudly that she was lactose intolerant.

"Are you from around here?" asked Remy.

Marlow looked around for a moment. All the locals here knew him, of course, but no one would blow his cover. The prospect of leaving the county forever with two beautiful UCLA grad students sure sounded better than real life in the bottom of a Crater.

He looked over at Mr. DWI First, Mr. DWI Second and Mr. Disorderly Conduct. Mr. Disorderly Conduct waved to him.

Marlow smiled at Remy. "No. I'm not," he said. "I was just stuck here for awhile. My car broke down and I'm waiting for it to get fixed."

Marlow wasn't a lawyer anymore as he talked with Remy. Although he was a USC Trojan to the core, he did the UCLA rap. He then talked about being a writer and pitched the Yazzie trial as a script. She was on the edge of her seat.

Remy was in "the industry," getting her Masters in film, while working for her dad's agency. She hoped to be accepted into the Directing Workshop for Women over at the prestigious American Film Institute by next summer. Jeannie was a graduate nursing student. Their goal was Vegas for the night, for a wild few days before school.

He stared at Remy, then across the room at Jeannie. He would never have had the guts to approach women in their league. It was just dumb luck that the drunk drivers had taken the last table. But now he had a chance. They liked him, or at least Remy did. It wasn't just the prospect of sex with one or both of them. He had this vision of hanging out with them in L.A., going to Hollywood parties, and swing-dancing or whatever was the cool type of dancing that people in Hollywood did these days.

Remy told him that her dad was a big time agent/producer who represented actors in commercials and then launched them into movies. He was "always looking for fresh faces . . . real people. . . ."

His face was still fresh, maybe not as fresh as it had been when he was twenty-five—his year of starving and taking acting classes learning about "sense memory—but, damn it, certainly he was a real person. He would write again, audition, and earn money by being a paralegal during the days, then party with these girls at night.

Remy smiled. "It's a long way to Los Angeles. We sure could use another driver."

Then all of a sudden, it seemed like the entire highway crew got up and went back to work.

"Hey, Remy," shouted Jeannie from across the room. She finally had her food. "I got us our own table over here. . . ."

Remy joined Jeannie at the other table. Marlow suddenly found himself gifted with superhuman hearing.

"What was that all about?" Remy said. "He was cute, he was nice, he was cool. . . ."

"He had that Ted Bundy psycho-killer vibe about him," Jeannie said. "The guy just totally creeped me out."

Marlow tried to wash his hands with the napkin, but whatever was on them just wouldn't come out.

"Round two," said Diana.

Nico had taken off his jacket as if waiting for her cue. He brought over a much bigger box than Van Leit's, and made it a point to show how easy it was for him to carry. He put his box on Luna's desk, right next to Van Leit's. This time it covered Luna's application for state health insurance.

Luna looked at Nico's arms. The boy had most definitely been working out since high school. She mentally calculated all the dumbbell curls Nico had done to get arms like that.

"The out-of-town guy," he said. "Felicia's boyfriend."

"What was his name again?" asked Diana.

"Brown" said Nico, with obvious distaste.

"Thayer Brown," added Van Leit.

Thayer Brown was a handsome guy, or at least he looked that way in the photo. The first picture was a driver's license photo, and the man looked like he had arranged for the DMV to light his perfect face perfectly. Luna had never seen him in life, because she avoided the limited nightlife of the area. Thayer was a liquor rep for one of the big distributing companies and lived over in Albuquerque.

Nico ran down the brief doomed romance of Thayer Brown and Felicia. They'd met at the 66 Stars on a night when Jeremy was out of town, and soon Thayer made it through Crater every Friday night and stayed the weekend. At that time, Jeremy was driving a truck on weekends, so he had no idea.

"So let me guess," said Luna. "Jeremy sees her at the 66 Stars and says 'I'm gonna kill you, bitch' in front of the same waitress?"

They looked at Luna strangely. She should have kept her mouth shut. "You don't know the story?" asked Diana.

Nico squirmed a little, as if he were telling a dirty joke in front of a bunch of sorority girls who kept begging him and begging him to tell the world's dirtiest joke. He pretended to protest for the briefest of moments.

"One of them nuclear waste trucks overturned on I-40, so the whole interstate was closed," Nico said.

He was smiling now. The man always brushed his teeth, and she'd been such a sucker for that smile in high school.

"Jeremy actually had a legitimate job for awhile. Imagine that. He was driving a rig and had to turn around at the canyon. He goes to the Crosswinds truck stop, cause he's running real low. He actually gasses up at the truck stop. . . ."

Nico shook his head at the sheer insanity of a local actually stopping at the Crosswinds and paying the extra fifty cents a gallon for fuel rather than gassing up at the old Mustang gas station in Old Town. The others followed suit.

Diana grew impatient. "Could you speed this up, please?"

"He goes back around to take a piss, must have opened up the wrong bathroom door by mistake, the ladies room. And he sees Felicia giving head to our boy Thayer. One for the road, if you know what I mean."

Luna blushed. "Witnesses?" she asked incredulously. "I mean to the um . . . act."

"We got a DNA sample," said Nico. "She was a spitter, not a swallower."

Luna stared, dumfounded.

Van Leit started laughing.

"Could you guys stop being assholes for at least a minute," Diana said. She was definitely playing grown-up today. "I'm totally serious here! Now let's get through this."

"I was kidding," said Nico after punching his partner a good one to the side. "We got a witness to what was going on—a woman named Yoko had seen them a few minutes earlier. . . ."

"Yoko?" Luna asked.

"Don't even go there," Diana said, and her expression stifled any hint of a smile on Luna's face.

Nico continued. "But when Thayer pulled up his pants and Felicia was on her knees, they had a pretty good picture. Well Jeremy pulls Thayer out, starts beating the crap out of him, but a couple of truckers saw it all and caught up with them. It took seven of them to hold him down. Jeremy is one strong and crazy . . . umm . . . MF. All the time he's going, 'I'm gonna kill you both. I'm gonna kill you both.'"

Nico pointed to seven eyewitness statements. "A couple of these guys have priors," he said. "All of them are from out of town."

"Don't worry about it," said Diana. "Felons can have good eyesight too. And we can subpoena all of them. Everybody has to pass through Crater sometime to get to somewhere else."

Nico lifted up another box and picked up another file. "A couple of weeks later, when everyone thought things had settled down, Thayer comes out of Felicia's and that's the last he's seen alive."

He took out a picture of the dark corner of the Crosswinds. Thayer was burnt to a crisp. He was kneeling.

Nico couldn't help but smirk. "He was dead before he got burnt. That's what they're saying now. The lab guys confirmed it. His pants were down, and he was umm . . . dismembered."

Nico frowned as he picked up another file from the box. "There really isn't much physical evidence linking Jeremy to this one. But. . . ."

He searched for another piece of paper. "We do have Jeremy's confession to Shark that he was the killer."

"Did he say that?" asked Diana.

"Not in so many words," said Nico.

"Then I think the two of us need to talk to Mr. Shark and remind him of his civic duty. He's got the eight year bitch coming up, right?" Diana asked. She looked at the files. With his prior felonies, Shark did have the habitual offender enhancement of a mandatory eight years.

"You got the eight year bitch on Shark, all right," said Nico.

"Why don't you have another chat with Mr. Shark," Diana said.

"Let's see if he can cooperate more fully this time."

"You got it."

"We can only fry Jeremy once," Van Leit said. "And we'll get him for killing mama for sure. Thayer's kinda the icing on the cake."

"We'll win on Thayer too," Nico added. "We'll just have to work a little harder."

"Two down," said Diana. "One more to go."

Marlow stood outside Felicia's house. It was a double wide and, like her mother's, it was boarded up and covered with yellow tape. Marlow had met Felicia once before, years earlier. He had been representing Jeremy on a parole violation—he couldn't remember which one. Jeremy's charges blurred together over the years.

Right before court, Marlow had seen this beautiful woman in a very tight low-cut cowgirl outfit sitting in the gallery, writing down notes furiously onto a yellow pad. The only tasteful item she wore was a small silver cross that dangled perilously over her cleavage.

At first glance, he thought she was an undercover reporter—"I pretended to dress like a small town tramp in the middle of nowhere!" Her outfit couldn't possibly be real . . . but there she'd been, writing away.

He had gone over to her, introduced himself as an attorney. She seemed mildly interested, but went right back to her notes.

"Are you a reporter?" he asked, hoping to uncover a fellow exile out here. "A writer?"

"Not exactly." She didn't look up.

That's when Smoky brought Jeremy in and put him over at Counsel table.

"Could you give this to my fiancé?" She'd asked, as she'd signed "Love always, Felicia" to the bottom of the note.

Jeremy laughed when he took the note from Marlow. He could read Marlow's look of awe. "Some guys just got it and some guys just don't," he said.

Marlow had stared at Jeremy as he read Felicia's letter. Jeremy kept making eye contact with Felicia. It was like there was a laser beam connecting the two of them. She blushed every time. He blushed too, which was a sight to see. Marlow worried that if he got in the way between the electron flow it would set off some kind of invisible alarm.

Jeremy had smiled when he finished the letter. Felicia must have written him something that could magically dissolve the handcuffs and leg shackles.

The judge had called court to order and the magic must have rubbed off on Marlow. Marlow made some routine parole violation hearing into performance art, and good art at that. The courtroom quickly filled up. The clerk came in from her window, the dispatcher from her radio, even a trucker who must have driven off the interstate. They just knew. A star was being born in the Crater County courthouse.

Marlow was so damn good, the parole officer even apologized for wasting the Court's time. During his entire speech, Felicia kept staring at Marlow rather than Jeremy. Unfortunately, once the shackles were off, she hurried over to Jeremy. She kissed him so hard, that Jeremy didn't even bother to say thank you to Marlow.

"Why can't I have something like that?" Marlow had asked himself back then. "Why the hell can't I have something like that?"

Marlow didn't know what to think as he stood outside Felicia's house this morning. He felt an overpowering mixture of sadness and guilt. God, he hoped that Jeremy hadn't killed that poor sweet woman, Felicia. She was the good girl the bad boys loved at first sight and she wasn't real good at pushing them away. Damn, she didn't deserve this!

Marlow cried for a moment. Then he remembered something about the canons of ethics. He had to zealously represent Jeremy no matter what.

No matter what.

His pager went off. He didn't even have to look down to know who it was.

"Round three," said Diana. "Felicia."

Felicia's crime scene photo wasn't particularly graphic. She'd been strangled then left for dead off a deserted road. She almost looked like she had grown tired one night and decided to take a short nap inside the yellow tape of a crime scene in the middle of the desert.

Felicia's murder was by far the weakest case. Shatrock had found her face down in a ditch by the side of the road, then had called in the varsity.

"Thank God, Shatrock didn't touch her when he got there." said Nico. "Or he would have fucked up the evidence."

"What evidence?" asked Luna.

Felicia's box was the smallest of all. There really were no physical links to Jeremy, other than the bloodstain from their fight two nights earlier. There had been signs of sexual intercourse, but the person must have used a condom. There were no signs of a struggle.

"Not only is it impossible to say whether the intercourse was consensual," one expert had written. "It is impossible to know whether she was even alive at the time it occurred."

Even the men shivered when they read that.

They did have some 911 tapes from a few days prior. Felicia had kept calling in, saying she was scared of Jeremy, but whenever a cop had gone out there, she usually recanted, said how she still loved him and besides it was her fault anyway with all of her running around. There hadn't been any marks other than the one time right before her mom had died, when Van Leit had found the blood. Jeremy's blood.

At the bottom of the box, there was a small pile of some personal belongings, including a diary. Luna was about to pick it up. Diana stopped her hand. "It's from high school. Thirteen years ago. I already read it. Jeremy said he wanted to kill her, even then."

"Thirteen years ago? That's really going to get admitted into evidence," Luna said sarcastically. "Could I see if I'm in the diary? Could I?"

Diana shook her head. "I want to put it on the evidence list, just in case. This is the sort of stuff we use at the penalty phase, *after* we convict Jeremy."

"I don't get it, Di," Luna said, after the four of them had gone through the nearly empty box. "Why are you even charging Jeremy with this one?"

Diana said nothing.

"Because it makes sense," said Nico. "Jeremy kills Sarah, he gets a cross tattoo."

"He kills Thayer, he gets another cross," said Van Leit.

"Felicia was the third cross," Diana said. That was explanation enough.

Felicia had been a grade higher than Luna, in Diana's class. She'd dropped out before senior year, when she got pregnant. Later, she had miscarried. Maybe it was Jeremy's, maybe it wasn't. No one ever knew for sure.

Luna had barely known her at Crater High. Felicia ran with the bad crowd, the dropouts like Jeremy, but still kept touch with the cool crowd, which was basically Diana. Once Felicia had dropped out, Diana had adopted Luna as her new best friend.

Luna had called Felicia a tramp to Diana a few times, just to get a rise out of her. 'Felicia's a tramp! Felicia's a tramp!' Luna recited to herself.

One look at Diana's face told her that it definitely wasn't time to bring that up now. Luna looked at the picture again. From the back, Felicia's hair looked exactly like hers. A shiver went through her spine.

"There but for the grace of God, go I," she said to herself. "Watch out for those bad, bad boys."

Nico and Van Leit moved the boxes off her desk.

"I talked with Barcelona," Diana said. She looked at the blank faces of the two cops. "She's the Attorney General. We've got to get these cases through grand jury next week. Then hopefully she can send some hotshot down from special prosecutions to help us out. We definitely can't handle these on our own."

"Are we going to do all these cases at the same time?" Luna asked.

Diana shook her head. "God I hope not! I figure once we get the first conviction we just drop the others. But if we charge all three, it will scare them into a plea."

Nico laughed. "This whole case is going to be open, open, open . . . then shut, shut, shut."

"Or shit, shit, shit," said Luna.

Marlow drove slowly as he headed toward the Discount Prison. The wind seemed to push the car more than the tires. He finally forced himself to stop punching the dashboard as he drove. What the hell had he been thinking? What had possessed him to answer the stupid page?

Then he knew. He had a chance at something better, even if it was a small chance. He didn't want to pass that up, even if it meant being trapped in the middle of the Crater.

The Discount Prison was half a mile out of town. It wasn't only the Crater County Detention Center—a profit-obsessed private company ran it for all the leftover felons from the overcrowded state, federal and even foreign facilities.

Marlow hadn't known the phone number when he first came here, because the Discount Prison wasn't listed under government or prisons, since it was run by a private company. The information operator had told him that the place didn't exist.

"How could a prison just disappear?" he had demanded.

She had said nothing, as if this were normal out here—a Bermuda Triangle in the middle of a Crater that didn't really exist. Finally, Marlow remembered the name of the corrections company that ran the place and the operator had offered up a number.

He had represented a few young Crater County drunks who had gotten busted on a Friday night and had to spend the entire weekend with federal detainees in on murder and terrorism charges. The young drunks had a traumatized expression when they came out, but wouldn't say a word. When Marlow had spent his one night in jail on contempt charges, he was put in maximum security and locked in a single room for twenty-three hours straight.

The final three hundred yards to the facility weren't even paved. "The Discount Prison," he said to himself. "Where we pass the savings onto you!"

It was a Discount Prison, all right. The underfed Discount guards waved him right through. He didn't even have to flash his ID or wait for the metal detector anymore.

Jeremy waited for him in the blank walls of the attorney visiting room. The guard smoked a cigarette, right in front of the "no smoking" sign. Marlow didn't remember the guard's name. Everybody called him Smoky, not just for his Nicotine Jones, but also because in size, texture and smell he really did resemble a young grizzly after a forest fire.

"Who died?" Jeremy asked by way of greeting when he saw Marlow's melancholy face. "You still moping over the late, lamented Mr. Yazzie?"

"Hey, I don't have to come see you every time you get lonesome. I'm your lawyer, not your girlfriend."

"Wrong thing to say," Jeremy laughed. "I don't know if you've heard, but I'm suddenly single again."

Marlow didn't know how to respond to that.

"By the way, I got my target letter." Jeremy handed it to Marlow.

It was the standard letter, "Greetings. You are the target of a Crater County Grand Jury" . . . etc. Three counts of homicide in the first degree and a handful of other counts, not that the other felonies mattered in a triple death penalty case.

Grand juries were rare down here. They usually had to go all the way to Albuquerque to do them. Marlow finished the letter and looked up at his client. He'd given it to Jeremy nearly every time they met, but it certainly couldn't hurt now.

"Time for my standard little speech," he said. "I can't reveal anything you say to me; however, if you tell me one thing and then testify in court to something else, well, I have to withdraw as I cannot present perjury. So do us both a favor and say as little to me as possible."

"Blah, blah, blah," replied Jeremy. "Blah, blah, blah."

Marlow grew annoyed. He had turned around for *this*?

"So what was so important that you buzzed me over here, so important that I had to drop everything, and I mean everything? You know I'm not officially your lawyer yet."

"That's why I paged you," Jeremy said. "I have money. Cash. Like forty grand or so I can have someone give you, on top of what the public defender gives you, which we both know isn't shit."

Marlow thought about it for a second. There was only one bank in Crater, so he definitely couldn't put it in there.

"I can't ask you where you got the money, I assume."

"You assume correctly."

Marlow didn't have to think any more. Jeremy had probably got it from a good drug deal or two while he was on the road and was trying to launder it through him. "Then I can't take it."

Jeremy laughed. "An honest lawyer, that's pretty rare."

"I do what I can."

They stared at each other for a second. "Do you have any idea how big this is going to be?" Jeremy said at last. "I'm going to be bigger than Manson! I'm the 'Alleged Three Crosses Killer.' They're going to study me in schools and make some Academy Award winning movie and shit about me."

Jeremy waited for a very long beat before smiling. "And how I was wrongly accused!"

Marlow was no mind reader, but Jeremy's forehead looked like a gigantic movie screen, running clips of Jeremy on the news, law students debating Jeremy's case and then a handsome young actor playing Jeremy in a movie.

Marlow stopped the flick before the final reel. "You know that you're probably going to be dead. The case against you is strong."

"This is my only shot," Jeremy said. "Once Felicia left me, I was already dead."

Marlow stared at him. "Huh?"

"Someday you'll know what I'm talking about."

GRAND JURY

Luna couldn't bike or run this morning. Diana wasn't leaving anything to chance and had ordered her to be ready, fully dressed out in front of the Mothership.

"Is that what you're wearing?" her mother asked when Luna walked in for breakfast. Luna had always spent more on running shoes than business suits, and today, as usual, it showed. "You look like the lesbian gym teacher chaperoning the school dance."

Ruth couldn't help but adjust her daughter's outfit until it fit just so, and she had to add just the right jewelry from her private collection.

Luna wanted to protest. Twice, she nearly pushed her mother's hand away. Then she realized that this would be her mother's only flesh and blood human contact for the day.

"I'm meeting with members of the International Women's Group at noon," Ruth said, after buttoning her daughter's back. "It's about the conflict between Christianity and Islam."

Ruth was actually dressed for the occasion. Because she had a web cam, Ruth dressed up, even for phone calls.

"You guys have some good speakers?"

"Someone from Oxford University," Ruth said. She handed her daughter a cup of coffee, this one from Kenya. "Debating someone from an Islamic university in Pakistan." She pointed to her computer, which was now set up on the dining room table. "And when you're in Albuquerque, could you stop and get me whatever it takes to correct Error Message E-12?"

Luna scanned the table. Her mom had already drafted up a few questions based on some scholarly articles she had downloaded.

Unfortunately the print had run out halfway through question two. Error Message E-12 meant another cartridge for the printer, or something like that.

Luna grabbed Ruth's hand before it made it to the pocketbook. "Don't worry Mom, I'll get it."

Diana honked her horn.

"Got to run!" Luna yelled on the way out.

"Wait!" Ruth hurried to the stove and pulled out what she called "sixteen-dollar burritos with Crater Green." She'd gotten the recipe from some joint in Santa Fe and had to have most of the ingredients shipped down as well. "Crater Green" was the local brand of green chile.

"Here's some for your friends too, dear."

Jonathan Manygoats had his clinic near the Navajo capitol of Window Rock, Arizona, a couple of hours away. Marlow had met Manygoats when he called him as an expert witness in the Yazzie case. Marlow had tried to use Manygoats' diagnosis of Yazzie's "spiritual conflict" to set the stage for the psychologists to talk about Yazzie's bi-polar condition and schizophrenia. It had actually worked. Twice.

He remembered first meeting with Manygoats, back at the Discount Prison, when the young medicine man had come all the way from Window Rock to visit with Yazzie. Manygoats had been wearing a nice olive suit and, if not for the ponytail, could have passed for a young cardiologist out for the evening rather than the Navajo nation's most famous medicine man. The "yuppie shaman," Marlow had first thought dismissively, but he couldn't help but respect the man's professionalism. Manygoats had offered him a crisp business card that read "Healer, Expert Witness."

Manygoats had waited outside for him after his meeting. "I sense that you are in a spiritual prison as well," Manygoats said. "I can help you."

"As an expert witness or as a healer?" Marlow had asked skeptically.

"Both," Manygoats had smiled. "If you get the state to pay my expert witness fee, I'll throw in a few personal healings for you on the side."

Manygoats had been a good expert witness and a good healer. Not surprisingly, he was also a "talk show shrink" and had a radio show where he talked about "imbalances." Marlow had wanted to hate him at first sight, but the man was so "right on" with his opinions. Marlow regularly listened to his late-night talk show out of Albuquerque when the reception was good enough, which wasn't often.

The third judge, Judge Chaffee from Tucumcari, had disallowed the medicine man's testimony in the final trial. For some reason, Marlow's body had disallowed the healings after that.

Marlow now sat in the sweat lodge, waiting for Manygoats to get to him. It was good to get out of Crater, even if it was only for a few hours. "Blessing ways" weren't cheap, but he certainly needed a lot of blessing these days. He prayed for a moment. Maybe the grand jury wouldn't indict Jeremy on any of the counts and this whole thing would go away. He wouldn't even have to turn around. He could just get back on I-40 and keep on going until he ran out of desert.

Manygoats, now in full regalia, entered the sweat lodge and nodded to him. It was time to begin.

The Lexus wasn't really comfortable for five, but the Crater County law enforcement community really was one close family. Diana drove. No one was ever going to touch her precious car. Van Leit, with seniority as sheriff, had shotgun. And by a 4 to 1 vote, Luna, as the thinnest, was stuck in the back seat between Shatrock and Nico. She glanced nervously at the closed windows.

They munched on the "sixteen-dollar burritos," as Diana continuously warned them not to get any of the exotic cheeses on the upholstery. Luna failed of course, but quickly wiped her spot away before Diana noticed.

"Can you cook as good as your mom?" Nico asked. "That's what they always say, you can judge what a girl will look like by checking out her mom."

"Thanks, I guess," Luna said. She couldn't cook at all. For six months, Luna had lived on protein powders and energy drinks while she was training for the trials. "I don't cook. I blend, defrost or dissolve."

Despite her mother's Kenyan coffee, Luna soon found herself nodding off after twenty minutes. She always got carsick when she drove, had since she was little. She'd stayed up late the night before watching a bad movie musical about Shangri-la. She worried that like the native girl, somehow she too would age a hundred years once she passed outside the magical cocoon of the crater walls.

It hit her right as they came to the invisible crater wall at the county line.

"Could somebody open a window," she said. "I don't feel so good."

She was fine when she got back in. Nico looked at her as if it was all a ploy to get the window seat, but he didn't say anything and took the middle with a smile.

Her head soon bumped into Nico's shoulder. Nico didn't move away. She was conscious enough to feel him gently touching her hair from behind. She didn't push him away.

Luna woke up as Diana slammed on the brakes where I-40 hit the outskirts of Albuquerque. Traffic was backed up for miles at the "Big I" interchange due to the dreaded orange barrels. She was still slightly nauseous, but when she glanced at herself in Diana's rear view mirror, she was only a little worse for wear, maybe only ten years older. Well, not really. After playing with her hair and touching up her make-up, most of the years disappeared. She couldn't help but notice a bulge in Nico's pants. She smiled at him.

There were three courthouses on the corner of 4th and Lomas—District, Metro and Federal. Each courthouse was a few stories high with a dozen or so courtrooms, and each *room* saw more cases than Crater saw in a year. The three courthouses sure didn't seem like a happy family as each courthouse fought for dominance. Federal was a massive brick box, and it looked like the overbearing father. District, with its weird mix of adobe on the bottom and curved atrium ending in a bright blue circle on the top, was the mother. Her old home of Metro was the thinnest and it looked like the wallflower daughter who hid in the corner.

"*Everything's up to date in Albuquerque*," Luna sung out loud as they pulled into the lot on 3rd street. She was paraphrasing the *Kansas City* song from *Oklahoma*. "*They gone about as far as they can go. They got a building there, that's seven stories high*," Diana joined in. "*About as high's a building ought to go*."

Diana laughed out loud. "Remember when we did *Oklahoma* my sophomore year?" She couldn't help but add, "When you were a freshman."

Then she lapsed into silence. High school plays triggered a memory.

No one knew them at district court, so the very big guards made them go through the metal detectors, right next to the common criminals and their families. Shatrock's belt buckle beeped, as did his metal tipped boots. A guard ushered them up to a courtroom on the third floor, at the base of the great round atrium with countless windows looking out to the Sandia Mountains.

Grand jury was uneventful. The courtroom was nicer and bigger, but it was just a courtroom, like any other. Luna had been scared that the Albuquerque grand jurors would be dressed better she was, but thankfully they dressed like slobs just like the regular folk back out in Crater.

After endless preliminary matters, Diana went first with Van Leit on the Sarah Sanchez case. She was nervous at first, but quickly hit her stride when she realized that the jurors kept nodding at everything she said, like they were bobble-head dolls. She called a few of the experts, who talked about blood and bullets and what not.

Luna went on next with Nico, testifying about the Thayer Brown case. Her mother had edited her questions, so they flowed in a logical manner. Nico gave the answers that they had rehearsed.

If it hadn't been for Ruth, Luna didn't know how she could have made it through. Nico smiled at her the whole time, even winking when he thought the jurors weren't looking.

Luna lost her place a few times. This wasn't like her daily grind of prosecuting traffic tickets in Metro, after all. But as long as she got back on track with the notes, she was fine. The jurors kept bobbling along.

Nico said all the things he was supposed to say and it was time to break for lunch.

They had lunch at a little dive on 5th and Roma called the Corner Café, where the special was Greek chicken with rice. They saw lawyers, judges and bail bondsmen all order the chicken "to go," and added a little of the famous "Crater Green" chile on the side. It was weird seeing other lawyers again. Luna almost wanted to go up and introduce herself.

Diana locked herself in the ladies' room at twelve forty-five. After a polite interval, Luna knocked on the door.

"You still alive in there, Di?" She could hear the sound of retching. The toilet flushed and Diana came out, only a little the worse for wear. Luna wiped a smudge off her face.

"You'll do fine," she said.

"Just trying to lose weight," Di said. "I want to be thin like you, Luna my love." Luna didn't know whether she was kidding or not.

After lunch, Di called Shatrock to the stand on Felicia's case. Luna could see why Di had been so nervous. The old cop stuttered a few times, and got across his points to prove the elements of the case. Shatrock made a lot of wild-eyed speculations that any half decent defense attorney would have stopped mid-syllable. Diana wasn't on her game either. She tensed whenever she mentioned Felicia's name. Luna passed her a few notes when she got bogged down.

But it didn't matter; the grand jury wouldn't fail to indict when they had two solid cases already, right?

Di finally rested and the grand jury shuffled out to their deliberation room. The "one big happy family" waited together at the table. A short time, later the grand jurors shuffled back in.

Still bobbling, they returned a "true bill" on all three counts. Diana pumped her fist in triumph. She looked like she'd been the one on trial and had just heard the magic words.

"Good work, Di," Luna said to her, giving her a hug. By the time they walked out into the great atrium, the sun had long since set. Luna shivered, even though she was still inside the building. They could all feel the warm air moving out of the mass of windows into the cold night.

It was dark when the "blessing way" ceremony was finished. Marlow felt a little better, a little more blessed. He gave his gift to the Manygoats, and got back into his car. He was going to call a contact he had at district court, but he knew it was unnecessary.

He knew.

Luna slept all the way back. She knew that it was good thing that she couldn't remember her dreams. As Diana dropped her back at the ranch, Luna shivered. She had forgotten the cartridge for her mother's printer. Oh well. She'd get it the next time.

SELECTION OF COUNSEL

Attorney General Barcelona clearly was not happy to see them as she ushered Diana and Luna into her office. Barcelona was a petite woman in her fifties, immaculately draped in the scarves of the Santa Fe style. She favored enormous heels and a very high chair so she could still tower over all she encountered.

Diana didn't like looking up at Barcelona as she took one of the very low chairs reserved for visitors. She had been rejected from the Attorney General's office seven straight times, a streak that stretched back to a summer internship at NMSU. She couldn't help but have mixed feelings as she sat in her low, uncomfortable chair. If she'd received a job offer here, she probably never would have gone back to being Queen of the Crater.

She was hardly queen here, or even a princess. The attorney general hardly looked at them. She kept staring at some files in front of her.

Luna was also a little intimidated in Barcelona's presence. She had been an intern in the civil division one summer, but Ross Peters must have gotten the "Don't hire Luna Cruz" mantra all the way to Barcelona. She'd also been rejected for every opening since.

Luna's eyes didn't look up at Barcelona. After a few trips to the bathroom, she finally felt over her morning car sickness. Instead of feeling older, she felt like a little girl out with her mother on a trip with the promise of a "big surprise at the end if you're good."

Her eyes eagerly stared out the window at the beautiful snow-capped *Sangre de Christo* mountains and the majestic southwestern architecture below. She watched a few Native American artisans walk by in their brightly colored vests. It was good to see contrast in a landscape for a change, instead of Crater's unchanging sea of gray land, gray buildings and gray people.

The Attorney General's office was in a sprawling two-story adobe building just south of the Santa Fe plaza. Right across the street was the state capitol building, the Roundhouse. Luna remembered doing "Youth and Government," playing the junior state legislator from the great county of Crater for a few days on the Senate side of the Roundhouse.

Meeting the Attorney General felt like a school trip, although she knew she wouldn't be able to sneak over to Señor Murphy's for piñon brittle.

"My hands are tied," Barcelona said after the last of the files. "Do you know how many death penalty cases we have right now?"

"We have three death penalty cases in one county," said Diana. "I have one staff attorney, Luna over here. She's done one year at Metro, but has never done a felony jury trial. I did Yazzie twice and got my ass kicked by Marlow, and that's back when I had a full office. You had to send us someone from special prosecutions to bail us out. You're going to have to do that again."

Barcelona forced a polite smile. "There are some political realities you have to face in an election year. My budget is stretched to the bone and all my top players have already been assigned."

There was a map with some pins in, showing the locations of all the special prosecutions going down in the state right now. Diana had some knowledge of the demographics of the state, and couldn't help but notice that they were all in politically important toss-up districts. It certainly didn't help that she and Barcelona were in different parties.

"I already told you this over the phone," Barcelona added. "I don't know why you even made the trip all the way up here."

Diana smiled. "I'm sure I'll think of a reason."

The state Public Defender's office was on the north side of the plaza, on Guadalupe Street. It was also in a two-story adobe building, but the building wasn't even a third of the size of the Attorney General's office. That was not an accident.

Marlow met with Carmelita Herrera, who was in charge of contract attorneys. Carmelita was a large woman, who evidently enjoyed each of the several bowls of hard candies she kept on her desk.

Marlow showed Herrera the three police reports. The dates were circled on each. "See, each crime took place on a different date. That's three separate crimes, three separate cases."

As if to make a point, he grabbed a butterscotch from one bowl, a jelly bean from the second, and a piece of piñon brittle from the third.

Herrera laughed. She picked up the indictment. "One indictment makes it one case. Flat fee. They can only kill him once, you know. You're lucky we're letting you have it as it is."

"Lucky?"

"You basically bankrupted the department's expert witness budget with Yazzie alone. First you had to put on that medicine man, Mr. Many-Sheep, to talk about Yazzie's evil spirits."

"It was Manygoats, and I was establishing that my client was bi-polar. I backed that up with the real therapists."

"You backed that up with real therapists, all right. What are you, an employment agency? How many shrinks did you have to get to try to prove bi-polar on that drunk? Shrinks don't grow on trees. Neither do investigators."

Marlow did the costs in his head. With the amount of preparation he'd have to do, he'd get less than minimum wage. Especially since he was going to have to do all the investigations himself. Shrinks and investigators didn't grow on trees, but apparently contract lawyers did. Marlow grimaced. If he was such a great lawyer, why did he always get screwed when it came time to be paid? Baby lawyers in L.A. got more for pleading shoplifters than he was getting on three damn death penalty trials.

"You knew what I was going to say, so why did you come all the way up here?" Herrera asked.

"I need any excuse to get out of Crater."

"I don't blame you."

"And besides, I have some friends up here I need to see."

• • • • •

Luna and Di walked by some galleries and passed the Señor Murphy's location at the gigantic *La Fonda* hotel. The hotel was a modern recreation of the ancient Taos Pueblo. The old Diana was back and it was like old times again. They got lost on the plaza a few times as they looked at the natives selling jewelry at the Palace of the Governors. Finally they had to ask directions in order to find the Coyote Café for lunch.

"Your tax dollars at work," Di said with a smile, checking to make sure she had brought her official county credit card. They both smiled as they sat down in the luxurious hardback chairs in a dining room that looked like one of the happier paintings of Frida Kahlo.

Luna looked at the menu. If her mother hadn't heard about the sixteen-dollar burrito from the Coyote Café, she might as well have. Suddenly Luna felt a tap on her shoulder. She turned around and was surprised to find Marlow.

"What the hell are you doing up here?" she asked. "Have you been following us?"

"I'll take the fifth," he said. "I had to come up here anyway, and I heard you were in town, and I knew this was Di's favorite place."

He looked over at Diana. Diana was not happy to see him, but couldn't resist his charm. "Why don't you join us?"

Lunch was delicious of course. All their meals involved *chipotle*, even though they weren't quite sure whether that was animal, vegetable, or mineral. They talked about everything but the case. Marlow and Luna finally established that they had both gone to the same Colorado-USC game and thus had both been in the L.A. Coliseum at the same time.

Luna looked over at Marlow for a moment and couldn't help but think that Nico had never left the state of New Mexico in his life. Neither had Diana, for that matter.

Marlow reached for his wallet, but Di put it all on her tab.

"We're doing plea negotiations," she said. "This is official county business."

After lunch, the three of them wandered through the Santa Fe galleries together. In one, they saw a bronze statue of a nude man that went for forty thousand dollars. "I know the artist who owns this gallery. She's a good friend of mine." Diana said.

As if on cue, an attractive woman in her forties, with a leather vest and red scarf, came over to Diana and gave her a hug.

"Do you want this one?" the artist asked. "You can complete the set."

"Forty thousand is more than you pay me," Luna told Diana with a smile. "And Mr. Bronze here won't do cross-examinations for you. Right, Di?"

Diana laughed. Luna laughed with her. It was good to have her friend back, instead of her boss. "Some other time," Diana said, and hustled them out the door.

They got candy at Señor Murphy's and Luna insisted that Marlow try the piñon brittle. By the second bite, he was a piñon brittle addict. Marlow and Luna had to pool their resources to get a second bar.

"I would go so totally broke if I lived here," said Luna. As they walked out onto the narrow confines of Old Santa Fe Trail, she saw galleries and boutiques in every direction.

Marlow stopped suddenly, a Eureka moment. "Well, there's a special store here in *Santa Fe.*" He pronounced the city's name in the traditional style. "A store that only the locals know about. It's right on Cerrillos Road, and if you want to find the real Land of Enchantment, it is the only true place to visit in all of *Santa Fe.* The Pueblo Indians who've been here for forty thousand years, the Spanish who came up with Coronado, they swear by it, and are forbidden by a sacred blood oath to tell of it to any tourist. It's the most popular store in the world."

Diana smiled an evil smile. She too knew of this special and magical place here in the heart of the City Different. She looked down at her county credit card, then over at Marlow. "Take me to this enchanted store."

The Santa Fe Wal-Mart was unusually crowded when they got there, and indeed filled with the real *Nuevo Mexico.* Marlow nearly stepped on a few boisterous children yelling in Spanish as they hurtled through the aisles. Diana got a shopping cart for the three of them and bought all the things they couldn't get back in Crater, which was nearly everything. Luna knew she had to buy something for her mother, but she couldn't for the life of herself remember what it was.

Next, they drove to the Santa Fe outlets (at Cerrillos and I-25) and searched for their "arraignment outfits."

Diana felt that often the arraignment outfit was even more important than the one for jury selection. "It's the outfit the TV stations show you in whenever they talk about the case. You have a bad outfit and they'll show it in your obituary."

She smiled. "I think the taxpayers want me to have the best damn arraignment outfit that their tax dollars can buy."

Marlow was about to protest.

"Hey at least I'm at an outlet store," Diana continued. "I'm saving my constituents money!"

Marlow went over to the tie tables. Diana had snagged all the store's clerks, so he was on his own. Luna went over and joined him in his quest for the perfect tie. They started on the cheap table, but quickly moved leftward to the prime real estate.

"This one says 'not guilty by reason of insanity,'" she said of a green and purple Jerry Garcia abstract number.

"Who's insane, the lawyer or the client?" he said, as he took the tie out her hands, and put it back on the table. As his fingers brushed against hers, there was the slightest spark from the Indian rug beneath their feet.

Must be the dry Santa Fe air, they both thought.

They finally narrowed it down to two ties, a conservative blue one and a wild red one. Marlow wanted to avoid the look of indecision in front of Luna, so he bounced a check and bought them both.

Luna looked over at him, and he knew he'd have to help her out with her potential arraignment outfits in the next store over. Luna had her mom's credit card at the place, so she was in the mood to spend. She felt momentarily guilty, but her mom wanted her to look nice, right?

Instead of hating the task, Marlow was awed by her beauty as she tried on each outfit. Luna had a running commentary about each suit.

"This one says staff lawyer for a 'French whorehouse,'" she said of one with a particularly short skirt. "But I do like showing a little leg."

"More like 'assistant staff lawyer,'" he said. "It's like Ally McBeal on acid."

She finally found a gray one, the right mix of style and substance, but she still felt uneasy as she twirled around. Marlow the ancient question "Does this make my butt look fat?"

"I don't know how I'm supposed to answer that," he said. "I have a duty to my client. . . ."

"Is that a yes?"

"Luna, I think it is scientifically impossible for your butt to look fat."

Marlow helped Luna with her packages as they left the store. They could hear the whizzing of traffic on I-25 as they went out into the parking lot. The sun had already set and the state workers were getting onto the freeway to take them to Albuquerque or Rio Rancho. Luna and Marlow were about to give each other a hug good bye, but stopped suddenly when they noticed Diana give them both a stern look.

"This was fun," she said. "We'll have to do this again in . . . about six months. Once we get back to Crater and do arraignment tomorrow, everything changes."

PRE-ARRAIGNMENT PLEA

Luna had tea with Ruth right before going to bed. Ruth swore that it had no caffeine, but Luna couldn't help but feel jumpy.

"What's wrong, Luna my love?" Ruth asked. Even after all the time away, she could read her daughter's body language.

"I met somebody," Luna said.

"You don't look that happy about it."

Luna looked at her mom. Did she really want to go into the whole Marlow thing? She didn't even know what the whole Marlow thing was, or what it could be, or much less what she wanted it to be. Her mother had always wanted her to find someone perfect, and no one ever had been.

"He's the lawyer on the other side of the case," she said at last. "That makes things complicated."

"Luna, even if he wasn't the lawyer on the other side of the case, things are always complicated with you when it comes to relationships."

They talked for the next few hours. Somehow her mother made her feel both better and worse at the same time. Better in that her mom thought Luna's birthright was a great life and great men—that doctor from South Africa, that movie producer, that lawyer who also wrote novels. Strangely, Luna also felt worse at the end of their talk, because she knew was so far away from getting this birthright. Ruth desperately wanted to turn her lonely house into the grand-Mothership. Luna couldn't help but blame herself for letting her mother down.

Luna did not sleep at all that night. Her mom must have been mistaken about the caffeine in the tea.

• • • • •

Marlow met with Jeremy right before lights out. Jeremy had paged him and he'd thought that it was a medical emergency. The guard had said something about Jeremy getting stabbed.

Marlow was almost disappointed to find Jeremy in good health. "Well?" he said.

"I just wanted to know something." Jeremy said.

"What?"

"Have you ever been in love?"

Marlow frowned. "Huh?"

"Love, love, love," said Jeremy, in that DJ voice, as if he were about to launch into a dedication to a lonely listener. "Have you ever been in love?"

"None of your business," Marlow replied, too quickly. "I have no idea why we're even talking about this."

"I'm talking about the kind of love where, for the first time in your life, somebody doesn't see you as a piece of shit."

"I'm still a piece of shit, so—"

"I'm talking about how a woman loves you so much that you start changing. You take a real job and start making something of yourself for the first time in your life, just to be worthy of her. You ever had somebody like that?"

"Not yet."

Jeremy kept going. "But then this woman, she's got a mother and, even though you've changed, this mother starts telling your woman that you're like totally a bad influence and shit. And this woman, this perfect woman, starts pulling away from you."

Marlow said nothing. Smoky finished his cigarette while pretending not to listen. Jeremy stood up and came up to Marlow's ear, almost whispering.

"So while you're away, your woman starts shacking up with this other guy, the type of guy that you can never be. Not just shacking up, but giving head to this asshole, right in front of your face. That probably wasn't the only one in town. Who the hell knows who this tramp had been with?

"And everybody in this whole town is laughing at you. And pretty soon, you lose your job because you're so pissed off and you're back on the junk again, back in that cave you thought you had left forever, but it's worse this time. Worse because you've finally tasted what life is all about."

Smoky had long stopped pretending not to listen as Jeremy continued. "So then you decide you've got to do something about it. Something that will change everything forever."

"How many times have I told you to watch what the hell you say in here?" Marlow yelled.

Jeremy shrugged and sat down again. "I'm just wondering if you've ever been in love like that."

"No, Jeremy," Marlow said at last, trying to keep a poker face. "I haven't ever been in love like that."

"Bullshit. You're in love like that right now and you don't even know it. With that new DA. I knew her back in high school. The late lamented Crater High. Go Comets!"

Jeremy smiled at Marlow for a moment. He gave a glance to Smoky, who threw him a cigarette and a match. He took one puff, then two. "By the way," he said in a very low voice. "Back in high school, before I dropped out. . . ."

Marlow leaned forward to hear him.

Jeremy blew smoke in his face. "Your girl Luna gave me the best damn blow job I ever had!"

Marlow surprised himself. Suddenly, he had his hands around Jeremy's neck and was squeezing the shit out of him. Smoky hurried over and separated the two of them.

Marlow took a breath. "Just a little privileged conversation between attorney and client."

Smoky backed off. Marlow looked over at Smoky. Smoky was a drinking buddy of Jeremy's, when Jeremy was on the outs. If it really did come down to a fight, whose side would he really be on?

Jeremy had somehow managed to keep his cigarette lit. He took another puff. "So I guess you're in love after all."

Marlow didn't respond. What could he say?

Jeremy laughed again. "By the way, I was just shitting you

about everything I just said . . . as far as you know. . . ."

"Then what the hell is this all about?"

"I want a real lawyer this time," Jeremy said. "Some emotion, real fucking emotion. Everybody's been saying 'don't get Marlow anymore. He's lost it. Yazzie's dead and buried now. And ever since that third trial, he's been moping around town whimpering about getting the hell out of Crater.'"

Marlow certainly couldn't argue with that.

"But I was here for the first two rounds where you saved that poor motherfucker's red ass. I was in court with you a few times on my own shit and I heard some things. Then when I was driving a rig and made it out to Tohatchi, one of them Navajo medicine mans, that real young one-the "yuppie shaman," you called him, well, he was blessing the rig next to me, some shit like that. When they started talking English again, the yuppie shaman was going on about how you'd gone all the way out there to get some kind of blessing that let you summon up the skin walkers or the waiting coyote trickster spirits, or whatever that shit is. That's what you are, the Trickster Lawyer."

"He's exaggerating." Marlow said, with a slight smile. "I had a bad back and I didn't want to spring for a chiropractor."

"I just wanted to mess with you a little to see if you still got it." Jeremy rubbed the skin around his neck. "You still got it. Now I want you to take whatever that is you got, and use it to save my ass."

"I will zealously represent you," Marlow said. He couldn't think of anything else to say.

"Tomorrow is the big day. There are going to be a couple of hundred thousand people out there," he said. "We get book rights, we get movie rights, we get everything. Tomorrow this poor nobody from Crater becomes 'Jeremy Jones—the Accused Three Crosses Killer!'"

"Well, Mr. Accused Three Crosses Killer, it's time for me to go." He didn't want to ask, but couldn't resist when he saw Jeremy's hand. "What's with the tattoo?"

"Just my way of getting in touch with my feelings," Jeremy smiled. "You should try it sometime."

ARRAIGNMENT

Luna's bike had something to say to her on next morning's ride—you will never make it out of Crater alive. The bike did not want to cross the county line and the winds kept increasing every time she got close to the invisible crater wall. Once she turned around, the bike magically came back to life and whisked her home.

There wasn't any coffee, Kenyan or otherwise, when she went over to the Mothership for breakfast, still in her workout clothes. She had totally spaced buying groceries at the Santa Fe Wal-Mart. Worse, she was supposed to get her mom that printer cartridge when she'd seen E-12 message flashing on Ruth's screen.

"I'd been ordering my groceries by Internet," her mother explained. "Now somehow, the whole computer is infected." Ruth giggled. "I tried chicken soup, but it got caught in the disk drive."

Luna felt instantly guilty. "I'm sorry I forgot, and I'm not going to get out any time soon. I'm pretty much stuck here in Crater for the next few weeks."

Ruth sighed. She suddenly looked much older. The Internet was the only way she could pretend that she wasn't stuck in Crater. The pain in her knees made travel harder with every day, especially in the mornings. Ruth didn't say anything, just walked a few more steps and precariously stepped onto a ladder, grimacing in pain as she reached for something. When she brought it down, she was all smiles again.

"*Chai* tea from one of my ambassador friends over in China," she said.

"Don't worry, Mom, I'll cook it up for both of us." Luna made a pot for two.

The two of them enjoyed their *chai* and talked about Ruth's trip to the Great Wall a few years ago. Luna looked at her watch. Diana would arrive any minute. She hadn't wanted Luna to ride her bike to work today. No second chair of hers would appear on camera in spandex and a sports bra.

"Got to change," Luna said.

Within moments she stood in front of her mother in the new suit. "How do you like my arraignment outfit? Got it in Santa Fe."

"Turn around," Ruth said.

Her mother didn't say anything for a long moment. Luna suddenly felt like she was twelve again, during the awkward tomboy summer when she nearly overdosed trying to bulk up on protein powder, as she started to learn about training. It was only two weeks, eighteen years ago, but Luna always thought of that twelve-year-old fat girl at times like this. What had her mom called her? Oh, yes, the lesbian gym teacher chaperoning the school dance.

"Mom?"

Luna turned around and saw that her mother was crying. "I know you really wanted to make the Olympics and you were so hurt when it all went wrong. But you look like a real lawyer now. I'm so proud."

Honk!

Diana had to honk only once. Luna hurried out. "I just wish you could see me in action." She slammed the door behind her and hurried out to the impatient Diana.

Marlow stared at the two ties, red or blue? He finally went with blue—Charlie Sheen in the first half of *Wall Street,* was the image he wanted. He hurried out to the car. Marlow's hands stumbled with nervousness. He fiddled with the keys in the ignition, but his car didn't start no matter how much he fiddled. Battery probably, but he couldn't think of anyone to call to give him a jump. He had defended the town's one tow truck driver on a DWI, a private case. The man still owed him a few hundred, but Marlow certainly didn't want to see the man now, drunk or sober.

He lived only a half-mile from the court yet it always seemed further than that. The wind in Crater was strange; no matter which direction you went in, it always seemed to be blowing you back toward the center of town as if reflected back off the imaginary Crater walls. He tied his tie as he walked, and it fluttered in the wind.

As Marlow approached the court, he could hear echoes of people talking. This would be big!

"Nice tie," one of the clerks said.

"Luna, you have excellent taste," he thought. He decided that he would wear the blue tie for the rest of the trial.

A crowd, a great majority of the county's population, had gathered at the Justice Center before dawn. They were all in their Sunday best; as this was the biggest deal to hit Crater since the Yazzie case. That case had made national news and had touched off the big debate about Native American drinking and driving. A national news magazine had even called Crater "Drunktown, USA" back then.

There was a debate among the women over newscasters. Some liked the cute guy from NBC with the tight butt and others were partial to that guy from CNN who had the broad shoulders. One guy had gone from covering Drunktown, directly to the United Nations.

They could see a news van come down from the freeway right as the sun rose. Somebody must be the early bird. A woman sighed when she saw it was only Albuquerque Channel 8. New Mexico's Most Enchanting Newscast just wasn't enchanting enough for the crowd. They waited for the rest of the vans to come. Then they waited a few more minutes.

Nothing . . . then more nothing. . . .

Several crowd members looked at their watches. CNN was really cutting it close, and Fox should have at least sent a chopper.

Channel 8's Stephanie Park Live staked out her camera position with her burly cameraman. She was no longer an anchor, just a reporter and the lowest one on the totem pole. She hadn't tested particularly well and had been exiled out to do big murder trials in the boonies. Her assignment was to shoot the pool footage and give it to the other channels, but none of them seemed that interested. The courtroom hadn't opened yet, so she had to set up outside.

Diana and Luna arrived. Diana wore her new arraignment outfit. Luna walked a few paces behind, as if hiding behind Diana. To Stephanie, Luna looked like a little girl, while Diana came across as a real woman.

Stephanie smiled at Diana. "We meet again."

"Is this it?" Diana asked. "I thought there would be more media."

"It's just me," Stephanie said. "Sorry."

Diana smiled. Perhaps this was better. They shook hands.

Stephanie set up a tight shot, With her pretty face, Diana actually looked better in a close-up than from the middle distance which revealed too much of her bulk. Diana gave a statement about Sarah and Thayer. When she came to Felicia, she cried a bit when she mentioned the "community's great loss."

Stephanie was a good judge of character. The tear was definitely real and would look great for the noon news that catered to the female stay at home viewers. "I still got it," she said to herself.

Once filming stopped, Diana went to the side and waited for the bailiff to open the court.

Smoky drove Jeremy up to the courthouse in the dusty white SUV. The crowd surged over to the van as if Jeremy was the second coming, and the SUV was a golden chariot. Stephanie quickly had the cameraman try to shoot over the heads of the swarm of people.

The door opened. Jeremy smiled when he saw the crowd. He waved at Shark and flashed his tattoo at him. Shark gave him a thumbs-up.

Marlow hurried over and joined Jeremy.

"Don't look so happy," Marlow said to him. Marlow couldn't help but remember when he had joked with a client right before a hearing in Albuquerque in order to ease the tensions. A reporter had captured the laughter on tape, made it seem like both Marlow and his client hadn't been taking the whole crime thing seriously.

"But it was definitely no laughing matter at sentencing," the reporter had intoned at five-thirty, six, ten and then at both seven-twenty-six and seven fifty-six during the local cut-aways the next morning. . . .

Marlow's admonition to Jeremy had little effect. Jeremy basked in the glow of his fans. Then Jeremy saw the single van, and the one solitary, weather-beaten camera from the local Albuquerque station. One van, one camera. So much for the Academy Award winning movie.

He was about to give a statement to Stephanie when Marlow hurried over, still out of breath from jogging over. "My client has no comment at this time," he yelled between gasps.

The courtroom still was not open. They all had to wait outside the door in a cramped courtyard.

The bailiff must have overslept and the judge was still nowhere to be found. Diana had some time to kill, so she went back over to Stephanie. "I don't get it. How come there's nobody here?"

"Let's face it," Stephanie said. "This case has no hook. Three poor Mexicans dead in the middle of nowhere. It's not particularly compelling to the national media."

Stephanie meant to whisper, she really did, but years of voice training made even her whispers came across loud enough for the crowd to hear. There was a hissing from the crowd. That had been the worst possible insult, "not compelling."

Jeremy heard her, as did Marlow.

"Not compelling?" Jeremy asked. "What the hell does that mean?"

"It means that no one will ever do a movie about your life," Marlow said. "She said you need some kind of a hook."

"Not compelling, not compelling, not compelling," Jeremy mumbled under his breath.

Marlow stared at Jeremy. He tried to read that forehead, but couldn't entirely succeed. The wheels in Jeremy's mind were turning. Something was up.

"I'll find a hook," Jeremy said. He looked over at Marlow. "You gotta help me here. You want this as much as I do."

Marlow didn't know if he wanted to ask Jeremy what the hell he was talking about. Somehow, he felt he already knew.

And Jeremy was right.

Jeremy spotted Diana in her arraignment outfit, an island of silk in a sea of blue jeans and flannel. "Is Diana's mother still in town?" Just as he said that, the doors opened. There was a crush of humanity toward the door. Most of the people outweighed Luna by a hundred pounds, and she found herself pushed closer to Jeremy, Marlow and Smoky.

"Does Diana have a boyfriend?" Jeremy asked her. She stared at him, not knowing what the hell he was talking about. Luckily, Nico came over and escorted her to safety.

Once the bailiff reluctantly opened the court, Luna looked around at her new home for the next few months. The main courtroom, Courtroom A, was halfway through renovation. With state and county budget cuts, it would stay "halfway" for at least another year. The trial would be held in horrible Courtroom B. Courtroom B had once been the county's only two racquetball courts when the justice center had doubled as a community center.

The wall between the courts had come down and a few windows had been put in. The room had been painted a nice earth tone. Luna still found herself worrying that a stray racquetball would bounce the wrong way and cream her in the head.

Diana joined her at the table. Nico and Shatrock sat at the tables behind her. Luna tried to joke with Diana, but her sophomore friend was long gone. Diana was her boss again.

Marlow and Jeremy sat at the other table. Right behind Jeremy was Smoky. Smoky had done this so many times before for Jeremy that they moved and stood together with an easy familiarity—an old married couple where the husband just happened to wear shackles and handcuffs.

Judge Benally had driven in all the way from Albuquerque. The county was still waiting for a regular judge of its own, since the last Judge Crater had retired three years ago. Benally was one of the three who made the long boring drive out here on I-40.

He had been Yazzie's judge in the first mistrial, before the state had wisely recused him from the second. The Judge was currently on the short list for State Supreme Court judges, so Diana figured it was wise not to recuse him again.

On first glance, Marlow could not have asked for anyone better. Benally, who was part Navajo and part yet-to-be-determined, had done legal aid on the Navajo reservation before getting to the bench. At fifty, he had a long gray ponytail, and a yin-yang tattoo on his gavel hand. Yin seemed to win, most of the time-whenever possible, defendants usually got probation.

The Judge was also famous for his "buts" during sentencing. He would go on and give a long-winded speech on how he would sentence someone to twenty years, *but* he would suspend the sentence to the *three hours* time served in booking.

On his first appearance before Benally, Marlow had an embezzler, an elderly woman, Juana Mendoza, who had skimmed a few grand off the town's annual bake sale. Marlow pled her straight up to all five counts. The woman had no record and had developed a little nickel slot problem late in life that led her astray. Marlow didn't mind spending a few weekends over at the Sandia Casino as part of his research to understand the woman's problems. At his urging, Juana had sold her car to repay every single cent of the money, and then gone to a twenty-eight day gambling program at her own expense.

Judge Benally went on about how the woman had betrayed the public trust and how her taking even a few thousand dollars was the same as the corporations taking billions. He was going to give the maximum time on each of the counts, something like a hundred years, and hoped she'd never get out alive—

Marlow didn't know that a "but" was coming. "That's total bullshit, Your Honor," he had yelled. "My client will die in jail!"

And then, right on cue, Juana had a heart attack that nearly killed her. She was given probation, of course, but Marlow did have to spend a night in jail at the Discount Prison.

The Judge most definitely had a "yang" side as well. It was rumored that he carried a loaded revolver with him to all the courthouses where there were no metal detectors, such as the courthouse in Crater. No one had ever tested his yang side to that point. Yet.

Luna heard some rustling in the gallery. This was supposed to be a closed hearing. She turned around to see Van Leit carry her mother up the steps and into the courtroom.

Luna flushed. "Mom, you don't have to be here, I'm not saying anything!" she said, after Ruth was seated beside her.

Ruth didn't reply. She didn't have to.

Luna was a bit disappointed that it was Van Leit who escorted her mother. The thought of Van Leit inside the Mothership somehow gave her the creeps.

"I'm fine," Ruth said after a minute, as if to reassure her daughter.

Jeremy stared at them, looked at her mother as if he had somehow seen her before.

Suddenly Luna felt very vulnerable. She took her mother's hand. "Are you sure you're all right here?" she asked.

"I'm fine," said her mother. "I wouldn't miss this for the world."

Marlow went over and shook Ruth's hand. "Your daughter will be a great asset to the legal community here."

"Officer Van Leit's been telling me all about you, Mr. Marlow," Ruth said. "So you'd better be nice to my daughter."

Marlow looked at her, then over at the smirking Van Leit. It was hard to tell if she was kidding or not. He took no chances and quickly went back to stand next to Jeremy.

Van Leit turned his smirk up a few notches. At least the man was sober for court.

The bailiff was an elderly gentleman named Quintana who was bent like a question mark. Quintana called the Court to order and everybody rose. This time, the judge was neither yin nor yang, just business. It was only arraignment, after all.

He called the case of *State of New Mexico* v. *Jeremy Jones.* Diana mumbled some things. Marlow then waived the reading of the charges and entered a plea of not guilty. A pre-trial date was set and a few preliminary discovery orders were signed.

That was it.

Smoky took Jeremy away before Benally banged the final gavel.

Marlow looked over at Luna in her new outfit. She looked amazing. He was about to say something to her but after a look at Diana and the courtroom dynamics, he thought better of it.

Luna looked over at Marlow. Diana had meant business with this whole "everything will be different when we get back" speech. She certainly didn't want to get on Diana's bad side right now.

"See you in six months," she said to him with a smile. He was about to help her with her boxes, but Nico came over and grabbed them.

"Don't want you seeing anything you're not supposed to be seeing," he said.

"If it's something I'm not supposed to be seeing then it's not going to be admissible, asshole," Marlow responded.

Nico shook his head and effortlessly picked up all the boxes in both of his hands. He didn't actually say, "See if you can lift this much, asshole," but he might as well have.

Back at Luna's office, Nico now had what seemed like hundreds of pounds of her property in the air. Damn, those arms looked good when they were holding her things. She wasn't surprised a few moments later when she found herself agreeing to dinner that night.

Marlow liked to eat when he studied. He'd always gained a few pounds studying at Denny's on Jefferson Boulevard during finals week at USC. He was at the Rustler's Steakhouse and had ordered the Big Bad Rustler steak, bloody with extra green chile, just like Jeremy would have. He went without the salad bar, which was an intimidating two dollars extra. He then tried to find the bottom of the bottomless glass of iced tea, as he delved into the nearly bottomless boxes of evidence.

As he went through all the witness statements, he read each one aloud and pretended to do all of the voices.

Marlow then got to the witness statement of Katy Baca.

"Jeremy said 'I'm gonna kill you, bitch,' to Felicia's mother, right as I was bringing them beer. Then he looked right at her and said 'I hope you got that, because I mean that and I never lie.'"

He tried to imitate Jeremy's voice "I'm going to kill you, bitch. I hope you got that because I mean that and I never lie."

Not quite right.

"I'm going to kill you, bitch. I hope you got that, because I mean that and I never lie."

Again. . . .

Back at the Mothership, Ruth wanted to improvise with her remaining groceries and spices to make something nice to celebrate Luna's first day in court as a real lawyer, but Luna would have none of it.

"I didn't really say anything, Mom," she said. "I'll just whip up something over at the guest house."

"But it's a start, dear." Ruth said "And—"

Luna stopped the conversation. "Mom I have to do something for you for all you've done for me. Before I forget. . . ."

She quickly found the computer company's technical hotline number to order the missing part. Unfortunately, the hotline was on Eastern Standard Time and the techs had gone to wherever they went for the night. She'd have to handle it tomorrow. She left a message after the beep.

Luna hurried over to the guesthouse right at seven. Nico was already sitting on her front step. He had turned the Corvette's lights off, and left it parked on the road. There was a full moon as they walked to the car.

Inside the car, she was seventeen all over again, going to prom with the cool senior boy. She never got carsick in the Corvette, maybe her lust for Nico acted as an antacid. . . .

Once more, she was a cross country runner and a drama geek, Diana was her only friend, and she sometimes wondered if that was because she was the second richest girl in Crater. The weekend before the prom, Diana had told her what to expect. She blushed even more when she thought about that night.

And Nico was a senior football stud in a rented tux. He had long flowing hair back then. She had her whole life ahead of her, all over again. She would be the Olympic champion and live in a mansion in the hills somewhere. It had to be someplace hilly, not flat like Crater. Nico would be a professional football player or a senator, maybe both at the same time.

Marlow, what's a Marlow?

The Nico of today was on his best behavior. He kept his hands to himself and tried not to say anything stupid for at least the first few minutes. A song came on the radio on the oldies station.

"Summer lovin' happened so fast," she sang along with Olivia Newton John.

"Summer lovin' got me some ASS," Nico sang with John Travolta.

Oh well, thought Luna, Nico was still pretty darn cute.

There were only a handful of restaurants in town, but Rustler's was the only one that didn't deep-fry everything and then smother it with cheese. The place was practically empty. The locals had gone to bed, and the travelers must have kept traveling. They saw Marlow in his booth before he saw them.

"I'm gonna kill you, bitch. I hope you got that, because I mean that and I never lie," he kept saying over and over again.

"I hope you're not talking to me," Luna called out.

Marlow was un-nerved and fumbled with his silverware when he saw her.

"Just getting into character," he said strangely. Then he saw Nico.

Nico made it a point to put his arm tightly around Luna's waist. "Well, Mr. Character . . . you were just leaving, right?"

Marlow called for the check, paid it quickly and then went out into the wind.

After a few quick shots with beer chasers, Luna had forgotten about the momentary unpleasantness. Nico told her quite clearly that Jeremy had been full of crap. He had never said anything about her virtue, her honor, or any of her body parts to Jeremy.

She looked in his eyes. He meant it. When he proposed a toast "to the best lawyer in Crater," she had to down another. Luna hadn't had anything to drink in a long time. At her size, she could barely hold her liquor, especially since she hadn't taken her mom up on her offer of a gourmet meal.

The "Rodeo Sweetheart" steak was surprisingly good, and she had to take Nico up on his offer of yet another toast, this one to "the lawyer with the best ass in Crater."

At about eight-thirty, the lights flickered off. Blackouts were not unusual in Crater. The Discount Prison was notorious for overtaxing the limited supply. The host of the restaurant quickly brought out candles and ordered them to drink some champagne so it wouldn't go bad.

On the ride home, she definitely felt buzzed. For a moment, Luna thought she'd been drugged, then she realized that she'd downed all those beers all by herself. Because of her legal training, she tried to compute her blood alcohol level, but failed utterly. She wanted to be that hot high school junior girl with the senior boy again. She nuzzled next to Nico's big left shoulder. He soon had her hand on his thigh and she didn't push it away.

The lights were still off all over town and the whole place had an eerie and quiet feel. The ranch was dark, of course. She thought about checking in on her mom, but the door was closed and everything looked in order at the house. Nico walked her to the door. He didn't attempt to kiss her. He just turned away and walked slowly, very slowly back toward the car.

He did look good in the moonlight.

"Where the hell are you going?" she asked. "I'm scared of the dark."

Soon they were inside her house and had lit some candles. Both of their clothes were quickly off. "So do I look better now or back in high school?"

Nico looked at her toned body. The swimming had definitely balanced out the running. The legs were more muscular, so they looked a little longer. The abs were even flatter and the chest was now a little higher from the hours she'd spent in the pool. He certainly didn't mind her streamlined look down below.

"No contest," he said, still in awe. "You look way better now!"

"Right answer." She looked at him. His years of bench pressing had certainly paid off. He wasn't the smartest guy, or the nicest either, but when she saw him naked again that sure didn't matter very much.

They did it in every room of the guesthouse, and in every position that they could remember. It had been a long, long time for her. With the exception of the spandex, she'd lived like a nun during her training. Yet for some reason, right at a moment of climax, she thought of Marlow.

Several times, she'd thought she heard rustling outside, as if someone were watching them. She swore she saw Marlow's face, lit up by the moonlight, looking through her window. It turned her on even more. But when she looked again, the face was gone, if it had ever been there at all. With another thrust, she was back in the moment again, back with Nico and it was wonderful. After the third climax, they took a deep breath and lay there. Luna fell asleep in Nico's arms.

CRASH!

At first she thought it was a dream, but Nico nearly dropped her as he shot up from bed. He got out of her and quickly put his pants on.

They heard three gunshots.

"That's coming from the Mothership!"

Nico quickly got his gun and put on his shirt. "Stay here," he said.

"Like hell." She grabbed a bathrobe and followed him across the yard to the Mothership. The door was open, swinging in the slight breeze.

"Mom!" Luna yelled. "Are you all right?"

She tried to flip on the lights. Still nothing.

Nico hurried to the bedroom with his gun drawn. He felt a breeze. Someone had escaped out the window. At first glance, Ruth looked all right. She was on her knees praying.

"I think it's all right." He lit a candle, moved forward a step, then froze.

Luna hurried in, stood for a moment looking, and then screamed. She had seen the three small, distinct bloodstains on the pillow. "Mom!" She hurried toward her mom.

Nico stopped her. "Don't touch her. It's a crime scene."

"Is she. . . .?"

Ruth wasn't moving. She was propped against the side of the bed. Nico didn't have to say anything for a long while.

Nico held Luna in his arms for a few moments, until she forced herself to look around and take in the sight of her dead mother.

"It's just like Sarah Sanchez," she said in total disbelief. "Just like Felicia's mother."

It wasn't just the alcohol that made Luna throw up. As what seemed like every ounce of food that she had ever eaten came up, she couldn't believe that this had really happened. She would never see her mother again. Her mother would never see her win, her mother would never see her married and somehow her mother would never be able to print. It was all her fault. All her fault. All her fault.

Marlow woke up the next morning with a pain in his hand. He couldn't remember why it hurt so badly. Then he looked down and saw the tattoo of a small cross between his thumb and forefinger.

Just like Jeremy.

MOTION HEARING

Luna swam for the next five months straight, coming up for air only a few moments a day. At least that's what it felt like.

After the funeral, she'd stopped biking. She didn't like the way her bike looked at her anymore. She had switched to swimming every day in the dirty pond locals whimsically called Crater Lake, although it seemed much more crater than lake. There were hot springs in the center of the lake, so the lake always stayed warm. Swimming just felt right. She liked the darkness of the dirty waters and the slightly sulfuric smell from the hot springs. Somehow, the dirt and acid had an exfoliating effect on her skin and on her heart.

There had been a brief flutter of activity in the investigation of Ruth's death, but there was no evidence linking it to anyone. Supposedly, a couple of prisoners had not been accounted for during the blackout, but it seemed unlikely that someone would break out of jail, do a killing, then break back in. Nico and Van Leit would always tell her that they'd heard some new lead, but the lead never led to anything.

There had also been a lot of media attention. The reporters couldn't help but point out that Ruth's killing mirrored that of Sarah Sanchez. When they flashed the two women's pictures side by side, Ruth with her good grooming looked like the "after" picture, while the slightly overweight Sarah looked like the "before."

Two days of news, then the story quickly faded. It had taken place in Crater County, after all, and Albuquerque had an even more shocking triple murder the next week. Luna certainly didn't give any interviews and, once it became obvious that the killer wouldn't be caught, neither did Diana.

Ruth's funeral had been a blur. Luna had sat there in the town's only cemetery as her mother was lowered next to her father. She'd had a rabbi come in all the way from Albuquerque, because her mom would have liked it that way. None of her mother's relatives had made it out for the funeral. Luna had lost touch with them long ago, so it was probably just as well. Her father's nurse from the clinic showed up, an Asian woman. She had always wondered if her father had had an affair with the woman, but didn't want to think about that now. . . .

Luna had never chosen between her parent's faiths, but she prayed that her mother had gone to a better place. She decided to sing a song for her mother. Her first choice was *Amazing Grace* but her mother had hated that, really hated that. Luna then tried her hand at a few Hebrew folk songs, but none of them worked either.

She finally settled on *Somewhere Over the Rainbow*. She could barely get to *"way up high"* before the tears engulfed her and she had to stop. She cried for three days straight, and then it was back to the lake. The only place she felt comfortable anymore was underwater.

Otherwise, there'd been an amazing lack of crime during those five months. Luna kept living in the satellite, her piles of papers and clothing getting bigger and bigger as the months passed. She had Nico board up the Mothership. The man sure did know how to pound a nail.

She went to work on Monday mornings. She went through the files with Diana, screening the petty thieveries and the drunk driving cases. In the afternoon, she stared at the wall and played on the Internet until it was time to go home. She had no idea what she did on Tuesdays and Wednesdays.

A judge came to town on Thursdays. She and Marlow would meet in the mornings in the courthouse hallway and resolve whatever was on the docket. They stared at each other for about five seconds a case, then knew exactly what to put in the plea agreement. She had better handwriting, so she would write it up. He would explain it impatiently to his client, have him initial every line, then sign it. She would sign it and give it to whichever judge had come for the occasion. Each judge made a point of carefully deliberating before saying the sentence for the day.

It was like clockwork. She'd utter the words, "We've achieved a plea and disposition in this matter, Your Honor," on the pleas and, "We ask that you impose the balance of the term," when the criminal screwed up. The judge would pretend to stare at the document for a good thirty seconds before signing off on the paperwork.

They would have lunch every Thursday at the Rustler and talk about the little they'd heard about the outside world. They'd invariably complain about some lawyer neither of them knew who had just won a million dollars suing someone for something or other. She'd complain about Diana, and tell stories about her high school romps with Nico. She complained about friends getting married, he complained about not having friends.

They often played "name the crime," as they looked around the Rustler.

"The waitress is a shoplifter, right?" Luna said one day about their server. "Or was that her sister?"

"I had the sister on a solicitation charge, one county over," he said. "They had a whole ring. Japanese tourists came here on sex tours. It was like a regular Pat Pong 1 in Bangkok over here for awhile."

Marlow knew about Pat Pong 1 from the writing underneath one of Jeremy's tattoos of a lovely Asian lass. Jeremy had never been there, but he had told him some crazy stories.

Luna stared at him until he started laughing. She quickly joined him. The idea of anyone having sex in the entire three county area was particularly amusing to both of them.

"You remind me of my gay friend I had in college," she said. "We always used to have lunch and laugh and laugh."

"Except that I'm not gay and I really want to have sex with you," he said in a way that could be construed as a joke.

She would always giggle when he made remarks like that. He would always groan that she didn't take him seriously. At the end of lunch, he would ask her out for the weekend and she would always say that it was "too early."

He'd always ask if she was all right.

She would always reply, "Not yet. I still miss my mother way too much. . . ." and she suddenly got the desire to be alone under the water again.

Then it was back to the lake for an afternoon swim in the acidic bath of Crater Lake. Then home to the satellite for two and half hours of bad television, then another hour or so of not falling asleep and listening to the Jonathan Manygoats radio show on the rare occasions when the outside radio waves made it over the Crater walls. The man was so right on.

She would go out for a drink with Nico every Friday night, catch a slight buzz, and then politely leave him at the door. Nico, for his part, would then head out to the 66 Tears and sleep with one of three different waitresses. She knew about it, but she didn't care. Sex and jealousy over sex were the last two things on her mind at this time.

Every Saturday, Luna took a really long bike ride—thirty miles to the nearest movie theater and saw whatever movie was playing, even if it wasn't in English. She bought her bare necessities for the week. She slept all day Sundays and read trashy novels in her waking moments.

Swimming was all that mattered. She soon got into a groove and clocked the same fifty minutes day in and day out. Lately, she had cut it down to forty-five. Her brain just couldn't handle one more lap.

Marlow had gone to Ruth's funeral, and he had wondered for a few moments if he was invisible. No one talked to him, much less acknowledged him. He sat in the back, away from the small crowd. Inside the bathroom, Nico gave him a good shove on the way to sink, but he didn't respond.

Nico had noticed a band-aid over the tattoo.

"Knife fight," Marlow had responded.

Nico hadn't laughed. It didn't matter. No clues had been found at the crime scene, and lawyers don't kill people, do they?

The next day, Nico and Van Leit had questioned him about his whereabouts during the night of Ruth's murder, just to rile him. Marlow showed them a copy of a rented movie as an alibi and that was enough for them. Van Leit had joked about the band-aid, but didn't bother to follow through on it.

They'd quickly gone back to their escaped prisoner theory. They even went over to the Discount Prison, and questioned Jeremy about his whereabouts. They tried to do it without Marlow present, but Jeremy wouldn't say a word until Marlow was at his side.

"So, do you have something to say to us," Van Leit had asked, "after making us wait for an hour?"

"I'm invoking the 'ain't saying shit' clause of the constitution," Jeremy had replied.

"There was a black-out for about an hour," Nico said. "You could have made it over there and killed Ruth, then made it back here and no one would have noticed."

"Don't you think it's more likely that someone on the outside did the killing?" asked Jeremy. "Maybe my man Marlow over here."

Marlow had abruptly ended the interview.

And that was it for excitement. Marlow couldn't make it on the diet of public defender misdemeanors alone, so he soon took paying cases all around the three county area. Unfortunately, when you live on an interstate, you have to subsist on speeding cases. He'd get about a hundred bucks to say, "We ask for a deferred sentence."

Usually he'd get the deferred sentence and court costs. Occasionally, someone went way too fast, thirty miles over. In those cases, the sentences weren't deferred and the clients paid the full fines and got points on their records. His clients would then say, "What the hell did I need you for?" and often canceled their checks.

Considering the miles he put on his car, the hours he'd wait for the judges or the defendants and, of course, the occasional canceled check, he was barely making minimum wage.

The biggest thrill he had was a death threat from a mentally ill transient woman he represented on a solicitation charge from the truck stop. She had seven kids, seven DWIs and seven teeth, so he was surprised that she had any takers. When he told the woman he recommended that she plead guilty, she warned him, "I can have you killed. My old boyfriend's a hired killer, and he'll kill you if I give him a blow job."

Marlow couldn't help but stare at the seven teeth. But the woman wasn't done yet. "Oh damn, he's out in Aguilar, and his truck got wrecked . . . I'll have to blow someone else to drive him to Crater."

As he and Luna had the woman committed to the state hospital, Marlow couldn't help but think that life was very cheap out here in the Crater. As he thought of the value of human life, he then thought of poor Ruth.

He put the thought out of his head as he sent applications to every job advertised in the *Bar Bulletin*. At some point, about three months in, he crossed the magic line from being under-qualified for the jobs advertised to being overqualified. On his 36th birthday, which he spent alone with some rented movies, he realized that he was officially not a member of the young lawyer's division any more.

He didn't go out in town Friday nights, because he wanted to avoid Nico and Luna. He went out to the 66 Tears every Saturday, hoping to see Luna there, alone. She never came. When she didn't come, he would ask the one attractive woman in town, Gianna Mendoza, to dance. She would dance with him once, then politely go off with her boyfriend. Marlow thought that the woman also saw Nico on the side and that pissed him off even more. He would then go home and watch *Saturday Night Live* and fall asleep on his couch right after the show's "Weekend Update" segment.

About once a month he would drive to Albuquerque, usually making it too late to hit the afternoon crowd and too early for the late night. He went out to the Eclipse Gentleman's Club in Albuquerque and even got the beautiful May Lee to give him her e-mail. He met her at UNM one Wednesday night and was disappointed that she wanted him to edit her term paper on the effects of a smoking ban rather than something having to do with sex. He made a vow to avoid Albuquerque altogether after that.

Other than his lunch with Luna, the highlight of his week was his Tuesday meeting with Jeremy. Jeremy had become the "cool friend" that his parents never would have let him hang out with. As for Jeremy himself, there was an initial rush as he read the stories in the paper about his case, but once the spotlight turned elsewhere, he soon found himself in the rut of jail life and jail drugs. It was as if the cell door clanged shut one night, and he woke up five months later.

Marlow found Jeremy entertaining—whether his stories were true or not was beside the point. Jeremy claimed to have slept with almost every woman in town, although he never mentioned whether Luna was one of them. Jeremy also mentioned that this was the world's easiest town to get laid in. "Maybe you could help me write a 'How to Get Laid in Crater' book," he often teased.

Marlow didn't argue. Half the time, he wanted to ask Jeremy to really write a book on "How to Get Laid in Crater," if it included a good chapter on winning the heart of a certain Crater County prosecutor.

Jeremy also claimed to have been in some type of "Special Forces" in the Marines "where the government gave me a medal for killing, instead of trying to lock me up."

It was during a Tuesday meeting that Jeremy reminded him that the six-month rule was about to run.

"They'll have to let me go," Jeremy said. It was hard to tell whether he sounded happy or sad about that. More like he was groggy, not just from the drugs, more like he had just woken up from a five month sleep.

Marlow was embarrassed that he had completely forgotten about the six-month rule. He'd put both the case and his life on hold. He hadn't filed a single motion since the funeral. Jeremy had become a friend in here; he had forgotten that he was also a client.

"I'll file it tomorrow."

Diana had enjoyed those five months, probably because she always managed to find a way to get out of Crater on "official" DA business. Diana hated to admit it, but after Ruth's death, she found she had suddenly become a hot commodity when she went to Santa

Fe for the government meetings. Somehow, business also took her to the desert when it was too cold in Crater and the mountains when it was too hot. That all ended when she got Marlow's Motion to Dismiss. She suddenly fell apart. She cited some "emotional stress" and booked herself into a twenty-eight day place near Tucson. She was set to leave on the day before the motion hearing.

So much for Diana being able to play grown-up, Luna thought. Diana gave no explanation for her behavior to Luna on the day before she was scheduled to leave. "I just can't handle things right now," was all she could offer to Luna at first. Diana didn't drink much, and certainly couldn't do drugs out here, so it must have been something else.

"Let's just say Felicia's death hit me a lot harder than I thought," she said. "And I can't really handle doing the case right now. I won't be much good for anyone."

"Hey Di," Luna tried to offer by way of rebuttal. "My mom just died!"

Diana began crying. She hugged Luna tight. "Luna my love, I am such a bitch, aren't I?"

"It's all right," said Luna. "What's really going on here?"

"I can't tell you until this is all over," she said. "But I need you, Luna. I need you to do this for me."

Luna was always a sucker for tears. "Okay, Di," she said. "I'll do it."

"Luna, I'm only going to be gone for twenty-eight days. All you have to do is get the ball rolling. I'll be ready soon."

Luna knew she would have to split the cases into three. All she had to do was win Sarah Sanchez's case, the easy one, and it wouldn't matter whether Diana came back or not. She also didn't want Marlow to bring in all the uncertainty inherent in the Thayer Brown or Felicia cases and confuse the jury so much that they acquitted on all three counts.

The motion hearing was on a Thursday. First off, Judge Benally signed Marlow's new discovery order, which basically allowed him to do anything he wanted, including "simulations," whatever the hell *that* meant. The Judge was definitely in his "yin" mode.

Next, Luna argued her Motion to Sever the three cases. She cited the venerable case of *State* v. *Rondeau*, which authorized the severance under the old rules, and carefully pointed out Committee Comments to the rules which said splitting the cases could be allowed under "judicial discretion." She spoke in a monotone as she read from the rule book.

Marlow began to argue that splitting the cases would prejudice his client and argued *State* v. *Montano*, an even older decision.

Benally smiled. "It is my discretion. That's why I helped write that rule. I always remember what my old football coach used to say. 'We play them one game at a time.' I'll sever the cases, but let you do one opening argument for all three in the interest of judicial economy."

"In that case, your honor, I would ask for three separate jury pools," Marlow said.

"Mr. Marlow, you want me to get three separate jury pools in this county? I don't think you've even got eleven people total without felony convictions who bother to register for driver's licenses so they can be in *one* jury pool."

"In that case," Marlow said, not missing a beat, "I would make a motion for a change of venue so that we could get three larger juror pools."

"You're making a motion *now*? Mr. Marlow, what have you been doing for the last five months?"

Marlow didn't answer.

"I'm waiting," the Judge said again.

"Uh . . . preparing for trial."

"Don't you think that maybe if you wanted a change of venue, you should have filed something earlier? And Ms. Cruz, I am amazed that you actually cited *Rondeau* for your case allowing severance. Couldn't you find a more recent case?"

Neither Luna nor Marlow bothered to respond. Benally was clearly in his yang mode now.

Finally, they came to Marlow's Motion to Dismiss. The rule

would run by next Thursday and the state had done nothing to move this case forward at all.

The Judge stared at Luna. Luna didn't know what to say. This was all Diana's responsibility. There was no way she could be ready by next week. She asked for an extension in light of Diana's illness or whatever the hell it was.

Benally smiled. "You did pass the bar, didn't you, Ms. Cruz?"

"Mum . . . yes."

"Then this case goes to trial on Monday," he said. "I look forward to spending a few weeks in your lovely town. But please be aware that I hate long trials and I do hate people who waste my time!"

As he rose, he looked at Marlow and Luna. "Counsel, please approach."

They walked up to him.

"I must say that never in my twenty years on the bench have I ever seen such shoddy preparation in a death penalty case from both sides. What the hell do you people do out here?"

PRE-TRIAL DISCOVERY

Marlow decided it was time to make up for five months of lost time. He got himself back into character on Friday night. He bleached his hair first, then spiked it with some "extreme gel" he'd had since Halloween back in high school. Marlow looked at himself. He could be a Marine, or perhaps one of those white gangster rappers that were always dodging bullets and dating movie stars. Now that he had bulked up a bit, he could almost pass for Jeremy's older brother.

He put on a black sweatshirt, black leather jacket and a hood. He looked down at his band-aid and took it off. He looked at the cross and felt alive again. Then he put on black gloves. If he was a white gangster rapper, then it was showtime at the Apollo.

Friday night, Luna cried as she went over the files. When she looked at Felicia's mother, Sarah, she saw her own mother, Ruth. The pain knifed her through the heart. She could just barely type a few lines before breaking into tears, so she settled for putting together the most basic outline of the elements of the three cases.

She talked with Diana over the phone. Diana was now in Tucson, and six-forty-five to seven P.M. was Diana's one monitored phone call for the night.

"I don't think I can do this by myself, Di."

Diana was little help. She talked about what Luna needed to do to "resolve her issues," or at least that's what Luna thought she heard. Diana kept talking. It sounded like she was trying to impress whoever was monitoring the call.

"'Resolve my issues?'" Luna interrupted, about five minutes in.

"I'm one the who has to come up with a *voir dire* and an opening statement while you find your inner child or whatever the hell you're doing."

"That's not fair, Luna my love," Diana said. "I've got some real issues I need to deal with here. You need to take emotional ownership of what is within your power."

Luna thought she heard whomever monitored Diana's calls say, "Good point," to Diana. Luna felt outnumbered. It was no use arguing.

"Well what do you want me to do?" she asked at last.

"Just be yourself, dear." Diana replied. The counselor abruptly drew her away from the phone.

CLICK!

Luna wished she had twenty-eight days worth of insurance to find her real self. She had no choice but to do what she always did when she was tired. She just recited her notes over and over again until she had something resembling *voir dire* of the potential jurors. She spent another hour developing a semblance of an opening statement.

Marlow didn't drive on this night. He didn't like carrying a bag with him, so he made his way though the back alleys of town on foot. This was nearly a fatal mistake. Crater was known for its big dogs and, in every yard, a new dog barked at him. Still he quickly realized that the dogs barked at everything. It took the sound of the dogs gnawing human flesh to actually rouse an owner out of bed to investigate.

When he got to the yard, he accidentally tripped over something, a bike maybe. The noise startled a neighbor, and his dog. A light went on, the dog barked, but soon there was only blackness and silence.

Luna's eyes finally gave out before her brain did. It took a moment for Luna to realize that she was still writing questions, but her eyes were already closed. It was time for bed, perchance to dream about *voir dire* questions and opening statements. She didn't shower, just plopped into bed with her clothes on.

She quickly realized that her brain did not want to write the questions in her dreams. She cried in her sleep. "I'm sorry, Mom," she said. "I miss you."

Marlow went to the window and pried it open with a screwdriver. The victim would be in the bedroom on the other side and wouldn't be able to hear. Marlow had little trouble lifting the window from its perch. Working out sure had its benefits. A little creaky, but still quiet enough. No one would hear.

A splinter hit his right hand, next to his wrist, in the area of exposed flesh between where the sweatshirt ended and the glove began. He wasn't bleeding enough, so he jammed the splinter in better. The blood flowed a little more. Good.

Marlow heard a car coming from the other direction. It sounded like Nico's Corvette. He looked at his watch. Shit. Inside the house, he crept past the stairs and toward the bedroom. The wooden floor still creaked a bit, but Marlow quickly found a carpet that deadened the sound.

Perfect.

He looked down at his watch. He was way too slow. Headlights shone outside. The car was almost to the driveway by now. He reached into his bag. There was the white rag for the chloroform. Then the small revolver. . . .

He opened the bedroom door slowly. The lights were off. He slid on the floor toward the bed. Which way would a killer go? Straight, a little toward the right.

He made it, then slid up and took the white rag and poured something on it. He leaned against the night table next to the bed to help himself up.

A drop of blood fell on it. Good.

Marlow looked down at the bed, then at the rag in his left hand. Bring it down! Bring it down! But he couldn't do it. He hesitated for just a moment. His arms tensed up. Too late!

Suddenly a flashlight lit him up good, just as the rag was about to hit.

"Freeze, asshole!" He didn't have to turn to know Nico's voice, and that it was Nico and Van Leit behind him.

"Freeze, or I'll blow your brains out," Van Leit said.

Marlow's muscles felt like rocks. He couldn't move even if he wanted to.

"What the hell are you doing in Sarah Sanchez's house?" Nico asked.

Nico lit a candle. The power had been turned off months ago. The light illuminated Sarah Sanchez's small room and the candlelight danced over a picture of Sarah and her daughter, Felicia, posing with kids at a day care center. The bed was empty, of course, but it had been made, as if its owner would soon be returning.

Marlow's arms finally rebelled, stretched out on their own accord.

"I said, don't move!" Van Leit said.

"Look in my bag," Marlow said.

"Lie on the floor, with your hands over your head," Nico replied.

"Do I really have to?"

"Fuck yes you do, you little puke," said Van Leit.

Van Leit pantomimed kicking Marlow, so Marlow reluctantly complied.

"I see a gun in here," Nico said as he went through the bag. "That's aggravated burglary right there! Twenty years."

"Look at the order, asshole," Marlow said. "It's next to the gun."

Nico shined the light at a piece of paper. "Pre-Trial Discovery Order," he read aloud, very, very slowly.

"Here let me help you with the big words," Marlow said. "Paragraph three. 'Defense Counsel is permitted to do reasonable simulations at the crime scenes.' Sarah Sanchez's home is a crime scene. I'm doing a reasonable simulation."

"I bet you do a lot of simulating," said Nico.

"Put down the gun," said Marlow. "I've got work to do."

The cops re-read the order as if looking for a loophole that would allow them to beat the crap out of Marlow. They couldn't find one.

"We're keeping an eye on you," said Van Leit.

Marlow did not respond. The cops glared at him for another minute, then reluctantly left.

Marlow picked up the candle and wandered around the room. He looked down at the drop of blood at the night table. One drop of blood. His drop of blood. He was confused.

He opened his bag and shined a light on Van Leit's original police report in the Sarah Sanchez case. A drop of blood was found on the dresser.

Dresser?

Marlow swung the flashlight around. The dresser was halfway across the room, on his left side. Jeremy was right-handed. There would be no reason whatsoever that blood from his wrist would end up on the dresser all the way over there while he was crawling to the bedroom.

Something wasn't right . . . there was only one way that a drop of blood could get there.

VOIR DIRE

For one of the very few times in her adult life, Luna missed her morning exercise. Since she could not swim, she tried to memorize the life histories of every single potential juror in the pool of forty-five. She even knew their birthdays. She had known most of them, of course, and had even prosecuted a few for various misdemeanors.

Julie Woodford, the woman who sold coffee in the courthouse, was definitely on the "out" list. Woodford was very conservative, always gave Luna a dirty look when she saw the spandex. Or perhaps it was Luna carrying a thermos filled with some exotic gourmet blend. Would Woodford vote to acquit in a death penalty case, just because Luna didn't buy coffee from her? Luna didn't want to put it to the test.

This had to be a "death penalty qualified" jury as well. Jurors had to say that they'd be willing to impose the death penalty if the evidence warranted it to get on a jury. Several of the jurors had left the death penalty box blank.

Marlow didn't even go over the juror list. All jurors were bad. Every single one of them would hate his client. And that woman he knew from the 66 Stars, Gianna Mendoza, would probably fry Jeremy because Marlow was a lousy dancer.

"Who hates you the least?" he asked his client in a morning meeting. "Just put an X down."

Jeremy noticed that a few of the people had left the death penalty box blank. "I guess all *these* people like me," he said.

"They'll probably be tossed," Marlow replied. He explained about death penalty qualified juries.

"Can't you do something about that?" Jeremy asked. "Get those people on!"

Marlow smiled, as he thought of something. "I can when the time comes."

"So do you have a theory of the case yet?"

Marlow smiled. "My theory is that you were set up, and you're such an asshole that you're still taking credit for the whole three crosses deal, just so you can be famous."

Jeremy smiled. He didn't say anything for a long while.

Marlow stared at him. There were times when he could read Jeremy. Now was not one of them. What the hell was Jeremy thinking?

"I like that theory," Jeremy said at last.

Marlow spent the rest of his morning with the Yazzie files. It was almost as if the old Navajo had come back to him in a dream that night and told him to look for some magic fetish in that lisping voice. Marlow couldn't help but do his Harrison Yazzie imitation.

Pretty soon the entire floor was littered with the remains of the Yazzie file all over the floor. He turned over page after page to no avail.

He checked his watch. Shit. It was time to go. He went to his car, still frustrated. He had a flat tire. Some local kid must have slashed it. Then he realized there were hardly any local kids, not anymore. He remembered that he had run over some glass yesterday. A broken bottle.

A broken bottle. That was it!

A broken bottle of Jack Daniels found in Harrison Yazzie's car just might hold the key to walking Jeremy Jones on murder.

Judge Benally called the case of *State* v. *Jeremy Jones* to order in the Crater County Middle School gymnasium. There was nowhere else to put the thirty-nine juror candidates (eight had called in sick, including the woman he had danced with at the 66 Stars), certainly not in the two converted racquetball courts that now constituted Courtroom B. The Judge sat on the tip-off circle, Luna to his right and Marlow with Jeremy and Smoky to his left. The juror candidates sat in the stands.

"Where's the media?" Jeremy asked Marlow, clearly disappointed.

"They can't be here for juror selection," Marlow couldn't help but rub it in. "You're just not compelling."

At the sound of those horrible words, Jeremy muttered something under his breath.

After some preliminaries from the Judge, Luna went first. She knew every answer from the questionnaires, but she had to get them on the record.

"Does anyone here have any moral qualms about inflicting the death penalty?"

"I do," said Jeremy. "I have some serious moral qualms."

One of the jurors chuckled. For one moment, Jeremy was not a triple murderer; he was once again the class cut-up. Luna sighed. No one wants to give a fatal injection to the class cut-up. She turned to Benally, as if expecting him to give Jeremy a warning. He didn't say anything.

Marlow took advantage. "I have qualms as well," he said. "Is that spelled with a 'q'?"

More jurors laughed this time.

Benally banged his gavel sharply. "Ladies and gentlemen, let's continue."

That's when Luna felt a panic attack coming on. She looked up at the crowd. Even though she knew these people, not just from their questionnaires, but from seeing them every day of the last six months, they were now strangers to her—hostile strangers. They laughed at her for being too stupid, for being too slow, for being a failure.

She was back in Boulder for the Olympic trials. There was a crowd at the Boulder reservoir, but none of them were there for her. Joelle Bouganville, the boat person from Haiti turned Olympian, was the favorite. She looked at the other women competing against her. Every single one of them had been a state champion from a bigger state than hers. Every single one had a more expensive bike. Every single one had learned to swim in a real body of water.

Who the hell was she to compete with these women, some stupid skinny, half-breed bitch from Crater County, wherever the hell that was?

Somehow her body kicked into gear and she had survived, even held her own. She made up some serious time on the biking, and at one point she was even in the lead during the run.

But then, on the hill going up Broadway, Luna's legs just quit and Bouganville and the rest of the pack caught up to her. She stayed with the pack right as it got into Folsom Field, CU's gigantic football stadium, to face every triathlon fan in America. When she saw those folks, they knew she was a fake, just a skinny little nobody from the bottom of a crater. They could see right through her.

Her body quit, right as she made it onto the field for the final lap. She started walking. No, it wasn't her legs. It wasn't her lungs. She just didn't have it in her. The pack drifted away and soon others passed her from behind. Luna walked past the finish line, dead last.

She heard booing in the stand. Sixty thousand people booing. She would realize later the booing was for the winner, Bouganville, who went by the *nom de guerre* of Boo Boo.

Boo! Boo! Sixty thousand people couldn't be wrong. Boo! Boo!

Bang! Bang!

It was the sound of Judge Benally's gavel back at the middle school gymnasium.

"Ms. Cruz, please continue," the Judge ordered again. "The last time I checked, jury duty was not a life sentence."

Luna looked down at her papers. All she would have to do is read the questions she had already written. Just as she had at the start of the triathlon, she went into autopilot.

"Ms. Plata, happy birthday, by the way."

"Thank you," said Corinne Plata ("waitress at the Rustler"

according to her questionnaire). "You have a son who is a policeman in Albuquerque. Do you think you can still be fair and impartial when listening to the testimony of law enforcement?"

"I can."

"Mr. Kellner ("retired miner"), your son is a cop up in Santa Fe. Same question."

"I can."

Much like the biking portion of the Olympic trials, Luna had no recollection of the next hour. She went through all the jurors and usually got all the answers she expected.

She also had to question the jurors on whether they knew the victims. There was a quick consensus: Sarah Sanchez was a saint, they didn't know Thayer Brown, and as for Felicia, they didn't come out and use the word "tramp," but she certainly had quite a reputation for getting around town. Many of the older woman disapproved.

"I know she slept around," said Jennifer Lithgow (a "retired homemaker and fitness consultant"), "but that didn't mean she should be killed."

"Thank you, Ms. Lithgow," was her only response.

There was a woman, a Lisa Chaves (no employment listed), who had more tattoos than Luna had ever seen. "Tattoos might be an issue in this case, Ms. Chaves. Can you be fair and impartial?"

"Yes."

From the woman's facial expression, Luna should have pressed the issue, but she was busy going down the line.

Finally she got to the death penalty exclusion. A few jurors said they still weren't sure what they would do. She was about to inquire further when Benally banged the gavel down.

"I think the state has exhausted the time provided," Benally said, "as well as exhausted the Court and the jurors."

There was a murmur of agreement from the jurors. Even after an hour or so, she felt she didn't know them any better. Luna expected them to start booing her for her performance.

Marlow stood up. Jeremy stood beside him. Both were dressed in nice blue pinstripe suits. For a moment, they looked like twins with their bleached blond hair.

Luna couldn't help but stare. There was something about Marlow now. He was turning into something else.

Marlow smiled at the jurors. The jurors smiled back at him. "My client has lived here all of his life," Marlow said. "Many of you know him."

The jurors nodded in agreement.

"I know several of you left the death penalty box blank," he said. "If you are not capable of voting for the death penalty, you can be excluded from the jury."

There was a look of disappointment from those jurors.

"My client's accused of three brutal crimes, and if he is found guilty of these crimes, it is your duty to put him to death."

Without hesitation, Marlow jumped into the crowd like a talk show host. He put his hand on Mr. Jones. "Sir, you left the death penalty box blank, but if my client's found guilty beyond a reasonable doubt, you could do it, right?"

"If he's guilty. . . ."

Marlow looked at him.

Jones smiled. "Beyond a reasonable doubt."

He went over to Ms. Plata. He didn't even repeat the question. "Beyond a reasonable doubt," she said, smiling.

He leaped over to Lisa Chaves, whom he couldn't help but dub the Illustrated Woman. "I couldn't sentence a man to death," she said.

Marlow frowned for a moment. He wanted the Illustrated Woman on the jury badly, but if she couldn't pull the trigger, even Luna could have her tossed for cause.

Suddenly the Illustrated Woman smiled. If this was a talk show, she now knew how she could get the free set of steak knives. "However, if his guilt was proven beyond a reasonable doubt, then I'd personally give him the juice!"

The audience laughed. Jeremy pantomimed dying and they laughed some more. Benally let it go on for just a second too long before banging the gavel.

Marlow turned toward him. "Your Honor, I like all these guys!

If I had my way, I'd have every single one of them on the jury."

Marlow's *voir dire* had taken all of four minutes.

Benally took the combatants into the boy's locker, which doubled as the Judge's chambers for this part of the trial. Luna had a notebook pad listing the pros and cons of each juror. Marlow had a short list that Jeremy had given him. Jeremy and Smoky came along behind him.

Quintana, the bailiff, read each name. Luna needed a few seconds to make her decision to keep the juror or strike the juror. She had a limited number of "pre-emptive strikes," then for the remaining potential jurors that she didn't like, she had to make an argument that a juror should be "struck for cause."

Jeremy just gave Marlow a nudge and a wink for the jurors. By the time it came to the Illustrated Woman, Luna had lost her pre-emptive strikes. She tried to strike the woman for cause. "She said she couldn't put him to death." Luna pointed out. "I don't think that—"

"*Au contraire,*" Jeremy said before she could get much further. "She said she could do it, all right. That is if you could prove me guilty beyond a reasonable doubt. She'd give me the juice herself."

"He's right," Marlow said.

"Thank you, Mr. Marlow," Benally said. "Please remember that you are the lawyer here, not your client, and I expect you to do the majority of the talking."

Jeremy smiled. He was about to make a joke, but thought better of it.

"I'll allow Ms. Chaves to remain on the jury." He smiled. "She does have the most interesting body art. The Court might focus its attention there, if Counsel gets too long-winded."

Benally called the jurors back into the gymnasium and told them who the lucky ones were. Luna was surprised. Back in Metro Court, people groaned when they were on the jury, it was a day of minimum wage work instead of being engineers or bankers. Here, each juror smiled when they were selected. The Illustrated Woman smiled the most of all. This was going to be the most excitement any of them had had in a long time.

Luna frowned. She was perhaps the only person in the whole courtroom who wasn't happy to be there. She looked over at Judge Benally. He wasn't happy to be here either. She looked at his black robe. She wondered if the rumors were true and if he really did carry a loaded gun under there. From his expression, she didn't really want to find out.

Jeremy was probably the happiest person in the whole gymnasium. He had a glow about him as if he were the bachelor who got to choose between twelve lucky jurors.

As for Marlow, he looked like he had woken up after a five-month sleep, ready to go. She used to look like that right before a race. Why the hell couldn't she be like that anymore?

The jurors left the gymnasium, chattering amongst themselves. "Jeremy is so cute," she swore she heard one say. "That defense lawyer is too," said another.

"Opening statements are tomorrow," Benally declared. "I want Counsel to meet and iron out all potential problems. I want this to be simple. I don't want a mistrial. If there's a mistrial, I'll have both parties wait for the next trial over at the Discount Prison."

Benally adjourned court. Smoky took Jeremy away, and soon it was just Luna and Marlow in the empty gymnasium.

"Is this our meeting?" she asked.

"This is our meeting about the meeting," he said with a smile.

Luna laughed slightly.

Marlow looked over at her. She looked so hurt and tired from all of this. So vulnerable. It had been only five months and she still wasn't over her mother yet. Hell, she still wasn't over the whole Olympics fiasco, whatever that was. He wanted to take her into his arms, to protect her from all the evil in this world. He wanted to tell her it would all be all right, even though it most definitely wasn't.

"You were great," she said.

"So were you."

"You're lying."

"I am."

She couldn't help but laugh. "Let's meet for lunch over at the Rustler."

"I think half the jurors will be there," he said. He thought for a second. Where could they go to get away from all of this. . . .

"Do you mind going to the Crosswinds?"

She smiled a guilty smile, as if he had asked her out to a motel. "Not at all. Probably a good idea."

"Give me a half an hour. I have to stop off at the bank."

Luna sat in the Crosswinds Truck Stop and waited for Marlow. She still felt the weight of the locals' taboo of the Crosswinds, like she'd snuck out over the Crater walls after curfew. She grimaced as she walked past the ladies room where Felicia had done the deed to Thayer, and Jeremy had done the deed, excuse me, *allegedly* done the deed back to him.

Her first prom, *the* prom, had been here at the Crosswinds. That had been the only breaking of the taboo in her lifetime. Well, the dinner part had been here at least. The Rustler had just had a suspicious fire, and there really was nowhere else to go in town. The fact that it was de facto forbidden only added to the fun. All the kids came here in nice dresses and pigged out an on all-you-can-eat buffet before the dance.

She was with Nico, the coolest senior stud. An amazed traveler had come over to them on that nigh—she in the pale blue dress, he in the rented tux. "Why are you two dressed so beautifully?"

"It's our prom," Luna had replied. "This is the big time for us."

She looked over at the hallway leading to the bathroom in the back. The one slutty thing she had ever done in her life was to take off her panties in that bathroom, then show them to Nico before throwing them over in the trash can on that magic prom night. She almost wanted to open the trash to see if they had somehow magically survived after all those years.

The tourist had taken a picture of them, little dreaming that this innocent girl in the baby blue dress wasn't wearing any panties. Luna remembered her momentary fear that the camera would see right through to her one moment of debauchery. Fortunately, the picture came out way too dark. Just as well. Luna kept it in her scrapbook anyway.

Luna thought about the night. After the dance in the gym, Nico had taken her to the back seat of the Corvette first. It was a cliché, but, as her English teacher Mr. Slevin had said, "Clichés sometimes work because they're often true."

Luna smiled as she remembered all the positions in the Corvette and how she had positioned herself with the prom dress still on. Then back to the Mothership, since her mother was gone. She'd indeed kept on her prom dress for the entire night, but with the panties gone, it didn't really matter, did it?

"I'm ready," she said to herself. It had been nearly six months since her mom had died. A decent interval had most definitely passed. "I'm ready."

She thought about going into the bathroom and taking off her panties.

Marlow went to the bank and asked to see Raymond Rossi. Rossi's office was in back, and Marlow felt as if he had left the Crater behind. Rossi's office was done up with perfect *feng shui*—stark white with Asian artifacts arranged just so. Rossi himself looked like a perfect example of *feng shui*, everything from his abstract tie to white mustache hairs seemed to be perfectly aligned with the universe.

Rossi was sixty, and had survived with AIDS for over twenty years. "A refugee from San Francisco," as he liked to say. Marlow didn't know the full story, just the rumors. Rossi had been an executive vice president of the bank's national office. He had displeased the boss and was about to be fired, and thus lose his health insurance for himself and his lover.

Somehow, he convinced the boss of his pressing need for continued coverage for himself and his companion. The boss had some sympathy, but not much. He had picked the worse possible place within the company for Rossi to go. That was Crater, of course. The lover had died rather than make the trip.

Every weekend, Rossi drove all the way to Santa Fe for medical attention and nightlife. During the week, he was as stuck in Crater as the rest of them.

Marlow had gotten him out of a few sticky situations with Van Leit and Nico, so Rossi owed him one.

"I need a favor," Marlow said, after the two exchanged pleasantries. He told him what he needed.

Rossi laughed. "That's a big favor. Is it really that important?"

Marlow didn't smile. "It's a matter of life or death."

"I'll see what I can do," he said as he scanned Marlow's list of requests. "If the big boys up in San Francisco office find out, it's not like they can send me any place worse than here."

Marlow met Luna in the Crosswinds cafeteria. They loaded their buffet plates. They both had big appetites and wanted to get their money's worth, at these exorbitant prices. They looked outside at the trucks heading off to parts unknown, like little kids at an airport. They played guessing games on what was inside each truck.

"Peaches," Marlow said.

"Peaches?"

"It's got a Georgia license plate. Georgia peaches."

"But if it's on the interstate, it's going to California," she said.

"They have peaches in California, so I'll say it's tofu."

"Maybe it's peach tofu."

They both laughed.

The mourning period is definitely over, Luna thought. And Diana is gone. If I play it cool, the two of us can get through this together.

She was the one who took his hand in hers. It was the most sexual act she had ever done, just touching Marlow's hand and rubbing her fingers gently across the knuckles. She remembered her athletic trainer at CU talking about "trigger points," how if you touched one part of the body, it triggered a reaction in another part. The masseuse had gone on to talk about triggering energy and aura or something like that.

Luna then moved her touch to the palm of his hand. She looked into his eyes then down below. She had triggered something, all right. Jesus, he might even be bigger than Nico.

He looked back at her with an anticipation that she had never seen before.

She hadn't felt like this since throwing the panties in the trash on prom night. Goosebumps ran all through her body. She rubbed his hand with a yearning that she didn't know she had.

That's when the band-aid fell off.

"Oops . . . sorry."

That's when she saw the tattooed cross.

OPENING STATEMENT

"Why the hell would he get a tattooed cross?" asked Luna in her cramped office. She was supposed to be ready for opening statements, but that wasn't going to happen now. Marlow and Van Leit sat on the boxes.

"I bet he killed her and then got the tattoo," said Nico.

"Why would he kill my mother?" asked Luna. "He only met her once."

"That one time with me," said Van Leit. "She was a bit of a bitch to him, if I must say so myself."

"Hey!" Luna looked at him. She could call her own mother a bitch, but this drunken asshole had better not.

"I'm still saying that he's copycatting Jeremy," Nico said.

"Copycatting?" Luna asked.

"Notice how he used to look like that old Indian Yazzie with his pony tail and Navajo spiritual shit," Nico said. "He kinda *became* his client."

"Now he looks like Jeremy," added Van Leit. "I mean, he doesn't wear glasses any more, he cut the ponytail and bleached his hair."

"It's his way of getting into character," Nico said.

"I'm just saying he's weird," said Luna. "Not that he's a killer."

"Well, he broke into Sarah Sanchez's house as one of those 'simulations,'" Van Leit said. "Maybe he's into simulations, whatever the hell they are. He killed your mother just like Jeremy killed Felicia's mother, in a simulation."

"Well if he really wants to be Jeremy, he's had five months to kill someone," said Luna.

"Who would he kill?" asked Nico. "If he wanted to kill a boyfriend, just like Jeremy killed Felicia's boyfriend . . . well . . . I'm the closest thing you've got to a boyfriend."

She didn't know what to make of that statement, "the closest thing you've got to a boyfriend."

"And you're still alive," she finally said. "Maybe it's nothing."

"So if I die," said Nico pretending to make a joke. "Then I guess you gotta worry about him coming after you!"

Nobody laughed.

Marlow stood in his bathroom, looking into his mirror. He still hadn't heard from Rossi. He now had no idea what he was going to do for his opening statement. So much for his theory of the case. He looked down at the cross and rubbed it with his finger. What would Jeremy do?

Judge Benally called court thirty minutes late. "I'm always on time," he had once joked to some impatient lawyers, "except when I'm not."

He was known for being one of the fastest judges, except for those "not" days. The "not" days were usually once a month, and then no one knew when he would begin, or when he would end, for that matter. He would often go into an office and do one telephone hearing, then another. Court could run all night.

There had been that glimmer of national media interest after Ruth's murder, but outside the Justice Center, there was still only the one reporter from the Albuquerque stations, Stephanie Park Live. Stephanie felt like Stephanie Park Dead from the drive out here at dawn to make it to court on time.

Luna didn't know what to say to Stephanie Park Live, so she politely waved her off. "I'll talk to you later," she said. Hopefully with her victory speech, although somehow she doubted that right now.

Marlow was a few steps behind Luna, and he didn't say anything to Stephanie Park Live either. For one brief moment, he had a deer caught in the headlights look and gave no comment.

Stephanie Park Live smiled. In her last few months as a court reporter in Albuquerque, she had dealt with the slickest of the slick lawyers. Seeing such naked fear on both sides was a refreshing change. It might even help her become Stephanie Park Live from Los Angeles.

Courtroom B smelled worse than usual. Having so many people in such a small place somehow intensified the old racquetball smell—sweat, rubber and old jock straps. Some of the women jurors had gone for perfume as a means of compensating. Unfortunately, Courtroom B now smelled like the basement locker room for an old French whorehouse.

Stephanie rapidly set up her TV cameras outside the glass wall of Courtroom B. She quickly got some great stock footage of the bleached blond defendant with spiked hair talking to the bleached blond lawyer with spiked hair.

Both parties were set, Luna on the left; Marlow, Jeremy and Smoky on the right. Marlow had re-bandaged the cross.

Luna stared at him. For a brief moment he looked so innocent, the guy with whom she had played "name the crime" with at the Rustler and usually lost. Despite his bravado, Marlow still sweated before a trial. She could see the stains underneath his suit. There was no way that a guy like that could have killed her mother. It was all just an act, right?

Judge Benally launched into the preliminaries about how what was said by Counsel was not evidence and, after a few more minutes, he called on her to begin.

Luna's opening statement was by the book, and that book was boring. She talked about the three victims in the case: Sarah, Thayer and Felicia. She went on about how each of them were killed, naming every element of the crime, right down to how each victim was indeed a "natural person." She used the phrase "and the evidence will show" before every sentence until it sounded like an involuntary nervous tick.

Luna took over thirty minutes to get through each element and each natural person. Stephanie had stopped filming after thirty seconds. The Illustrated Woman looked like she'd had a rough night of it last night, and her eyes were closed.

Luna noticed that a few other jurors were about to follow the Illustrated Woman's example, and ended by saying "The evidence will show that Jeremy Jones is guilty of three counts of first degree murder. And we ask that you follow the evidence."

Then she sat down. When she was a freshman in high school, she used to have a temper tantrum when she'd done badly. She was about to do that now, but she quickly clenched her fist under the table as if she could squeeze out all her frustration. It didn't work, of course, but she maintained her composure.

She looked over at Marlow. Every ounce of nervousness was now gone. Even the sweat stains had magically disappeared.

Stephanie and her cameraman had noticed it as well. "It's like he's six inches taller." She made him adjust the shot. "This is weird."

Marlow's voice sounded different as he spoke. It was deeper, a baritone. "Ladies and gentleman of the jury, I'm the defense attorney and my name is Jeremy Jones."

Stephanie got that on tape. "Huh?" she said to the cameraman.

"I am Jeremy Jones," he said again. "I am on trial here."

He walked over to the jurors. He pointed at the Illustrated Woman. "Your name is Jeremy Jones," then he smiled at the camera and at Stephanie. "You're on trial here. All of us are Jeremy Jones. There's a little bit of Jeremy Jones in all of us."

"Even her," he pointed toward Luna. "As the representative of the great state of New Mexico, especially her!"

Luna was very uncomfortable. She suddenly felt everyone look at her. She was in Folsom Field again shuffling slowly to the finish line, this time without her underwear. She knew she should object. This was emotion, not evidence.

He walked back to the podium. "When our society puts one person on trial, it puts all of us on trial. If we don't respect his rights, we don't respect our rights. We live in the greatest nation on earth, and despite its faults, I believe in our system. Jeremy Jones' guilt must be proven beyond a reasonable doubt. Because if you convict Jeremy when there is even the slightest doubt in your heart, you convict me and you convict her." He pointed at Luna again.

"And most importantly, you convict yourselves and you convict America."

And that was it. Two minutes. Stephanie Park Live would be able to run the entire opening statement for the noon hour news.

After Marlow sat, Judge Benally banged the gavel. "Excellent openings," he said. " We'll resume after lunch with the state's first witness."

STATE'S WITNESS: CHARLES "VAN" VAN LEIT

Marlow met with Jeremy in the holding cell in the Justice Center. Smoky had brought Jeremy a sandwich from the gas station across the street. Marlow looked exhausted, as if the four minute opening had taken as much out of him as Luna's half hour, along with her sleepless night of research.

"Not bad," said Jeremy.

"The sandwich or my opening?" asked Marlow.

"Both. So what are you going to do for Van Leit? And your theory of the case—"

"I don't know yet about Van Leit or the theory. I thought I had something, but it doesn't look like it's going to work out."

Marlow avoided Jeremy's gaze. How do you ask your client if he left a bloodstain on the dresser while killing a sweet old lady? Was Jeremy being set up? Jeremy sure didn't act like it, but with Jeremy, you could never tell.

"You look like you want to ask me something," Jeremy said.

"I don't think I can."

Jeremy smiled. "You know why Yazzie is dead right now?" Jeremy asked after a moment.

"Enlighten me."

"It's because you were a pussy."

Smoky chuckled for a moment. Marlow wanted to slug them both right there, but didn't.

"You're like a thermometer," Jeremy said. "I can see your forehead get red right before my eyes. I like that in a lawyer."

Marlow said nothing.

"I'm just a stupid ass criminal, and you're Mr. Big Time

Lawyer and I can read you like a book. Just think what Mr. Big Time Lawyer could read from a drunk-ass cop?"

"I guess I don't have anything to ask you," Marlow said.

Jeremy put his sandwich down. There was still a half left, which he hadn't touched. "You want some of this?"

Marlow shook his head. He wasn't sure whether Jeremy was talking about the sandwich or whether "you want some of this" was an implicit challenge toward something else.

He didn't like Jeremy playing him like a trumpet. It was time to go. "I'm just going to eat over at the Rustler," he said. "I like the company better over there."

The entire courtroom had moved over to the Rustler by the time he'd arrived. There seemed to be a line between defense and prosecution and it was drawn right down the salad bar. Luna, Nico and Van Leit sat on one side. Marlow quickly sat on the other. The jurors had a back room to themselves.

He was surprised that Stephanie Park Live came in and joined him at his table. "This is just for the pleasure of your company," she said.

He accepted. She was attractive, and besides, it might make Luna jealous.

"How'd you get so good?" she asked him, within earshot of Luna. She touched his arm, although there seemed to be something forced about it. He pushed it away, but barely.

"I used to be an actor when I was at USC," he replied. "I try to get into character."

"Kinda like De Niro," she said.

"Kinda," he replied.

Marlow's phone rang. "Just bring me whatever you got," he said into the phone. "I can't talk now."

Luna indeed felt a twinge as Marlow chatted up Little Ms. Live. She sat closer to Nico and made it a point to touch him on the shoulder a few times.

Van Leit had gone nuts at the salad bar. The sign said, "All you care to eat," and he was in a very caring mood. He must have had more bacon bits than lettuce. Van Leit had claimed that he was on his new special diet, but he had put together the most fat-filled salad in American history.

At least he hadn't ordered a drink with lunch, although sobriety didn't seem to agree with him.

"Are you ready?" she asked him.

"Ready, willing and able," he said. "Once I finish eating."

Luna was nervous. She made Van Leit go over his testimony in between mouthfuls that somehow kept getting on his mustache. It was simple and it was to the point. There really wasn't any difference between doing the questioning in a death penalty case than in a DWI, she thought to herself. Just get the cop talking, but don't let him talk too much.

She couldn't help but look over at Marlow and Stephanie Park Live. Had Marlow shrunk again? Stephanie Park Live was barely five feet tall, and she seemed to tower over him as they sat in the booth together. The sweat stains were back under Marlow's arms.

Luna smiled as the shoplifting waitress brought him his iced tea. Marlow had since defended the waitress on a failure to yield to oncoming emergency vehicles. Deferred sentence.

Luna met Marlow's eyes across the room. She couldn't read him, and he abruptly looked away when someone came over.

Raymond Rossi went over to Marlow's table. He nearly bumped into Van Leit who had gone back for another trip to the salad bar.

"Hey Raymond, mind if I make a deposit?" Van Leit leered. Van Leit pantomimed some unspeakable acts with both of his hands.

Raymond Rossi said nothing. As the only banker in Crater, he had to be nice to everyone in town. Well, polite anyway. Even to a jerk like Van Leit who would run him out of town on a rail.

"It has been such a pleasure working with you, Sheriff," Rossi said. "You are so good at keeping your balance positive." He walked away briskly without further explanation.

Van Leit looked at him quizzically then sat down with Luna and Nico.

Luna looked at Van Leit. Something told her that the sheriff now devoutly wished that he had never, ever said an unkind word to Rossi. Rossi was a banker. What could he have on Van Leit, a bounced check?

Luna looked at her watch. Time was a wastin'. Marlow had not come back out by the time they left. She watched Van Leit nervously play with his mustache one more time. That must have been one hell of a bounced check.

Once Benally started late, he was indeed late all day. The courtroom was empty. Jeremy and Smoky were in the holding cell, the jurors were in the library and the Judge was taking calls.

Luna and Marlow stared at each other in the empty courtroom at one o'clock. There was nothing to say. She wanted to make small talk, but from the look on his face, he was like a werewolf with a bad moon just starting to rise. He talked to himself and recited something softly, even practiced hand movements. He had a manila envelope that had been given to him by Rossi. What the hell was in that envelope?

She forced herself to look down at her direct examination of Van Leit. It was good, but something was missing. Then she remembered. Her mother wasn't there to correct it, one more time.

"Damn, I miss you, Mom," she said out loud.

She went into the hallway. The entire hallway belonged to her. There were the eyewitnesses to Jeremy's threats and the criminalistics folk who had come down from Santa Fe.

"When do I go on?" Mr. Ballistics asked.

"I think after me," said Mr. DNA.

"I got to get back to the lab," said Mr. Blood Splatter.

"I don't know," she said, a tired ringmaster at the three ring circus. "And remember I'm splitting the cases up. You'll go on for each case,"

Mr. Ballistics gave her a look. "Remember we're on the clock and I still haven't been paid yet."

"Talk to the Judge," she said. "We're running on his time."

• • • • •

Finally, Benally called court to order at one-forty-five. Smoky brought Jeremy in, and the two looked relaxed, as if they'd smoked a joint or two in the holding cell. There was another short delay as the Illustrated Woman was brought to court, reeking of cigarettes. She gave a nod to Smoky. Raymond Rossi now sat in the back. Van Leit glowered at him.

"Will the state kindly call the first witness?" Benally asked in mock politeness.

"We call Sheriff Charles Van Leit."

Van Leit took the stand. He wasn't nervous; he had testified in a million cases over the years. Luna noticed a bit of ranch dressing on his cheek. She gestured toward it on her own face and soon he had removed it before anyone had noticed.

"Detective Van Leit, could you describe the events of August fifteenth?"

"I received a call of a domestic disturbance at Felicia Sanchez's residence at about nine P.M. She told me that—"

Marlow rose "Objection, hearsay. That was clearly being offered for the truth of the matter asserted."

Luna felt rattled. She hadn't expected Marlow to actually object. She quickly regained her composure.

"Officer, please don't go into the specifics of what she said. What did you observe?"

"She looked like a typical domestic violence victim. She'd been in a fight with her boyfriend. She'd scratched him and drawn blood. I took a sample of the blood."

"What did you do next?"

"Felicia was hysterical. She said something about how Jeremy was going to kill her mother for keeping them apart."

Marlow had been a little slow, and hadn't objected in time. "Motion to strike," he said. "Hearsay being offered for the truth of the matter asserted again."

Judge Benally smiled. Yang time. "The jurors will disregard the statement of Felicia's that Jeremy Jones was going to kill her mother. The statement by Felicia Sanchez that Jeremy Jones wanted to kill her mother, or that the mother was trying to keep them apart is inadmissible hearsay. It is as if it never happened and was never offered for the truth of the matter asserted. Get Felicia's statement that Jeremy Jones wanted to kill her mother completely and utterly out of your mind."

There's an old law school quip that admonishments like that were like letting a skunk into the courtroom and telling the jurors to disregard the smell. In a converted racquetball court with minimal ventilation, the stench was now overpowering.

Luna smiled. She had scored one point. It would now be downhill from here.

Yet Marlow did not look troubled. Not one bit. He still had that damn envelope.

Luna plugged away. "What did you do next?"

"I called for back-up. For Officer Nico Walters. He was out of town and running late. I tried to call Sarah Sanchez and there was no answer. I decided to proceed to the other residence, the Sarah Sanchez residence, on my own."

"How long did it take you to get there?"

"Sarah Sanchez lived approximately five minutes away from her daughter."

"And what did you observe when you arrived?"

"A window was opened, some splinters were there. I noticed some blood on the window."

"Then what did you do?"

"I took out my weapon, and kicked in the door."

Van Leit took a pause, just as Luna had instructed him too. Now all the jurors focused on him. "I was too late."

Luna felt a semblance of an electrical shock coming through her system, but she suppressed it. Too late, just like she'd been too late for her mother.

"What did you find in the bedroom?"

This should have been her moment, but Luna underplayed it. She glanced over at Marlow. He wasn't going to object. Good.

"I saw Sarah Sanchez dead. She was on her knees on the floor as if she was praying."

Luna quickly had Van Leit's photographs admitted as state's

evidence and published them to the jury. Luna couldn't handle looking at Sarah's picture. She still saw her own mother, so she passed the photos face down to the jurors.

The jurors made audible gasps as they saw the dead body and the three bloodstains. Van Leit took them through each picture, shot by shot.

Luna also introduced a diagram of the crime scene done up in blue magic marker. She had Van Leit go over to the diagram.

"What else did you observe?"

"I found some blood smudges on the dresser," Van Leit said. "It was Jeremy's blood."

Luna recoiled. He wasn't supposed to say that since he had no personal knowledge. It was the experts who tested the blood, not him. She took a deep breath and waited for Marlow's objection. Marlow said nothing.

"And how did you know it was Jeremy's blood?"

Again, she waited for Marlow's objection. Still nothing.

"I collected it myself and sent it to the crime lab," Van Leit was on a roll. "They personally told me that it was Jeremy's blood. One hundred percent match."

That was a hearsay objection, and also an expert opinion by a lay witness, but still nothing from Marlow.

Luna spent another hour on his subsequent investigation, but she didn't remember much of it. She felt relieved.

She looked over at the jurors. They had long stopped looking at Jeremy as their cool neighbor. Luna had reminded them that a woman was dead and her killer sat right in front of them. She sat down. She didn't feel triumphant yet. More relieved. She had done everything she had wanted to do. If this was a race, she was right on pace.

Marlow got up. There was no doubt, that it had been a bad moon indeed. Oh shit, Luna thought to herself.

Stephanie Park Live started filming again. "This is going to be good," she said to her cameraman. "Do not turn away from this guy for one second."

Marlow walked right up to Van Leit. "Sheriff Van Leit, could you please describe the evidence you collected at Felicia Sanchez's residence?"

"I told you about the photos and the—"

"Sheriff, I believe that you are a bit confused. I was talking about *Felicia's* residence. When you made the domestic violence call over there earlier in the evening."

"She had scratched him pretty good, so there was blood all over the walls."

"And you collected this blood?"

"Yeah, it was evidence. I didn't want to wait for the crime lab guys to come all the way from Santa Fe and have there be no evidence. Felicia might have cleaned it up or something. . . ."

He looked directly at the jurors. "You know how it is in domestic violence cases."

"Please strike the officer's statement," said Marlow. "It calls for an expert opinion by a lay witness."

Marlow was now making up for lost time.

"Stricken," said the Judge. "Jury will completely and utterly disregard the officer's opinion on domestic violence between the defendant and one of the victims."

Marlow had just let another skunk into the courtroom, Luna thought to herself. She had barely touched on the domestic violence and now the jurors had something else *not* to think about.

"Let's continue," said Marlow. "Was the blood still wet?"

"Yeah, in one place, Felicia scratched him pretty good and Jeremy must have bled quite a bit."

"And you took a bit of that wet blood?"

"Yeah."

"And you took a sample of that wet blood with you from the house?"

"Yes," said Van Leit. "I'm not going to leave evidence lying around. You'd make some bogus 'chain of custody' argument."

Van Leit was cocky now. He loved busting Marlow's balls. He had him dead to rights now. The jurors loved it.

"So you took those samples with you when you went on the call to Sarah's house?"

"Yes."

"And you were alone when you got to Sarah's house, weren't you?"

"Yes. Officer Shatrock was off duty and Nico Walters was on his way,"

"So you were alone when you found the body?"

"Yes."

"How long was it before the other officers arrived?"

"Ten minutes max."

Marlow walked over to the diagram that Luna had prepared. "Let's refer to the diagram. You said that there was blood found on the dresser, over here."

"Yeah."

"And you said that Jeremy must have been bleeding a lot."

"Yeah."

"Don't you find it strange that the only drop of blood would be all the way over here at the dresser?" Marlow asked.

"I don't know. You'd have to ask Jeremy. I don't know how he bleeds."

"Shorter and better answer," Marlow said, as if the talk of blood excited him.

"Huh?"

"Your answer is either 'yes, it was strange,' or 'no, it was not strange.'"

"Ummm . . . yes, it's strange."

"You didn't find any blood over here at the nightstand?"

"No."

"If Jeremy had been crawling, don't you think there would have been blood on the carpet?"

"Maybe he cleaned it."

"How about Sarah's window?"

"What about it?"

"You didn't find any blood on the opened window from when the killer did his escape?"

"No blood . . . maybe he cleaned that too."

"So after he cleaned the carpet, and the nightstand, and decided to escape out the window, he came back in and then he deliberately left some blood over at the nightstand."

Van Leit stared at the diagram, confused. "You lost me there, Counselor."

"I'm lost too," Marlow said. He pointed to the jurors. "And so are they."

Van Leit mumbled for a second. "Well he went over there, either before or after he killed her. That's when he bled. That's my um . . . theory of the case."

"Your theory of the case? I think a better theory is that you planted the blood at the scene of the crime, Sheriff. But you were too stupid to plant the blood in the right place!"

Luna knew she was supposed to object. "He's badgering the witness."

Judge Benally banged his gavel. "No badgers allowed in my courtroom. Mr. Marlow, that's quite enough unless you have laid a foundation."

"Permission to lay a foundation, Your Honor."

"Proceed."

"Sheriff, do you recall the case of *State* v. *Yazzie*?"

Van Leit scowled. "Yeah. . . ."

Luna stood up. Where was this going? "Your Honor, relevance?" She glanced down at her pocket list of rules. "Ummm . . . Rule 402?"

"I'm laying a foundation," Marlow said.

"Counsel, the state has already taken a good deal of the Court's time for the day. How much more foundation do you wish to, umm . . . lay?"

"Your Honor, I will complete this case in seven questions."

The jurors looked at Marlow, amazed. Stephanie had her cameraman zoom in on Marlow's face.

Benally showed no emotion. He remembered how passionate Marlow had been during the first Yazzie case. Quite frankly, he was glad to see the old Marlow back.

Complete this case? Luna thought. Doesn't he mean complete the foundational questions, or perhaps complete the cross-examination of this witness?

Suddenly Luna felt a shiver run down her back. She looked at Marlow. He meant "complete the case," all right.

"Question one, you were the investigating officer on the Yazzie case, weren't you? The first one on the scene?"

"Yes, I was."

"Question two, and in that case you found a bottle of Jack Daniels, correct?"

"Uhh . . . yeah."

"Question three, I understand your normal drink is a cheaper whiskey, Wild Stallion, five-ninety-nine a bottle, correct?"

"It's all I can afford on an honest cop's salary."

Marlow opened the envelope and pulled out some kind of financial document. "Your Honor, I'm not offering this document into evidence, nor for the truth of the matter asserted. I'm just using them to refresh the witness's recollection, which is allowed under the rules."

Luna was still flipping through her rulebook.

"I'll allow it," the Judge said.

Marlow held up some records from the bank, credit card records.

"Question four, then why did you purchase a bottle of Jack Daniels for nine-ninety-nine on the night of the Yazzie incident?"

Van Leit said nothing.

"You purchased the Jack Daniels bottle after the call came in and before any officer would have joined you on the scene."

Marlow looked over at Luna. "I'm sorry, I wasn't asking a question. I believe that Counsel should object."

Luna was dumbstruck; she didn't even find whatever rule Marlow wanted her to object under. "Objection," she said with a whimper.

"I'll withdraw my statement, as long as you don't hold that one against me."

"Proceed," said the Judge. "You have only three more questions left."

"Question five, did you plant that bottle of Jack Daniels on Mr.

Yazzie? Or were you drinking on the job?"

That was arguably two questions of course, but everyone was too much in shock to notice. Marlow waved the papers a few feet from Van Leit's face.

Van Leit now had a look of flat-out panic. He was screwed either way, especially with that damn camera running.

"I'll repeat question five. Did you plant the bottle of Jack Daniels on Mr. Yazzie or were you drinking on the job?"

In actuality, the answer was both. He had been drinking on the job as usual, and planting a bottle on a presumably drunken Indian in a car crash just seemed like the perfect way to kill two birds with one stone. He had thought planting cheap Wild Stallion would have just been too obvious, because everyone in town knew it was his favorite bottle, and the Indians always seemed to go for the good stuff on their last rides, right?

Damn it! That faggot Raymond Rossi was out to get him. Rossi was there in the court, smiling right at him. What had Rossi just said at the Rustler, "You keep your balance positive?"

As the only banker in town with less than twenty businesses at best, Rossi could find out everything. Everything he had ever paid for, and the fact that he never tipped even. And there it was on official bank stationary. He had done nothing illegal at the bank, of course. He was dumb, but not that dumb. It's just that when you drink, you don't always have cash and check cards are so damn easy.

Van Leit looked like he had the wind knocked out of him. He forced a smile. Yazzie was dead, right. It's not like they were going to bring him back. It would still be okay, right?

He didn't even look at Luna. Her head was still down, lost in the rules. Instead he stared down Marlow. "I take the fifth amendment."

"Your Honor, I have established that this witness has a pattern of planting evidence. This would be admissible under Rule 608 as it goes to his character, or lack thereof. I have laid my foundation. Sheriff Van Leit, you are under oath."

There was a long pause. "Question six. Did you take the blood sample from Jeremy at Felicia's house and then plant it over at Sarah's house?"

Luna knew she was supposed to say something. But what? "Objection! That would be, umm . . . more prejudicial rather than, umm . . . probative."

Benally looked at her and waited for an explanation.

None came.

"There's no basis to that objection," he said. "Defense Counsel just asked a question that I think we would all like to hear the answer to. And clearly the witness's character when it comes to planting with evidence would be very probative indeed."

Van Leit glanced nervously over at Luna for guidance. She offered him nothing. But him planting a drop of blood was no big deal. Everybody knew that Jeremy did it! One little smudge on the dresser wasn't going to count for jack shit in the big case against the little puke.

"I take the Fifth Amendment," he said at last.

"The 'ain't saying shit' clause," Marlow added. He winked at Benally.

Van Leit kept his composure. Still, no big deal. They weren't going to throw out his testimony on the light of one smudge of blood. Outside in the hallway, he could hear the rustling of the veritable army of experts who were going to come in and help give Jeremy the fatal shot, three different times. There was a long pause. Van Leit started to rise.

The Judge turned to Luna. He was about to ask for her re-direct, but Marlow wasn't done yet.

"I'm sorry, Your Honor," he said. " I was one question off, I completed my cross examination in six questions. Then since I have one question left. . . ."

There was absolute silence.

"Question seven. Your Honor, since we have established that this witness has tampered with evidence before, would you dismiss all the charges against my client?"

Marlow produced a pile of Xeroxed copies of Supreme Court cases and handed a stack to Luna. Luna jumped up, after glancing at one of the decisions that said something about "material facts."

"Your Honor, the blood is not a material fact!" she shouted. "You can't drop this whole case on one technicality!"

"Technicality?" Marlow yelled. "The constitution is not a technicality. And the blood was clearly a material fact. The state's entire investigation comes from the illegally planted blood. That smudge is the only reason Jeremy Jones is sitting here next to me in handcuffs!"

They argued heatedly back and forth for five minutes. Then Benally finally banged his gavel.

"I'm going to take a brief recess," he said. He did not like that the camera was now focused clearly on him.

After Judge Benally and jury had left, Jeremy turned to Smoky. "I didn't think it would be this easy."

Marlow sat down, utterly drained. "It's not this easy and it's not over."

Luna had to face the criminalistics team who had hurried into the courtroom. They grew more and more incensed with every minute that Benally made them wait.

Stephanie Park Live reported on the "breaking story," but after reporting that the Judge was deliberating a motion to dismiss, there was nothing to add. Yet she still had to do it live every half hour.

Finally, right at four-forty-five, as if he wanted to wait until the last possible moment, Benally returned to the courtroom. "This case troubles me deeply. One thing is certain: I am not excluding the blood that was found at Felicia's house. There is no evidence whatsoever that Officer Van Leit planted the blood over there."

Luna nodded.

"However, when it comes to the blood found at Sarah's house, it's a different situation. I'm sure an officer planting a smudge of blood happens all the time. With an independent witness, I have little hesitation in overruling defense Counsel's motion to dismiss. It would be easy to bolster the detective's testimony. We would have independent grounds to avoid the fruit of the poisonous tree."

Both Luna and Van Leit looked at each other with relief. Van

Leit smiled. "I told you, no big deal."

Marlow showed no reaction. He knew what was coming.

Judge Benally waited a good long moment. "*But*, there is no independent witness to the blood found at Sarah's house. Felicia Sanchez is dead. She cannot back up the statement of Sheriff Van Leit that there was domestic violence and that Jeremy Jones intended to kill her mother. All we have is the testimony of Sheriff Van Leit and that is suspect at best. He tampered with a crime scene, thus all evidence he discovered at the crime scene would indeed be the fruit of the poisonous tree."

"Poisonous tree?" Van Leit. "What the fuck is that? You know the little puke did it!"

Beanlly looked at him with daggers. "Do not try my patience, Sheriff, and I use that term loosely because I'm sure you will not be sheriff for very much longer."

Van Leit backed down. He'd heard the rumors about what Benally could do if he was mad. Out of all the people in the room, he stared at Luna with the most rage. She had let him down somehow.

Benally banged his gavel. "Take this man into custody immediately on the felony charges of tampering with evidence and obstruction of justice."

Smoky came over and put the cuffs on Van Leit.

The Judge looked somewhat relieved. He would get out of Crater sooner than expected. "The state's entire case is one drop of blood found at someone else's house. I will indeed throw out the case of *State* v. *Jeremy Jones* on the first count—the murder of Sarah Sanchez."

Jeremy turned to Smoky. Smoky moved to release his shackles. Jeremy glowered at Van Leit and whispered something that no one could hear. Smoky fiddled with the key for a second.

Van Leit kept staring at Luna. "It's all your fault. You were supposed to know what the fuck you were doing! It's all your fault!"

Benally banged down on the gavel.

"Excuse me, but there are two other murders yet to go," Benally said. "Both of which carry the death penalty. The defendant is most certainly to remain in custody."

Benally postponed the trial for the week. "I want to see if there's the possibility of settlement. No offense. I may like the town of Crater, but I am no fan of I-40. I do not wish to return to this town for a trial that could most certainly be avoided."

Luna looked over at Marlow after Benally had left. The bandage was now definitely off the cross.

IN THE DISTRICT COURT
14th JUDICIAL DISTRICT
COUNTY OF CRATER

STATE OF NEW MEXICO, PLAINTIFF

vs.

JEREMY JONES, DEFENDANT

COUNT II

FOR THE MURDER OF THAYER BROWN,
A NATURAL PERSON

WITHDRAWAL OF COUNSEL?

Luna couldn't think of anything else to do on a night like this, so she went out to Crater Lake for a few laps. It was a full moon and she loved the way the moonlight glistened in the waters. She certainly couldn't stay at home after what had happened. She wanted to go to the one place that her pager wouldn't work for the inevitable call from Diana. The lake stayed so warm, even in the winter, because of the hot springs. She liked to think that the real reason was some kind of magic spell that protected the waters.

Luna had been swimming here for the last few months and hadn't noticed so much as a wrinkle or a sag in her muscle tone, even as her workouts had stagnated. Maybe she couldn't discount the magic after all.

Her goal tonight was simple: she would keep swimming until she could no longer move, as if each lap through the dirty waters would somehow cleanse her latest sin. A sort of baptism via the Australian crawl. She just didn't want to think about what had just happened earlier that day. Luna momentarily thought of going home to get a bathing suit, but she needed a total cleansing. Let the magic do its work.

The water was cold around the edges when she dived in. So much for the hot springs. Once she reached the center of the little lake, she did feel soothing warmth. Ever since they had done the musical *Camelot* in high school, she had dreamed about being the Lady of the Lake with the enchanted sword. Excalibur? No, that was the sword in the stone, right?

Luna had fallen asleep while reading the *La Morte d'Arthur* in "An Introduction to the Classics for Non-Majors" class at CU, but she did know there was a Lady of the Lake with a sword. She just wasn't sure whether the Lady had given the sword to Lancelot or Arthur.

The waters grew colder again as she reached the other side. If there was a magic sword at the bottom of the lake, its powers only seemed to work around the center. She turned around and did another lap, then another. . . .

After a while, her body grew more and more tired and her extremities tingled with the cold. Hypothermia? But you couldn't get hypothermia in an enchanted lake, she thought to herself. Luna's brain kept playing visions about the Lady and the enchanted sword. Her body didn't want to go past the warmth in the center of the lake. Maybe if she just floated here in the middle, it would all be all right. The magic would work its way with her. Lancelot would come . . . or Arthur. . . .

He had done nothing wrong, Marlow kept telling himself. After the day's event, he wandered around nighttime Crater on foot. He was way too restless to stay at home and watch TV or play on the Internet.

He remembered gloating after the first Yazzie mistrial, but his few USC friends had cautioned him. "They can always re-file, right?"

Here the state still had two more chances to fry his client, so he wouldn't gloat, couldn't gloat.

"I did nothing wrong," he said out loud to the Crater wind. The wind was in an especially foul mood tonight, and begged to differ.

Well, Mr. Wind, he had never offered the bank document into evidence. He had made no assertion whatsoever about its contents. Marlow had simply held up a bank record with numbers on it. It had been his own credit card receipts for the past two years. He had never said it was anything otherwise.

Luna had been too timid to object and now it was too late. He had a duty to zealously represent his client and could never reveal the secret to her. Why couldn't she be a better lawyer? Why couldn't she grow up and stop moping around her life? He wanted a worthy adversary.

But she wasn't his adversary, was she? Damn, he didn't want her to stay on the other side forever.

The wind subsided for a moment, as if giving him an opening. He would go for it. He called her home phone with his cell. Luna hadn't looked right. He was just calling to check up on her, right?

No answer. Is she all right? Fear shot through his entire body.

He walked over to the driveway. There were no lights on in either the Mothership or the satellite. He knew Luna swam, and Crater Lake was just over the ridge. Maybe she's out night swimming. If he could swim, he'd do something like that to wash it all away, or maybe he'd drown himself.

The wind must have agreed with him. He felt the wind change direction, blowing him away from town for a change. Right toward Crater Lake.

Although he had once been a die-hard skeptic of most things, after Manygoats he really felt that there was an order in nature. "Listen to the wind," Manygoats had once said on his show. "And you will listen to yourself."

Marlow listened to the wind and headed toward the lake. When he got to the top of the ridge, he could see the female body floating in the middle of the lake.

The body drifted, face down.

Oh shit!!!

He called 911. "I think there's a woman floating in the middle of Crater Lake. I think it's Luna Cruz!!!"

911 took way too long. Marlow had made it to the lakeshore. He was going to go in, had started taking off his clothes. He had grown up by the ocean, yet water terrified him. Tidal waves, sharks, or as novelist John Irving had called it, the mysterious Under Toad.

He took a few deep breaths. He would have to defy the Under Toad and swim out there. He touched the water. Freezing. Marlow started wading in. He had never been much of a swimmer. Not much of a wader either. Suddenly, he couldn't see her in the darkness. Had she drifted . . . or gone under?

Marlow scanned the lake for Luna. Where was she? Luckily the county's one ambulance came in the next instant. Nico's Corvette was right behind, its sirens flashing. The ambulance flashed a spotlight until it found Luna. She still floated, but had drifted closer to that part of the shore.

Nico did not even wait, just dived into the water. He swam out to Luna. Nico had done swim team, just to be with Luna that one semester. Those big arms really pushed him through the water. Luckily, the current had pushed Luna closer to shore and he made it there in moments. He pulled Luna to shore and gave her mouth-to-mouth. For a moment there was nothing, then she coughed up some water and took in a few deep breaths.

Marlow struggled to get his pants on as Nico carried Luna in his arms into the ambulance. Nico gave him a dirty look before the ambulance doors slammed shut.

Luna woke up in the High Desert Regional Hospital a few hours later. Nico was at her bedside. She gave him a kiss on the cheek.

"You saved me," she said, still groggy. The lights of the medical equipment glistened off his metallic sheriff's star, then flickered against the walls like enchanted candlelight. "You're my knight in shining armor."

He gave her a present and it smelled delicious. "While you were out, I went into the cafeteria, and whipped up your mom's recipe for sixteen-dollar burritos."

She gulped them down. The boy could follow a recipe all right, even with hospital ingredients. Sixteen-dollar burritos? What a bargain. Right now they tasted like a million bucks a bite.

"Thank you," she said and kissed him again on the lips. She was just a bit delirious and kept on going on about knights and ladies of the lake. Nico had no idea what she was talking about. He just caressed her hand. He knew something about trigger points too.

Marlow tried to get into High Desert Regional, but hospital security blocked his path.

"You're Sam Marlow?" a beefy security guard asked. Marlow nodded. "We have very specific orders not to let you in."

"But—"

The security threatened to arrest him, and together they were much bigger than he was. He didn't want to push it. He turned and walked out.

The next morning, Luna had to undergo a psychological evaluation to rule out suicide or "suicidal ideation" before the hospital could release her. Dr. Marianne Romero was the one who drew the short straw, and had to come all the way down from the state mental hospital in Las Vegas, New Mexico ("the other Vegas" as she had to remind out-of-staters). Dr. Romero was an attractive woman in her thirties, who looked more Gypsy than Latina. She asked Luna why she was found in the middle of the lake without any clothes on, which certainly looked like suicidal ideation.

Luna told Dr. Romero about triathlons and how in stressful moments she often took to athletics as a way of wiping away her pain and loneliness. She had not had any suicidal ideation, just wanted to think about something else besides losing the case.

Luna sounded somewhat convincing, but more like she wanted to convince herself. She wanted to keep going on about her life. Dr. Romero had a kindly face and was an excellent listener. Without her mother or even Marlow or Diana, she hadn't had a chance to be with a good listener in a very long time.

Unfortunately after exactly seven minutes, Dr. Romero stopped her before she could really start talking about how badly she missed her mother.

"Do you have any other family?" Dr. Romero asked.

"My father died when I was a little girl," she said. "I didn't really know him since he worked all the time in his clinic. His car got hit by a drunk driver, right on I-40 by the county line."

Dr. Romero expected Luna to say that she had become a prosecutor to avenge his death or something like that.

Luna surprised her. "I've always hated cars. I think that's why I run or bike everywhere I can."

That didn't sound right to Dr. Romero, but that wasn't enough to stop her from checking the sanity box. "I'm satisfied that you're not a danger to self or others," Dr. Romero said at last. "I will give you a satisfactory discharge."

"That's it?"

"That's it."

"Don't you want to know about what's going on in my head?"

The Doctor said nothing as she looked at Luna's face. Normally Dr. Romero dealt with mentally ill criminals, sex offenders mainly. It was a bit of a relief to see someone who didn't drool for a change. This girl looked a little more lost than usual, but she was a lawyer and should be able to deal with it. Dr. Romero usually had little sympathy for what she called the "wealthy un-well" and their "issues of abandonment."

Dr. Romero gave her another half-hour then said abruptly, "I'm sorry, but I'm out of time. I suggest you see a therapist over in Crater for a follow-up. I think you should be in counseling to deal with your grief issues."

"I don't think you understand, Dr. Romero," Luna replied. "There are no therapists in Crater."

Dr. Romero didn't have time to offer any suggestions before she was paged. She flipped through her messages. Some multiple child molester back at the state hospital had attempted a suicide. She'd have to hurry back up there to the lockdown unit.

Luna bent up to give the doctor a hug, but the she was already out the door.

Nico had waited at her side the night before, and now he was waiting outside. Once the doctor left, he came back in and gave her another burrito. "I figured getting shrunk would make you hungrier."

Luna laughed. "You read my mind."

An administrative nurse came in and gave Luna few forms to fill out and then it was time to check out.

"Take me home," she said to Nico. "You've been wonderful."

Marlow had waited in the parking lot, all night and through the day. He stayed in the clothes he slept in, still crumpled and dirty from taking them off at the beach and throwing them in whatever it was that passed for sand there.

He kept hoping against hope that the damn Corvette would leave, but it never did.

What did he want to tell her so bad? He was sorry for what had happened? It was all his fault for making her look so bad? It was all his fault.

Marlow realized that Jeremy had been right from the beginning, right from the moment he had lost his temper when Jeremy said, "You do love her."

He did. He knew that he had loved her from the minute he saw her from the top of the cliff, and thought she was something out of a Navajo vision. No, he had loved her from the minute he heard her talk, right after the first interview with Jeremy. He didn't love her for what she was, he loved her for what he hoped she could become. What did he call it, love at second sight? He could never leave this town, not until she was his.

Unfortunately, her being his was definitely not in the cards for tonight. After a few hours, he saw Nico and Luna leave together and head toward that damn Corvette. He wanted to approach them, right there and then, but he couldn't. He could tell that Nico was packing some serious heat.

He was scared of Nico, even when the man was unarmed. Why couldn't he be more like Jeremy? Jeremy had never been scared of anything. Jeremy would know how to take care of an asshole like Nico.

It was dark by the time Nico pulled the Corvette into the ranch driveway. Her medication had softened the ordeal of the ride He walked her to the door, and did his usual suave move of giving her a peck on the cheek, turning away, then ambling slowly as if he really intended to make it to his car.

Luna looked at the dark shape of the Mothership. She heard a coyote howl at the waning moon. She was hardly a roadrunner who could outrun the coyotes anymore.

"Nico," she said after a moment. "Could you stay with me? I just need to be held tonight."

Nico had somehow wrestled her keys out of her hand and opened the door before she had gotten to the word "just."

He built a small fire in the fireplace and "just held" her tight in his arms.

"You're my knight in shining armor," she said still a little woozy from the medication. She loved the image of Lancelot, could not let it go. "Just hold me some more."

He poured her a drink and they "just held" each other tighter. Slowly he rubbed her back, caressed her hair. He touched all of her triggers at just the right points.

Nico undressed her slowly. He'd been having the same fantasy ever since he'd seen her back in the holding cell in her tight little outfit. Jeremy had indeed been right about those long ago days when the two of them used to smoke joints together and bitch about women and things they had always wanted to try.

"Someday I want to take Luna and. . . ." he had said to Jeremy back then.

Jeremy's words in the holding cell had triggered those thoughts again. Now was Nico's last, best chance.

"There's something I want to try," he said.

"Anything. . . ."

Marlow's Saturn couldn't really trail a Corvette on the interstate, of course, but he knew where they were going. He was tired and he just wanted to go home, but he felt those Crater winds pulling him toward the satellite.

When he saw the Corvette in the parking lot, he almost kept going, but the winds made him stop. He opened his window. He heard blood-curdling screams coming from Luna's bedroom. It sounded like Nico was doing something terrible to her. For a moment he wanted to bust down the door, but he had to be sure he wasn't interrupting anything. He went around to the window and could not believe what he saw inside.

Oh my God!!!!

"Isn't that illegal in this state?" he thought to himself. He tried to turn away, but his face was glued to the windowpane.

Luna's face was a strange mixture of pleasure and pain. Nico apparently was very gifted in certain areas. At least he wore a condom. Marlow couldn't watch it anymore. He felt a hemorrhage of his heart, his brain, and his soul. He couldn't even stand there anymore after he heard another scream of pain, then an undeniable one of pleasure. The Crater winds must have known he couldn't take another instant. They suddenly blew him away from the house. Blew him right back to his home.

As he washed himself in his bathroom, he wondered if he could ever look at Luna the same way again. He kept washing and washing as if somehow that would make it all go away. He looked down at his single cross. There was always room for two more.

SETTLEMENT CONFERENCE

When Diana got back to Crater, she'd been through just fourteen days of her twenty-eight day program and that certainly wasn't enough, either mentally or physically. Diana's program was one of those where they knock you down, then pick you back up. Unfortunately, she'd just been through the knocking down part. She was definitely not happy to be back, while still mentally flat on her back.

Luna was still a little sore when she sat down in Diana's office. She'd brought an extra pillow with her from home and had put it beneath her on her chair. The morning's caffeine made her squirm even more. Nico had surprised her by busting into the Mothership and salvaging the most delicious coffee from Tierra del Fuego. He had then run over to the store and made her the first decent breakfast she'd had in a long time, a breakfast version of her mother's burritos.

"I've only got five bucks," he said. "I'll have to improvise."

"Maybe I could learn to like this," she thought to herself. He had improvised fairly well.

She still felt a little confused, a little unsure. Had it been the drugs from the hospital? No, she had agreed to Nico out of her own free will. She had wanted him. She could have said no. She *should* have said no, but it was now too late. She tried to sum up what it was about Nico that prevented her from truly loving him. It was that he was too "hard," in all senses of the word.

Diana's labored breathing quickly brought her back into the moment. Diana looked back at Luna. She couldn't decide whether to be angry or understanding. She felt guilty for abandoning Luna, but, Jesus, the girl had just blown the biggest case in the history of Crater!

"I understand how something like this could happen, Luna my love," Diana said to her. "I shouldn't have left you alone."

Luna shuffled uncomfortably in her seat. "I'm a big girl, Di."

"Big girl?" Luna was back to being the freshman again. "Well, big girl, how the hell could you let him blindside you like that?" Diana asked.

"Van Leit?"

"Not Van Leit," Diana replied. "Van Leit is a stupid, drunken crooked cop. You should expect that from him. But Marlow, he smiled at you and you got all weak. You lost it."

"I didn't lose it." She grimaced in pain again.

"Stop squirming!"

There was silence between them.

"We'll have to plead this thing out," Diana said at last. "I don't think either of us is up for counts two and three."

She dialed Marlow to set up a settlement conference.

Marlow told them over the phone that any settlement conference would have to take place with Jeremy present. Jeremy was the guest of honor. Since the Discount Prison was undermanned for the day, they would be unable to transport Jeremy to the DA's office. The conference would have to take place in the meeting room right there in Cellblock 1.

He was very surprised that Diana accepted his terms. She must be really scared, he thought to himself. He had never heard of a DA going to a prison, discount or otherwise, for a settlement conference.

He prayed that Jeremy would accept the terms and quietly go do the remainder of his natural life in jail or whatever the hell they would propose. Please Jeremy, take the damn plea. Plead to the death penalty even, so we can just get this damn thing over with.

Marlow wanted to get out of there that badly. The last DA before Luna had taken a job at the adult bookstore a few exits over on the freeway and worked as a janitor, or so the story went. He'd even settle for that as a way out. At least there'd be less direct client contact and he wouldn't have to save all the paperwork. Without Luna, he'd rather sweep up after the perverts than spend another minute stuck in the Crater.

Luna and Diana went over to the Discount Prison. Diana cursed the dirt roads as the dust engulfed the shiny skin of her yellow Lexus. In all their years in town, neither of them had ever been out here before. Important witnesses were always brought to them, or they'd send a cop out to talk with the unimportant ones.

The two women were both extremely nervous, so they brought Nico along with them as a sort of big, bald bodyguard. Diana nearly stalled the car a few times. Luna noticed that Diana's foot kept shaking.

Smoky worked the gate and made sure a female guard frisked them really well. Luna was still a bit sore, all over her body. The burly female guard brought out her pain with every grope.

"We're all on the same side here," she said when the guard got a little too personal.

"Are you sure?" the guard replied. "I see Jeremy every day. I've never seen you out here before."

The guard was just as personal with Diana. Diana was in her grown-up mode and showed no emotion. She gave the guard a polite smile when it was done.

Marlow arrived just as they finished up. The guards waved him through. He smiled at them all.

"We'll meet in the interview room in Cellblock 1," he said. "It's this way." They were definitely on his turf.

Smoky guarded the meeting room after seating Jeremy next to Marlow. Right as he was about to light up, Luna stopped him. "Do you mind?"

He gave her a dirty look and lit up anyway.

"What are you going to do?" asked Jeremy. "Arrest him for smoking?"

Jeremy got up and offered his hand. Diana made a point of not taking it, as if it were radioactive. There was some serious bad blood between the two—way beyond prosecutor and defendant.

Luna did not shake hands either, just sat down. Jeremy smirked at her too.

Luna was in agony on the hard plastic chair. Marlow wanted to throw up with every wiggle. He avoided eye contact with both her and Nico.

"Well?" he asked. He focused his gaze on the only person he could stand at the moment, which was Diana.

"Well you pretty much know what I've got," said Diana. "I'll drop Thayer Brown. You have to plead to Felicia."

"And?" said Marlow.

"Life without parole."

"I was hoping for counseling," Jeremy said. "On account of my anger management."

Marlow looked at Jeremy. "What?"

"We can throw in counseling," Diana said. Hoping against hope that Jeremy wasn't going to make a scene.

She was wrong, of course.

Jeremy waited for a moment, with one of those dramatic pauses that he seemed to favor, before responding. Everyone looked at each other. Maybe this whole case was going to go away, and they could all finally move on with their lives.

Once he started to speak, they each knew that Jeremy wouldn't let them go.

"I can't plead to life without parole," Jeremy said at last. "I admit that I was mean to Felicia. Very mean. Instead of life without parole, I'd like to plead to five years probation with the stipulation that I go to anger management counseling. I'll pay for the sessions myself, assuming you give me some time to come up with the first payment, as I am unemployed right now."

Smoky laughed.

Diana kept her composure. "I'll give you life *with* the possibility of parole—that's out in twenty years. You still get to do something with your life."

Jeremy wanted to go on about "doing something with his life," but Marlow interjected. "How about two counts of second degree murder, concurrent? That's eighteen years, out in nine. Your last two cases could go either way."

Diana wavered. This whole case would be over. She'd still have two murder convictions, and Jeremy wouldn't be out until she was long gone for sunnier climes. She'd take some heat, but who was going to run against her out here? The only other lawyers in the county were Marlow and Luna.

She was about to say yes and get the damn thing over with. Suddenly Jeremy stood up. Another dramatic pause. . . .

Oh shit, Marlow, Diana and Luna all said simultaneously to themselves.

"If this was Albuquerque," Jeremy said. "I'd take that deal. I'd probably even plead to the first offer on the table and I'd already be on my best behavior and busting broncos at the Honor Ranch for the rest of my life. It's actually better than life on the outs."

A recent "Channel 8 Exclusive" had shown the Honor Ranch with its inmate cowboys, and made it indeed look like more a Clint Eastwood movie—more of the good, and less of the bad and the ugly that Channel 8's viewers expected for their convicts.

Marlow covered his head with his hands. He knew what was coming. Jeremy kept going. If he was the devil's DJ, he was now spinning muzak, the music that played in the elevator going down to the depths of hell.

Luna made eye contact with Marlow. She tried to read him, but failed utterly. He looked enraged. Did he know about her and Nico?

He knew, damn it!

Just the way he avoided her eyes so quickly, made her know that he did. Suddenly she felt dirty. It would take a much bigger Crater and a much bigger lake to wash away what had happened that night. She wanted so much to make the last night with Nico never happen. But it did happen, and Nico gave a smirk toward Marlow. She knew what that smirk meant—a wolf pissing on the earth, marking his territory. Marlow made eye contact with Nico. He pissed right back. This wasn't over yet between the two of them.

"And I keep asking myself. . . ." Jeremy's muzak continued.

Luna watched the two men stare at each other. Maybe Marlow

had been hanging with Jeremy too long, because this sure wasn't the guy she used to have lunch with on Thursday. He no longer reminded her of her witty gay friend back at Sewall Hall, the old freshman dorm at CU, Marlow now looked dangerous, like a cornered animal.

As an athlete, Luna recognized someone getting psyched for the big game, and that's where Marlow was right now. What was his game anyway? His real game?

Nico stared down an angry drunk with a kitchen knife once a week, sometimes two in a night, so he was no wimp. Those big arms had thrown a lot of big men against the wall. He'd trained at the police academy and had taken a self-defense course every semester at the academy. Despite Marlow's recent weight training, Nico could still take him.

But then again, emotion could go a long way, and Marlow certainly had lots of that. Who do I want to win? She asked herself. Arthur or Lancelot?

Jeremy finally wound down, fifteen minutes later. "So my answer is that I formally and officially reject your plea offer."

There was silence as the lawyers finally came back into the room mentally. Jeremy looked around. "Did you guys hear anything I said?"

Diana hadn't had enough therapy in the fourteen days to hide her anger. "I think we're done here."

Marlow stood up and opened the door for them. "Since it's been months, I'd like to re-interview the witnesses."

Diana smiled. "Sure, but we do it at my place." She was already out the door when she turned. "Luna, are you coming?"

MORNING WITNESS INTERVIEWS

It seemed like no time had passed when the witness interviews began the next morning in Diana's office. If anything, the emotions between Nico and Marlow had intensified over the night.

Diana kept looking absent-mindedly at a watch that wasn't there. She hadn't had a watch in months. "I keep thinking that it's going to turn up," she said.

At least Luna felt comfortable when she sat down. She had politely declined Nico's invitation for a return engagement. The jury was still out on the whole Nico thing, although this morning he'd brought her flowers, just to mess up her head even more. When did he get so sensitive, she couldn't help but wonder?

As for Diana, she looked like she had absorbed a little from the program and had indeed taken control (the exact phrase was "Taking Ownership") of her life, at least for the moment. Luna noticed that Diana's left foot shook even worse with nervous tension.

"You okay?" she asked Diana, as they went up to get another cup of coffee for everyone. "You're supposed to be the grown-up, I'm supposed to be the immature one."

Diana laughed. She must have learned some kind of relaxation technique because her foot stopped shaking when they sat down again.

Caffeine injected, Luna and Diana sat back as Marlow questioned Nico about the first night at the Crosswinds and then the discovery of the body. Marlow was on a "fishing expedition," as they called it in law school; he asked Nico over and over again about the most mundane details. He tried to get into Nico's head.

Nico wouldn't bite. He was no Einstein, but he was a helluva lot smarter than Van Leit and he was stone cold sober. He remained calm the entire time, even after he related Jeremy's discovery of Felicia and Thayer in the bathroom for the tenth time, and the fact that no speck of DNA was found on Thayer's body to link him to Jeremy.

Every time Nico talked about Felicia's infidelity, Marlow looked rattled. He couldn't maintain eye contact with Nico, and didn't even dare look over at Luna. He kept bringing up the "no DNA" thing, over and over again until it became a mantra.

After Nico repeated yet another witness's statement that Jeremy had said out loud that he wanted to kill Thayer Brown for fucking his girl, Marlow had to excuse himself. He looked sick.

"What's the matter, Marlow?" Nico asked. "What's up your butt?"

That hurt Marlow badly. He had to sit down. "I'm done with him," Marlow said, utterly defeated. "Shark's next, right?"

"It'll take him a little time to get here," said Diana. "Shark is always late. Why don't you give us about an hour?"

Luna looked over at Diana after Marlow left. Maybe the tide had turned.

Diana gave Luna big hug. "We got him."

Diana and Luna had another cup of coffee when they were alone. It was from Ruth's private stock, from a Hawaiian island that neither had ever heard of. They could practically taste the volcano as the hot liquid went down their throats.

Diana glanced down at her empty wrist again, then looked over at the wall. "We've got some time."

"If you have a day left to live," said Luna. "You might as well live in Crater."

"Because it will feel like forever!" Diana said.

They both laughed.

"Are you going to keep on swimming?" Diana asked as a way of making conversation. Her relationship with Luna had been strained of late; it was time to heal the wounds, time for the sophomore to take the freshman under her wing again.

"I think it's time to start running," Luna said. "It's the final leg of the triathlon you know. So far, bad things have happened with the other two."

Diana laughed. "Bad things have happened with the other two. What do they say—trouble comes in threes."

She suddenly stopped laughing.

Marlow got back to their office long before Shark arrived. He had nowhere else to go. He read magazines in the lobby rather than talk to them. There was an article in *Cosmo* entitled "Can You Change Your Bad Boy?"

He shook his head, but read the article intensely as if it held the secret to the case. As the minutes passed, he still could not look at Luna at all. He focused all his attentions on Diana.

"How was wherever you were?" he asked Diana.

"It was good," she said. "I needed some time for me."

"I need some time for me as well," he said. "But ever since I started this case, there isn't a me anymore."

Diana didn't really feel comfortable with small talk. "Luna, could you page Shark?"

"I just did."

Luna paged him again. Another fifteen minutes passed. Diana gave her another look, so she paged him again. Shark finally showed up after the fifth page. There was a rumbling from outside to announce his arrival. Shark now had a shiny new Harley.

"Didn't hear the page," he said. "Sorry I'm late."

Diana growled. She had nearly violated him for being an hour late, calling in for a parole officer. She gave him a dirty look.

"Had to make a house call." He indicated his new bike out the window, as if he was trying to offer an explanation for his tardiness and the bike. "Business is booming!"

Diana wasn't satisfied, especially when he nearly took up the whole office as he sat down, spilling over the small seat in all three and possibly four dimensions.

"How's the ink?" he asked Marlow. There was an awkward

moment as Marlow reluctantly showed him the tattoo. He took Marlow's hand in his and looked down at the cross. He shrugged. "Not one of my greatest moments, but the customer is always right."

They quickly got to the heart of Shark's testimony. Marlow had to look at Shark directly when he posed the questions and it was not a pleasant experience. Shark talked about the final tattoo and Jeremy's words to him. "He said the reason he was getting the crosses was to get in touch with his feelings. He was crying."

Marlow remembered when Jeremy had said those exact words to him. "Getting in touch with my feelings." This tattooed biker freak actually came across as a credible witness. Shit.

"Did he actually confess to you?" Marlow asked. "Did he actually say the magic words, 'I killed all three of them,' 'them' being Sarah, Felicia and Thayer?"

Shark looked over at Diana, and pretended he didn't hear Marlow for the moment. What were the words she had used when talking to him over the phone? Obstruction of justice, interference with a police investigation, and harboring a felon? He couldn't remember all of them. The only word he could remember was the word "felony," which she had said at the end. And the words "habitual," "offender" and "enhancement;" which just so happened to be abbreviated as "the eight year bitch."

Diana was an eight-year bitch all right.

Marlow repeated the question, looked directly at him and spoke slowly, distinctly and very loud. "Did he confess?"

Shark stopped himself from looking at Diana. He stared at Marlow. "Yeah, he did."

Marlow looked down at Shark's statement "Then why did you say that—"

Suddenly he looked down at the statement. Shark had written it up himself and even his handwriting looked like the work of a master tattoo artist. It flowed and circled around. There was a second page, marked "Addendum" from an additional interview that Nico had done with Shark. Marlow hadn't bothered to read through it in the ream of other data. Jesus, he was getting as bad as Luna.

Sure enough, deep within the addendum, in Shark's scribbled hand were the words, "He said that he had killed all three of them." He listed all three names in case there was any doubt what he meant.

How the hell had he missed that?

Marlow sat down, stunned.

"Life with parole is still on the table," Luna said.

"I'll talk to my client," Marlow replied.

"Let us know if you still want to do the phone interviews in the afternoon."

AFTERNOON WITNESS INTERVIEWS

Marlow had to meet Jeremy over lunch at the Discount Prison. Lunch was the highlight of Jeremy's day and he certainly wouldn't give that up to meet with his lawyer.

Marlow looked around at the other prisoners as he followed Jeremy through the line. It was green chile stew today. It was always green chile something, since the prisoners had an "Honor Farm" out back, which was far less nice than the Honor Ranch up in Santa Fe. The green chile actually was quite good, and the prison shipped it in cans across the entire country under the brand label "Crater Green."

Even most of the locals didn't know that Crater Green came from the prison. Marlow didn't always want to know what went into the yellow cans.

Some inmates smirked as Marlow waited in line. "Fresh white meat," a few of them said, not quite under their breath.

Jeremy would turn around, they would get a glimpse of that serpent tattoo and they would stop in their tracks. Marlow wondered why. Jeremy didn't look quite as menacing as he did before he was arrested. He'd quit working out, and maybe even gotten back on the junk. He was definitely thinner and paler. Jeremy just had a half-dozen years of street rep to back up his attitude. He was in for three killings, so he got his respect that was due.

Marlow did not even want to think what Jeremy had done to some of the other cons in here or what Jeremy could do to him, before some lazy guard like Smoky actually bothered to come over and break the two apart. Marlow looked over at Smoky, still puffing away between hacking cough attacks. Smoky might not even bother to break it up at all.

"I still think I can get it down to two counts of second degree," Marlow said. "Cap of eighteen and, if you're good, out in nine."

"Don't tell me you're scared again."

Marlow looked at Jeremy. Jeremy was about to launch into one of those long speeches again. He now knew the character well enough that he could do the speech himself. He also knew his vulnerable points that Jeremy would hit: Nico, Luna, Nico *and* Luna, in that order. He knew Jeremy would end by teasing him about his manhood.

Nico and Luna . . . that was motivation enough.

The whole process had taken only a few moments, but Marlow was extremely effective at convincing himself, he could probably do the speech better than Jeremy.

"You got me," he said to the amazed Jeremy who had barely opened his mouth. "If you want two more trials, you got them."

"Why stop at three trials?" he asked.

Marlow stared at him. Did Jeremy have another cross tattoo on his other hand? He couldn't tell. Jeremy had so many tattoos, he couldn't keep track.

He slurped some stew, took a chug of ice water to wash down the heat of the Crater Green, and then turned to leave. He saw an inmate with "weasel" tattooed across his forehead on the way out. Weasel muttered something about "fresh white meat." Something got into Marlow and he gave the weasel Jeremy's serpent stare. He didn't even need the tattoo to back it up. The weasel scurried away.

Luna hadn't bothered to remember the names of the afternoon witnesses. They were all truckers from out of town anyway. All of these interviews had to be done by telephone; they were all on the road right now and didn't stop in Crater unless they had to.

She tried to imagine what these folks looked like by the sound of their voices. The baritone that talked about seeing Jeremy drag Thayer out of the bathroom was probably heavy-set. Probably wore a baseball hat and a T-shirt with an American flag that said "United We Stand."

Marlow had started out gung-ho, but his bravado wasn't much good over the speakerphone. He tried to bait them by forcing them to acknowledge that one Jeremy Jones had managed to fight his way out of the truck stop against four of them. He then settled into a series of routine questions and always ended by saying "You didn't actually see the murder of Thayer Brown, did you?"

He made each witnesses repeat their "no" over the static.

"How many more of these do we have?" he asked Diana. He still couldn't bring himself to acknowledge Luna's presence.

Just as well. Luna didn't really want to look at him either.

They had done four baritones—all truckers, and Luna imagined *all* of them with baseball hats and "United We Stand" T-shirts. That was it.

The final phone witness was a woman named Yoko Wagatsuma. Luna just couldn't picture an Asian woman trucker, so her mind shifted to clichés. Would Yoko be a petite geisha, or would she look something like a sumo wrestler? She had made a run all the way out to Barstow, so was running on Pacific Time. They would have some more time to kill.

Diana started to look at her wrist one more time, and then finally looked over at the wall clock.

"Come back at six," she said. "Hopefully we can finish this up then."

EVENING WITNESS INTERVIEWS

Marlow decided to go home, take a nap. Diana stayed behind to do some work. As for Luna, something bothered her about Diana's missing watch. It had been months yet she had never replaced it, because it was some kind of family heirloom. Luna remembered that Diana had lost it before she started traveling, so it must still be in town. Everyone in town would know that it had "DC" engraved on the back. No one in a small town would be stupid enough to keep the prosecutor's watch. So Luna would have to go out of town, or the next best thing.

Luna headed over to the Crosswinds and after a few questions went to the small room marked "Lost and Found." A petite Anglo woman stood guard over her as she pawed inside a gigantic crate.

There were a lot of watches. Finally, she saw the engraved one that said "DC."

"Where did you find it?" Luna asked. It couldn't have been in the bathroom, even a cop as stupid as Shatrock would have seen it there.

"It was at the salad bar," the woman said. "That's what they told me." She didn't have any idea how long it had been there, but it had been several months.

Luna handed the woman twenty dollars.

The woman smiled. "Enjoy your watch."

Luna was puzzled as she walked out of the Truck stop. Why would Diana come to the truck stop to eat a wilted salad when you could get a much better (and cheaper) one at the Rustler? And why wouldn't she come back to find her watch?

• • • • •

Luna kept the watch in her pocket as they all gathered for Yoko's interview. Once Yoko began talking in a high voice, Luna switched her vision of Yoko to geisha. The image of a geisha going to a truck stop bathroom, even a relatively nice one like the Crosswinds, was hard to picture.

Yoko was a truck driver who had been doing her regular route between a horse ranch in Amarillo direct to a pet food factory in Flagstaff. She passed through Crater every few days. She had been there earlier than the other witnesses and was the only one who had been inside when Thayer and Felicia had their little adventure.

"The door was closed," Yoko said. "It said 'out of order' on it, but I had been driving all night and I didn't even see it. I just pulled the door so hard that it opened right up."

Luna now thought of her as a sumo wrestler in light of her strength.

"It was dark in there and the light was out. I tried to turn it on but it didn't work. When I heard what was going on, I just left. When someone else came in, I gave them a look, but they still went in."

"Someone else came in?" Marlow said. "That wasn't in your statement."

"Just some woman," Yoko said. "No big deal. I didn't get a good look at her. Just a woman. She was already inside in the dark. Then I went out, tried to find another bathroom. It was an emergency for me, if you know what I mean."

Marlow wasn't sure what she meant. Luna knew instantly. She turned to give a knowing glance to Diana.

Marlow had kept going. "Do you know if that other person was in the bathroom when Jeremy came?"

"Nah . . . I went to the bathroom on the other side. When I came back that's when I saw that big blond guy pull the other guy out and beat the crap out of him and say he would kill them both. Then, when all the truckers came, he made his way out the door and then the cops came."

Marlow was so intent on trying to stare down the speakerphone that he hadn't noticed Diana stiffen as Yoko kept talking. Luna sure noticed. Diana always seemed to get nervous when Felicia's name came up. The foot kept shaking more and more intently.

Back in high school the boys had always joked that Diana had a hard-on for Felicia.

Jesus!

Eureka!

Suddenly the whole thing made sense to her.

Everything!

Luna already knew that Diana had been at the truck stop eating that very overpriced, wilted salad. Luna now knew why. Afterward, Diana must have gone into the bathroom with Felicia and Thayer doing God knows what. She could read it in her eyes, read it in the way her back was held up so straight and in the way her foot moved up and down like an epileptic seizure. That explained why Diana had wanted so badly to charge Jeremy with Felicia's death and why Diana had had the nervous breakdown, why Diana had tried to get out of town before the trial started, and why she had never gone back for that damn watch. It wasn't substance abuse or emotional trauma. It was something else.

She made eye contact with Diana. Diana kept a poker face, even if her foot betrayed all that she was holding inside. Was Diana also having an affair with Thayer? No, Diana barely knew Thayer. Luna remembered Diana's reaction to her asking why she was charging Jeremy with Felicia's murder.

Luna suddenly thought back to Crater High. Go Comets! There had been some awkward moments between the two of them. They'd first kissed her freshman year. Just two girls playing "spin the bottle" during a sleepover at the Mothership. Diana had said something about a sophomore showing a freshman the ropes. Diana had played around the outside of her T-shirt. "This is how a boy will touch you," Diana said. She'd also touched the outside of her bike shorts.

"What does it feel like when a boy touches me?" Luna had asked innocently, "Show me."

Diana had demonstrated to her, but it was all on the outside.

Two years later, right before her junior prom, it had grown a little more serious. That was right after Felicia had left to have her baby. Luna thought. The baby that never came. With Felicia gone, Diana was suddenly her best friend all over again.

Her mother was still able to travel in those days and was in Bora Bora or Pago Pago—some exotic island with a double name. Diana had spent the night with her at the Mothership. They'd slept in her mother's bed, shivering together in their underwear on a cold Crater night.

Diana had a woman's body already but, as a cross-country runner, Luna still felt like a young girl. They'd talked all night about Luna's big night with Nico coming up. Diana wasn't going to prom. She had a pageant or something coming up.

Girl talk. Just hours of girl talk, holding hands, drinking some exotic brandy stolen from her mother's liquor cabinet. Luna didn't think Diana even mentioned Felicia, other than that she had screwed up her life. Luna had called her a tramp.

Diana had said nothing. And Luna had been a little brat and said over and over again, "Felicia was a tramp! Felicia was a tramp!"

They'd wrestled a little, but it was all in fun, right? "Take it back! Take it back!" Diana had said. Diana had always been much stronger, and she choked her a little, just in fun, right?

"I take it back," Luna had said.

Diana had suggested drinking games after that. Luna had licked a few drops of the brandy off Diana's large breasts and Diana had followed suit by licking it off of her small ones. They played around a little more, as Diana demonstrated some of the things that Nico would do to her for her big date, fingered her down there once or twice. Both of them giggling. But it was just two girls messing around, right? She had passed out from the brandy before things had become too serious.

The next morning Diana had gone off to her pageant, and she had gone to the prom. And after the night with Nico, they'd never slept over again. She'd told Diana about the night and things had never been the same. She'd forgotten all about that, but that was just girl stuff, right?

Felicia was a tramp, Luna had said. Well she was. . . .

Take it back! Take it back!

She had choked me really hard, Luna thought. Was that what this was all about? Diana taking it back?

Luna brought her attention back to matters at hand as Marlow continued questioning Yoko. He had her describe her itinerary for every single one of her comings and going through Crater, and the contents of each load of her truck.

Luna watched Marlow in action. Even his mannerisms were Jeremy's now. Unfortunately, he'd picked up one of Jeremy's worst traits—when he was on stage, the one where the whole world revolved around him.

As Marlow spun further and further away from the night in question, Diana relaxed a bit. Marlow didn't notice.

Luna's mind raced through every possible scenario. Let's assume that Diana was having some kind of affair with Felicia while Felicia was having an affair with Thayer. Two affairs sounded unlikely but, hey, Felicia had always been a tramp, right? No one would ever know if Diana was there for a confrontation or a threesome. It didn't really matter, because Jeremy broke up that threesome for good. Somehow, Jeremy didn't know that Diana was there. He surely would have taunted her with it by now, if he did.

Could Diana have killed Thayer just to cover up the evidence? It was dark in the ladies room, so Jeremy wouldn't have seen her. Apparently, this Wagatsuma woman didn't get a good look at her either. The only people who would have known about Diana would be Thayer and Felicia. Everyone in the world thought Jeremy had Thayer in his bull's-eye. Perfect timing for someone to take care of him. Once Thayer was gone, could Diana then go out and kill Felicia as insurance, or maybe just for breaking her heart?

Luna looked over at Diana. Diana had been her best friend. But that was as a Crater High Lady Comet. How well did she know her as the district attorney of Crater County?

Meanwhile, Marlow had managed to get Yoko thoroughly confused. He kept harping on the fact that she had failed to pick Jeremy out of a photo array. She was now so confused, it was hard to say if she now hauled horsemeat for dog food, or dogmeat for horse food. Satisfied, he called it a day, abruptly hanging up on poor Yoko.

"Call Benally and tell him that we start up again on Monday," he said.

"Monday it is," said Diana. She swore for a minute. "We'll have to get all those subpoenas out for those truckers."

"That's your problem," Marlow said. "Not mine."

He left without even looking at Luna.

Diana let out a sigh of relief. "Thank God that's over," she said, just a moment too early. Marlow looked back, then kept going.

Luna looked at Diana. "Di, we've got to talk."

"We can do that tomorrow."

Luna looked at her. "Let's talk now." She handed her the watch.

Diana had an expression that was impossible to read.

"Fax those subpoenas out and come by the house tonight." Diana put the watch back on her wrist. She looked at it and couldn't help but smile. "Let's say around eight-thirty."

JOINDER OF PARTIES

That night, Marlow went out to the Crosswinds. Time for pre-trial simulation number two. He took a look around before gathering up the courage to enter. It was actually a pretty nice, modern truck stop and, with the mobile homes around back housing the crews, it was practically a city in itself. At night, it looked like a human colony on the moon, especially with the old refinery lit up in those ghostly green lights.

He had crossed the invisible line into the building to see Luna, but by himself he still felt the full-force of the Crosswinds taboo. He felt that all the out-of-town travelers were looking at the hick from Crater who was too stupid to get out of there.

Marlow suddenly knew why this would be a perfect place for an affair. Only five minutes from home and he didn't see a single familiar face. The entire employee crew, right down to the janitors, had changed since he had been here with Luna.

You might as well be in another county inside the Crosswinds. He tried to picture Felicia and Thayer. Maybe they'd snuck into one of the mobile homes used to house the employee crews. Thayer came through here all the time, so he probably had a connection. No one had mentioned anything.

He hadn't known Thayer, so he couldn't figure out what he would think. Thayer and Felicia have a quickie in one of the mobile homes out back. Thayer gets ready to gas up. Felicia is so overcome with the impending loneliness that she drags him into the ladies room for the infamous "one for the road" before mean old Jeremy comes back. He had to search for the ladies' room. It was down a hallway around the corner—not in clear line of sight from the cafeteria.

So then Yoko comes in, strung out from hauling horsemeat or whatever it was. Marlow has even less of a lock on Yoko. All he knows is that she was in a rush—has to go to the bathroom, or something like that. She doesn't see the "out of order" sign and, in frustration, pulls open the locked door. It must have been a pretty bad emergency, because she pulls really hard.

So Yoko walks in on the sounds of a sordid scene. Lights are off, but she can tell just by hearing, or smelling. Then Yoko nearly runs into someone coming in while she's on the way out. He had absolutely no clue who this next person was, this "someone else." Why the hell would Ms. Someone Else want to go into a bathroom with two people already in there?

He couldn't think of a reason without more information, so he turned his attention back to Jeremy. Our hero comes back from his truck-driving gig. Marlow assumed that Jeremy knew Thayer's car from seeing it around town, and he knew what was going down in the bathroom. Either fate or the Crater winds had drawn Jeremy to the Crosswinds at that particular moment on that particular night.

Marlow walked back out the door, pretended to see an offending car. He then looked around as if spying for two people who didn't want to be spied. An elderly couple gave him a dirty look.

"Do we know you from somewhere, partner?" the old man asked, not entirely friendly, and certainly not someone he'd want for a partner.

"I'm rehearsing a part for a movie," Marlow said. He stared the man down. The man melted before his eyes. Damn, it was fun to be Jeremy.

He then looked for the ladies room. He went around the corner. Would Jeremy be able to hear the sounds on the inside? Probably not, but Jeremy would just know. He just knew.

Is Ms. Someone Else still inside? No way to know. There's a maintenance closet in the bathroom. Maybe she hid in there when Jeremy came.

Jeremy drags Thayer out, says, "I'm going to kill you both . . . blah, blah, blah. . . ."

"Watch where you're going, pervert!" A young woman came

out of the ladies room and bumped into Marlow. He had given her a dirty look without even realizing it. She hurried away, terrified of him.

Jeremy then fights his way out when the four truckers grab him. Marlow looked around the Crosswinds. The truckers tonight were some pretty rough customers. Jeremy must have had his hands full, yet had still come out swinging, come out on top. Marlow smiled to himself. At this moment, he just knew he could take on all comers in a giant truck stop cage death match.

Marlow didn't want to break character. He left the truck stop and walked behind the building. There was one of those cut-off corners of the building, almost as if the architect wanted to cheat his client out of a few square feet of space. The shadows formed strange shapes in strange colors because of the ghostly lights of the abandoned refinery behind him.

He tried to think where Jeremy went after he left the truck stop. Jeremy disappears for two weeks. No one knows where Jeremy went. Then out of the blue, he visits Felicia and then boom! Sarah is killed. The next night, Thayer comes in from out of town to be with Felicia. And boom! Thayer ends up here, in this corner.

Marlow felt some strange electricity as he looked at the discoloration in the dirt in the corner. Here's where someone, and he hoped to God it wasn't Jeremy, put a burnt and dismembered Thayer for his final moments on top of this earth.

There were much better places to dump bodies in Crater County, especially if you didn't want them to be found. It would have been impossible to bring a body into the ladies room, past all those people. This would be the next best thing. One could literally throw a body out of a pick-up truck in a matter of seconds. Late at night, no one would be the wiser. No video cameras out here. If you wanted to dump a body to send a message, dumping it here sent a message loud and clear. There was no doubt in his mind that someone in the building that night had killed Thayer.

Who was he kidding? Looking down at the corner, he knew in his heart that it had to be Jeremy. If he were Jeremy he sure as fuck would have killed Thayer Brown for what he had done. Had to! And this is where he would throw the body. Had to.

And at that moment, he really *was* Jeremy. He looked down at the discoloration of the ground in the corner. He took a great deal of satisfaction. Those dark particles were all that remained of someone who had fucked the woman he had loved.

He had triumphed. He felt like the alpha wolf that had just vanquished the ambitious beta, then had devoured him whole and spit out the gristle in this corner here for the rest of the pack to see.

Marlow knew he had to break character now, but it had grown harder with every day of the trial. He thought back to days of hypnosis when he tried to stop grinding his teeth at night. Think of a happy place, the hypnotist had said. His mind raced to one of the few happy moments of his adult life, one of the few moments when he thought that life would really work out—that moment when Luna had taken his hand over in the truck stop, just that one moment when she touched the palm of his hand and he felt her warmth pulse through all of his nerves, all of his veins.

His mind wandered from the moment. No, don't go to the next instant, he told himself. Don't go to the moment when she saw the cross. Just stay at that perfect moment when she touched the palm of his hand, and ran her finger down the slope of his thumb. Just touched. . . .

His breathing slowed. He felt himself diminish slightly. He was a Marlow once again. Was there any defense for Jeremy? He tried thinking like the analytical law student who had scored in the 95th percentile on the LSAT, rather than the lawyer who pled traffic tickets to pay the month-to-month rental on a broken down house.

There had to be someone else to blame. He now had three suspects other than Jeremy: Yoko (a reach), Felicia (a real reach), and the mysterious third woman, Ms. Someone Else. But why the hell would she want to kill anybody, whoever she was?

Luna did get the truckers' subpoenas out by the end of the afternoon. She faxed them to the various trucking companies all across America. The fax broke down a few times halfway though a subpoena. She punched it a few times in frustration.

Why did she have a bad feeling about this?

To calm down, she went out for a long run that evening. She had an hour to kill before seeing Diana and she might as well get in a couple of miles. Luna liked running most of all, despite what had happened at the Olympic trials. She still did have fear when she ran in the twilight, however. She wore an elaborate mirrored outfit to reflect headlights, yet she always worried that some drunken Crater driver would take her out. Luna always ran as far off the road as she could, and she still worried. She must have passed five sets of wooden crosses along the side of the roads.

She made it a point to shower before going to see Diana. She knew about Diana and smell.

Diana's "Crater Ranch" was on the south side of town. She had inherited from her family, now that she was the last of the Craters. She lived alone.

Before going in, Luna looked at the rocky landscape that made up Diana's xeriscaped front yard. Even Diana didn't have grass in front because of the expense and her yard looked like one of those resorts in Arizona. Luna hesitated. She didn't own a gun or a knife; didn't think that Diana did either. She picked up a narrow sharp rock, practically an arrowhead—from the xeriscape as some kind of protection. If Diana tried anything, Luna had the natural arrowhead as a good luck charm, and perhaps a weapon as well.

Luna rang the doorbell of the nice Santa Fe style home. "Come in," Diana's voice came in from the intercom as the door clicked open. "I'm outside at the pool."

Crater Ranch might as well have been in Santa Fe. Luna felt as if she was passing through a gallery—each room contained artifacts, paintings and sculptures. She even saw something from the sculptor who did the forty-thousand-dollar bronze man, except it was a bronze woman.

"My tax dollars at work," Luna joked to herself.

Diana had a nice courtyard surrounding the pool, protected by an impossibly high adobe brick wall. For a moment, Luna thought that this was probably the only place in the entire county not subject to the Crater wind. Then she saw some tumbleweeds in the pool. No place was safe.

The hot tub looked free from debris, however. Diana sat in whirling waters, a clear drink in her hand. She was topless. She'd always claimed to be big-boned rather than fat, and that was indeed the case. Luna admired Diana's magnificent boob job.

"Your tax dollars at work," Diana said proudly.

"We gotta talk," Luna said to her.

"Come on in," Diana said. "The water's fine."

There was no place to sit down, and the hot tub sure looked inviting after her long run. She thought about the Lady of the Lake, and realized that she couldn't drown in three feet of water, now could she? She didn't have a bathing suit, but that had never stopped her before. And it was just her old best friend Diana, right?

For one brief moment she thought of undressing, but she still felt cautious. She had her jog bra and shorts and they would survive the water. She felt Diana look at her as she took off her sweatshirt. It was a cold night, and her nipples were already hard from the wind. She automatically thought back to those two nights in high school.

Luna couldn't help but flex for Diana. She had worked hard for her body. Diana had just paid for hers.

"Turn around," Diana said.

Luna obliged.

"Damn," Diana said appreciatively.

Luna looked back at Diana. If Nico was too hard, Diana was too soft. But then maybe "soft" was what she needed right now. She didn't know what to think any more. She hid the arrowhead in her spandex.

After some hesitation, Luna got into the hot tub. Diana poured her a drink. Luna was scared it was alcohol, but it was water. At least she hoped it was water. Diana didn't move closer to Luna. She looked at Luna as if she weren't sure whether this was business or pleasure.

Luna moved to the other side of the tub, as if to answer. "This is business, Di," Luna said. She waited another minute. "I need to know about you and Felicia."

Diana said nothing.

"I know you were there that night at the truck stop," Luna said.

Still nothing.

"You've got to withdraw, Di," she said. "Jesus Christ, you were a witness."

There was a long break. Diana got out of the pool and put on a towel. Her good cheer must have gone down the hot tub drain. Luna stayed put. The swirling water felt too good on her aching muscles. She wondered why she had brought the arrowhead after all.

Diana took a deep breath. "Felicia and I had a thing back when we were in high school. Not anything sexual really, just a *thing*, because she wasn't really gay. And she left me for Jeremy. He knocked her up. Jeremy!" She spit his name out.

Luna noticed the look in Diana's eyes. "I go away to Las Cruces, down to NMSU for school, then onto UNM for law and get on with my life and then come back here after all that time, because I had nowhere else to go. And she's my friend again. My only friend, before you. But before anything can happen, she's back to Jeremy again!"

"What about Thayer Brown?"

"What about Thayer Brown?" Diana replied. "I didn't know the man, but at least he wasn't Jeremy."

"I don't get it."

"Going back to me was too big a step. Felicia was pretty much totally straight, but she always seemed to hold out a glimmer of hope for me or maybe I was kidding myself all along. She took a baby step away from Jeremy, and that was Thayer Brown. Perhaps she wanted someone who could take Jeremy in a fight. We were supposed to meet at the truck stop. Nobody from here goes to the Crosswinds so it's the perfect place to talk things over. Just talk."

Diana stopped to think. "I got there a little early, ate a salad, then had to go to the bathroom."

"And Felicia was already there with Thayer," Luna said. Luna hoped that Diana would give her the sordid details, but Diana wouldn't budge.

"So once that Yoko woman left, it was the three of us," said Diana. "I tried to turn on the lights, but they didn't work. We talked for a few moments, just talked, okay?"

Luna thought Diana sounded a little too defensive.

"Then Jeremy comes in," Diana continued. "It was dark and I hid in the maintenance closet before he saw me. He was totally focused on the other two. He grabbed Thayer and pulled him out. I stayed in there, hid in the closet for another hour more, and the rest is history."

Luna stared at Diana for a second. The story didn't totally jibe with Yoko Wagatsuma's. Was there something else going on that night? Why would Diana just happen to go to that bathroom?

Luna looked over at Diana, who sat there with a towel around her shoulder. Could Diana kill Thayer and then try to set up Jeremy? She certainly hated Jeremy, and she must have absorbed something about evidence from being a DA, even by osmosis. She could have set it all up. . . .

Luna looked around the courtyard. She was very much alone, except for the tumbleweeds in the pool. And those walls were very, very high. Diana walked around behind her. Luna kept thinking to herself, trying to put the pieces together. With Thayer gone, Diana would have had to have taken Felicia out too. And there was motive enough—jealousy.

"What about Felicia?" Luna asked. "Did you kill Felicia?" Luna couldn't help herself. She was sixteen again. "Because she was a tramp?"

Suddenly, her head went way down under the swirling water. Oh my God, Diana wants to drown me! She tried to reach for the arrowhead, but it had already fallen to the bottom of the hot tub. And Diana outweighed her by nearly sixty pounds. Luna gasped for breath and swallowed chlorine. Her body rebelled. Diana wasn't that soft when it came to Felicia. Luna should have remembered that. There were no thoughts about the lady and the lake and the sword and the stone this time.

For a moment, Diana sure felt serious. Finally—after a moment that felt like an eternity—she let Luna up and threw her a towel.

"If you think I killed Felicia—" she said.

"I'm sorry, Di. I didn't mean it." She waited for a second. She knew what Diana wanted her to say. "And I take back what I said about her."

Diana looked at her again. "I loved her."

"I take it back," Luna said. "I really mean it."

Diana looked satisfied. They were both in high school again. "I really did love her," Diana said with a glimmer in her eye. "She loved me, even if it wasn't a sexual thing for her. I tried to help her get away from Jeremy in high school, but I failed. And then I got a second chance and it looked like it was all going to happen. I could have saved her. She should still be alive right now. You didn't know Felicia. You didn't know a fucking thing about her!"

Diana was right. She didn't know a fucking thing about Felicia. Diana started crying. Luna waited a long moment and then put her arms around her. Diana hugged her back. They were cool again. It was just like the pillow fight. Diana's foot had stopped shaking.

"If you ever say anything bad about Felicia, or say that I killed her," Diana said between sobs. "So help me God, I will hold your head under for real next time."

They held each other for a few more minutes, not saying a word, but then the winds began howling outside, the mercury dropped a few more degrees and Luna knew it was time to go.

"We're cool?" Diana asked Luna.

"We're cool," Luna replied.

Luna put her clothes back on and headed out the door. She'd let the arrowhead lie at the bottom of the tub. When she was halfway home she realized something. Diana might not have killed Felicia. Diana certainly had not killed her mother, or Sarah Sanchez. And most of all Diana loved her like a little sister, perhaps more than that. She knew that in her heart. But Diana had said nothing about whether she had killed Thayer.

Not one damn thing.

EVIDENTIARY CHALLENGES

The next afternoon, Marlow talked with Raymond Rossi in his office. As Marlow looked around the stylish office, he thought that maybe there really was something to this *feng shui.* The office had been rearranged since the last time to best catch the rays of the sun at this time of the year. He really did feel some positive energy passing through his body. He actually felt like he had broken character, if only for a moment.

Rossi did not look well; his medications were sometimes at war with each other. But as always, Rossi made the best of it. He played his computer as if it was a grand piano. Marlow sat in a comfortable chair.

"I could get so busted for this," Rossi said as he punched in a few keys. He stared at a few pages of data. "This Wagatsuma woman came here pretty regularly and always stopped at the Crosswinds and bought the buffet for nine-ninety-nine." He turned over a few more keys. "She did spend the night here at the motel when Thayer Brown was murdered. Do you think she did it?"

"I don't have to think that. It's called raising reasonable doubt."

"I don't understand you lawyers," he said. "You know Jeremy did it."

Marlow shrugged. He didn't know what he knew any more.

"Did you know the lawyers in the bank's San Francisco office make about six times what you make?" Rossi asked.

"But with cost of living, it evens out, doesn't it?"

"That makes it four times as much, and they own property which is going to appreciate every year. You don't own anything and even if you did. . . ."

Marlow shrugged again.

"I could probably pull a few of the strings I have left to see if I could get you a job out there. Hell, paralegals make three times as much as you."

Marlow thought about the Bay Area. God, it sounded much better than here. "If you like it so much, why aren't you back there?"

Rossi smiled. "I've learned to survive anywhere. I can even get you a job at a bank out there. You'd make more money as a teller—twice as much."

Rossi had just offered him not one, but two ways out of here. He would never have to be Jeremy again, or the criminal after Jeremy. He had a sick feeling in his gut that this had gotten way out of his own control.

The winds kicked up outside. Marlow wondered if they would let him leave. He looked down at his tattooed cross. Once the needle had pierced his skin, it had been too late.

Marlow laughed. "This isn't about money. And besides I kinda like who I am."

"Like who you are?" Rossi said. "I don't think you have the slightest idea of who that is anymore."

Marlow didn't argue.

Rossi focused his attention back on the computer screen. "I better get off before one of the security overrides hook on. Is there anyone else you want me to look up? See if they were at the Crosswinds that night?"

Marlow thought for a moment. If only he knew the identity of Ms. Someone Else.

Diana had brought in brownies for the day, and she and Luna munched as they organized the various witness interviews into a semblance of a murder case. They were friends again, and it was almost like the high school slumber party all over again, without the experimentation of course.

"I'll take Shark, you take Nico," Diana said, as if they were sisters splitting up a doll collection. "We split the truckers. You do two and I'll do two."

"Don't you think they might recognize you?"

"I was a woman at a salad bar six months ago," she said. "The only one I'm worried about is Yoko. She looked right at me. We split the criminalistics guys."

They made a few phone calls. One of the truckers had done a run up the Alaska Highway. They'd have to fly him down from Fairbanks.

Diana checked the budget. "The air fare costs as much as my boob job."

"We don't really need him," said Luna. "And besides, he's only one witness. You got two nice new boobs."

They both laughed. "They're worth it, aren't they?" Diana asked.

"Definitely."

"I do love you, Luna my love," said Diana. "But not that way—"

"I know."

They went through the other truckers. They couldn't reach any of them. Hopefully, they'd be able to appear telephonically. It was going to be touch and go.

"What about Yoko?"

Diana stiffened. "I'm going to be sick for that one," she said. She gave a slight giggle. "I'm going to go to my doctor's appointment at the clinic. He's in town that day. I'm sure he'll tell me to stay home with some Valium for the rest of the morning. Are you cool with that?"

"Of course."

"I can come back in the afternoon and do Shark," Diana said.

"I didn't think he was your type."

They both laughed. Luna still wanted to know what the hell had been going on in that ladies' room, but Diana would never tell.

"Are you cool with this whole thing?" Diana asked.

Cool with this whole thing? Luna still didn't know what "this whole thing" meant. Diana may have been there, but there was certainly a reasonable doubt as to whether anything more had gone on. But she looked over at her friend. Diana still was the sophomore, and she was still the freshman after all.

"Sure, I'm cool with it," she said.

Nico had called her for dinner. She had pinched her gut—after her little stay in the hospital, Nico's cooking and now Diana's brownies—she'd gained a pound or two. Dinner with Nico was out. Weight gain wasn't the only reason, but it was good enough.

It was time for an afternoon jog. She liked the self-reliance of running, even though the winds seemed nastier than when she was on a bike. She headed out towards the moto-cross park again.

Marlow had decided that maybe it was time for some serious cardio. It had worked for Luna—look at what amazing shape she was in. He already had the leg strength from the squats on the Soloflex, but maybe getting outside would be the way to clear Jeremy out of his head for at least twenty or so minutes a day. He knew that Luna ran past his house every day at five-thirty, rain or shine.

It was five-twenty-five, so he pondered the case against Jeremy for the murder of Thayer Brown. Jeremy was going down for Brown. There was no real physical link, but those four witnesses in the truck stop and that damn confession to Shark would be enough to put the lethal injection in right there. He just wanted to throw in the towel.

He checked his watch. Right on schedule, Luna came down the highway. Damn, she was fast. He let her pass. She was so intent on her run that she didn't even wave. That pissed him off. He didn't know what got into him. He started to sprint. The Soloflex had indeed given him leg muscles that he didn't know he had.

Luna saw a figure from behind. Oh My God! Marlow. When did he learn to run? He was much faster than she expected. He's gaining on me! Her legs howled in pain. She had been over-training as always, and some of her muscles must have stayed behind at the last hill.

Marlow knew he had about one good minute of adrenaline in him, before lactic acid forced his legs to turn into stone. He now went into a dead-on sprint to catch Luna. His warp drive was on.

She could kill him in long distances, there was no doubt about that. But if he put every ounce of energy into it, if he took all energy away from life support and put it into warp drive. . . .

Luna's legs began cramping. She'd already gone a mile or two, and the wind had taken a lot out of her. Marlow came closer and closer. Damn, he was really sprinting now.

What had she said in high school to that stupid girl from Laguna Acoma High who almost took her at the finish of the state finals senior year? "You can't catch me, bitch!" Luna said out loud.

She deliberately slowed, then once he got within a few feet of her, she sprinted again. He collapsed onto the dirt, utterly spent. She went a few dozen yards more just to prove a point. He didn't follow; he stayed on the ground gasping.

"Give up?" she asked.

He could barely move. "I'm way too young to have a heart attack," he said between gasps.

"Are you all right?" she asked. He sure didn't look it.

She thought for a moment then came back over to him. He really was on the verge of a heart attack.

With great effort, he lifted himself up. He tried to pretend that he'd been faking the pain, but he couldn't quite pull it off. "You win," he said.

"I always do," she lied.

"What did you say to me?" he said. "I heard you say something."

"'You can't catch me, bitch.' I used to say that when I was in high school. I tried to say that in college, but the bitches started catching me."

He couldn't help laughing, but the expenditure of oxygen nearly turned him blue. Finally, after another moment, and then another, he caught his breath. She gave him a hand up. They didn't say anything more, just started walking on the dirt road. They headed in the vague direction of Hell's Hills, although they both knew that they wouldn't make it by nightfall.

"We only have a few more weeks of trial," he said, when he finally had enough oxygen saved up. "Hopefully after that things can get back to normal."

"When have things ever been normal?"

She looked over at him. Even though his hair was dyed, and his glasses were gone, she still saw a remainder of that funny nervous guy who had joked with her after the first meeting with Jeremy. He definitely had more of an edge with the weight training, but that wasn't it.

He now had the slightest whiff of "bad boy" to him, and that turned her on more than she cared to admit. But then she saw that damn tattooed cross again.

"Why did you have to do that? Get that cross?"

Marlow felt very uncomfortable for a moment. "I have to sort of become my clients in order to defend them. It was my way of becoming Jeremy."

"Do you really want to be Jeremy?" she said. "Marlow isn't such a bad guy."

He looked at her. He wanted to say that Marlow was a nobody who couldn't get laid at a whorehouse, because the whores would ask him to edit their term papers instead. He stopped himself, gathered his thoughts. "I wasn't thinking. I had no idea that it would offend you. I'm sorry."

She looked at him. He really was sorry. She looked into his eyes. No, this poor panting slob hadn't killed her mom. How could she have thought that even for an instant? They kept walking for a few more dusty miles of dirt road. She walked a little faster than he. As he stared at her from just behind, he made an amazing effort. He somehow managed to get Nico out of his mind, and out of Luna.

But the moment passed. He had to ask. "What about you and Nico?"

"I don't know," she said. "I don't know."

They stayed silent for a moment. The winds decided that they should keep heading outward. They got closer and closer to Shark's.

"You're all I have that stops me from becoming him," he said.

"Huh?" That was certainly a weird thing to say.

"I went over to the Crosswinds," Marlow continued. "Just to really try to see the world through Jeremy's eyes. And for one brief moment in the back—right where the body was—I felt like I really was Jeremy."

She definitely felt uneasy now.

"But then you helped me get back," he said. "Back to being me."

"I did?"

"I thought of you, just the two of us holding hands that one day . . . you know how in hypnosis you're supposed to think of a happy thought, a 'good place' in your life."

"I'm a good place in your life?" That was weird and sweet at the same time. She looked at him for one more moment. The jury was still out on Marlow.

But then he did the absolute best possible thing he could do at that moment. He started humming the old Beatles tune. "*Oh you, you got that something. . . .*"

There was a pause. Then the jury reached its verdict. "*I think you understand,*" she hummed back.

"*Yeah you, you got that something,*" he said.

"*I wanna hold your—*"

Before she could say the word "hand," he put his finger to her mouth. "Shhh. . . ."

They had come to a small wooden cross at the side of the road. It had been the cross she'd passed the day of the arrest, blamed on a drunk driver, and had never thought of again, even though she passed it nearly every day.

"Do you know where we are?"

She shook her head.

"This is where Felicia died," he said. "Or I guess where she was dumped."

She stopped for a moment. She expected to shiver, but she didn't. This was just a piece of ground with a wooden cross in it. If there was a spirit, she couldn't feel it. Instead, she thought about how her bike had locked up around here.

"Sometimes I wish I could be like you," she said. "I never get into my cases like you do. Being a prosecutor is just a job for me."

"That's why you keep losing," he said.

"It's not over yet," she said.

"That's why you keep losing," he said again. "You work hard. You're smart. I saw that from the first moment I met you. I didn't even know about the Olympics, but that all fits in too."

"The Olympics?"

"That you choked."

"I didn't choke," she said. Although she couldn't think of a word to describe walking into a stadium at the finish of a race, when everyone else was running full speed.

"Well someday, I want to teach you how not to choke."

"And you know this. What have you ever won?"

"I got a hung jury, not once, but twice, on a drunken Indian who killed two of his family members. And I walked Jeremy Jones on one murder so far. Those are wins."

She laughed. "Okay, those are wins."

The winds blew them away from Felicia's cross, almost as if Felicia's spirit didn't want the two of them around for more than an instant. They turned around. They were a long way out here. It was getting dark and they didn't want to be this far out at this time of night.

"Okay, I choked," she said at last. "And I choked on Sarah's case, too. Those records, they were bullshit, right?"

"I probably shouldn't tell you this, but those were my annual statements," he said with a smile. "You should have challenged that."

"I won't choke next time," she said.

They stared at each other. He wanted to kiss her, more than anything in the world. She was becoming the woman he had always thought she could become. What was this, love at third sight?

"We only have a few more weeks to go," she said. For a moment, she thought about Nico and Diana. Damn, she'd been a slut the last few days. If Nico was too hard and Diana was too soft, Marlow at this very moment was so very just right.

Oh, what the hell. She leaned forward and closed her eyes.

The winds had other ideas. Suddenly, she coughed on some dust. She didn't have to look up to know what had kicked up that dust.

Marlow stopped too. He knew what the dust meant.

Nico's Corvette pulled up to them. "What the fuck are you doing?" he shouted.

"We're just walking," she said.

"I'm not talking to you," he said. "I'm talking to you, asshole." He turned toward Marlow and gave him a push. He then grabbed Marlow's tattooed hand and showed it to Luna.

"Look at this, Luna," he yelled, putting the tattoo right next to her face. "Look at this!"

She didn't do anything.

Nico pulled out a sealed manila envelope. "You know what's in here? It's proof that he killed your mother. I got direct fucking evidence proving that this lawyer right here is a psycho killer, just like his boyfriend Jeremy!"

Nico pushed Marlow hard to the ground. Marlow felt something snap. Nico towered over him, ready to kick the living crap out of him.

"Come on, pussy boy!" Nico shouted. "Make your move!"

Marlow was about to get up then noticed that Nico had a gun. It was still holstered, but he didn't know if Nico was a reincarnation of the Sundance Kid. He did know that cops got away with questionable "self-defense" shootings all the time, especially in towns like Crater.

"Both of you stop it!" Luna yelled. She hadn't seen Nico's holstered gun. She looked down at Marlow as he wiped some dirt out of his eye. She saw that damn cross staring her right in the face, and saw that manila envelope in Nico's hand.

There were two Marlows she thought. She may love the one who had just been walking with her, but there was the other one that wanted to be Jeremy. She looked in Marlow's eyes as he lay on the dirt. He had that rage and longing in those eyes. He looked at them both like an animal waiting to strike. In that moment, she indeed saw Jeremy sitting there, not Marlow. She looked at that damn tattoo one more time and couldn't help but think of her mother.

"Let's go, Nico," she said. "Take me home."

Unable to resist the cliché, Nico kicked a little sand in

Marlow's face. He opened up the Corvette for Luna and got in the other side.

Marlow choked on the dust.

WITNESS UNAVAILABLE

The next morning, Marlow met with Jeremy in the interview room at the Discount Prison. "What's wrong with you?" Jeremy asked. "You look like shit."

Marlow had started crying by Jeremy's fourth word. Crying right there in front of his client, something that no male defense attorney can ever, ever do. One of the unwritten canons of professional responsibility in New Mexico that should be posted over the signpost of the doorway into every courtroom and every jail was "no crying in criminal defense."

"She doesn't want me," he said between sobs. "She wants Nico."

"So Nico's her boyfriend now?"

Smoky giggled, as if the word "boyfriend" was a private joke between him and Jeremy. Marlow could barely muster a "yes."

Jeremy looked over at Smoky. "Yo Smoky, go out and get a joint, okay?" Smoky went down the hall to the cigarette machine, even though he already had one in his mouth.

Jeremy and Marlow were now very much alone. Marlow kept sobbing. Jeremy then slapped Marlow the hardest he'd ever slapped anyone in his life. Marlow stopped for a second. He tried to contain himself. Jeremy slapped him again. "Look around you. I can kill you right here, right now."

Marlow looked around. He noticed that Jeremy had unscrewed a table leg and had made a makeshift club. It must have been unscrewed for a long time. Jeremy could have killed him a thousand times before.

"I've got nothing to lose," Jeremy said.

Jeremy lifted the wooden club over his head. Marlow whimpered from the anticipated blow. Nothing. . . .

"If you think I'm going to give you one of my long speeches, you're wrong. I've got other plans for you. It gets kinda lonely in here. . . ."

Marlow looked around the small room. He was very much alone and the cameras in this area weren't working. This really was the Discount Prison and they hadn't paid their electric bill this month.

Smoky guarded the door all right, but guarding it *for* Jeremy, not *from* him.

"Anyone ever tell you that you have a cute butt?" Jeremy said. "You been working out?"

Marlow closed his eyes. In Marlow's mind, the whole thing happened in an instant, even more savage than he could possibly imagine. Jeremy had nothing to lose. What were they going to do—execute him for a fourth time?

Marlow opened his eyes. Jeremy hadn't moved an inch, just kept staring at him from across the room. Jeremy was hesitating, sizing him up, seeing if he'd fight back.

Marlow stood tall, straightened his back and clenched his fists. He still had one chance to salvage the moment before the unthinkable happened for real. His eyes were now dry. He took a good look at Jeremy for the first time in awhile. Maybe Jeremy was indeed back on heroin here on the inside. He was definitely diminished, while Marlow had kept on getting stronger from the months of the Soloflex machine.

For the first time in their attorney-client relationship, Marlow thought he could take Jeremy in a fair fight. Nico may have had the advantage of a gun against him, but man-to-man, Marlow thought he could easily take Jeremy.

"I'm not your bitch, Jeremy," he said at last. "I'm your lawyer."

Jeremy thought about it for one more second. "You know what I can do to you? Inside or on the outs?"

"Yes, Jeremy, I know." The fists stayed clenched. Marlow finally felt a little more secure. "Jeremy, do you really want to trust some other contract lawyer who will plead your ass to death row two times?"

Jeremy said nothing.

"They don't make movies about criminals with shitty lawyers," Marlow added. "They're not compelling."

Jeremy avoided eye contact for another moment. The devil you know is better than the devil you don't, he thought. He had done eighteen months after his first public defender had pled him out. With Marlow, he at least had a fighting chance of making it to the last trial. And if Jeremy didn't make it to the last trial, what was the point to this whole thing?

"Then start acting like that lawyer and not like that bitch I just saw." Jeremy said, putting down the club. "Now get the fuck out of here, and don't come back until you're a man."

Marlow knew what he had to do.

The envelope had been empty, but Nico had sworn that he did have some stuff back home that she really had to see. He had dropped her off, and she didn't even utter a word as he did his walk back to the Corvette.

"I'll get it all to you first thing tomorrow morning," he had said.

"You do that," she said, letting him drive off.

There was no call from him first thing in the morning. In his absence, Luna and Diana worked on perfecting the other witness interviews all day. They still were having a terrible time getting the truckers. They had conceded the Alaska one, and only had a definite commitment from Yoko. The other three were up for grabs, all over the country, and would most likely be done telephonically.

By the end of the day, Diana suddenly looked nervous. "We might have to do this with just Shark, Yoko and Nico for our lay witnesses."

"We'll be fine," Luna said.

"Call Nico," Diana said. "Just to be sure. And maybe we'll finally see this magic envelope he promised you."

Luna dialed his home, office and cell. All three said "unavailable at this time."

· · · · ·

She didn't do a run that night. She tried all three numbers before she went to bed. Still "unavailable at this time." She had trouble sleeping that night.

Heidi Hawk was on the first day of her two weeks of duty at the Crosswinds truck stop before she could finally transfer to her next gig, closer to home at the truck stop near Gallup. She had drawn the short straw and she was the one who had to take a smelly load of spoiled cheese back to the dumpster.

As she walked around back, she gagged on a smell. Was the refinery running again? She stared at the empty spires and tanks. Nothing. She then looked down and saw the burnt remains of a man, stashed in the corner of the building. She screamed.

Light had finally broken after Marlow came out of Shark's the next morning. He held his hand as he looked down at the second cross tattoo, right next to the first. He looked down at his watch. The Discount Prison was about to open up for visitors. He could now face Jeremy.

DISMISSAL WITH PREJUDICE

Luna came to an awkward realization just as Nico's very closed casket was lowered in the ground. She didn't love him, never had, and now never would.

She cried not because she missed him, but because she didn't. Someone had asked her to sing *Amazing Grace* at the funeral, but she had politely turned her down. She thought about the old Byrds song that came from the Bible, *To Everything There is a Season,* or whatever it was called. Now was not the time to sing.

Stephanie Park Live was there, of course, filming from a very discreet distance. Diana had talked to Stephanie, somehow managing to convince her not to even attempt to interview Luna. Stephanie had reluctantly complied.

Stephanie's newfound restraint didn't carry over into her reporting. She told her loyal viewers that Crater's murder rate now rivaled Detroit's. "Murder County, USA" she called it. She went on about a "Three Crosses Copycat" who copied the handiwork of the "Three Crosses Killer." She flashed to pictures of Sarah and Ruth, then pictures of Thayer and Nico.

"Who will be the third cross?" Stephanie asked. Before closing off, Stephanie did show one bit of restraint. She didn't show a picture of Luna.

Crater County hadn't been compelling, but once white people started dying, "Murder County" had finally become a compulsion for the national media. Some new faces from some rival networks were out there as well, but they didn't hesitate to show Luna's picture. A fairly famous cable talk show host even hosted a show from Crater . . . well, from Albuquerque, where there was a working studio. The host had Dr. Romero from the State Hospital go on about the Copycat's "narcissistic personality."

"The Three Crosses Copycat Killer's profile sounds like a male over thirty, underemployed, probably a loner," Dr. Romero had said. "This is his way of getting attention, of feeling powerful, after suffering severe setbacks in life."

There was a caller on line 1. "That sounds like everyone in Crater."

Luna ran into Van Leit at the funeral. He was out on bond. It looked like charges would never be filed against him, after all. "We don't have the judicial resources," Diana had said. He was on administrative suspension, but the word on the street was that he would be officially back on the job once Jeremy's cases were resolved.

Van Leit sat with Shatrock. She looked at Shatrock, that big fat doofus in the cowboy hat and spurs. Shatrock was now the chief law enforcement officer for the county, until Van Leit got his job back.

God help us all, Luna said to herself. She hid her reluctance as she shook their hands and wished them both luck. She stared at Van Leit one more time. If Nico had stayed alive, he would be sheriff, and Van Leit would have no chance of getting his job back. With Nico gone, it was now a foregone conclusion he would.

Van Leit had once had access to the files, and would easily be able to set Nico's death up to mirror Thayer's. Van Leit might have been sheriff, but he was a sheriff of shit, and knew that he was a laughingstock outside the Crater's walls.

And then, Van Leit had told her it was all her fault when he got arrested. She stopped herself before she went any further. This wasn't the time or place for thoughts like this.

At the wake in the church's social hall, Luna talked with Diana. "Are we still going to trial with Thayer Brown?"

"We have to," said Diana. "We still have the truckers, we still have Yoko. It's still a winnable case."

Luna shook her head. "Our primary detective is dead."

Diana glanced over at Shatrock. "We'll be able to get his notes in as a hearsay exception, but we're going to have to rely on Shatrock to do so. And then we'll have to rely on Shatrock as pretty much the only witness on Felicia's case."

"Shatrock's not the primary on Nico's case, is he?" Luna asked. "I mean the case of Nico getting killed."

"Dear God, no. I called down special investigations from the Attorney General's. Barcelona sent me down one agent. Some guy named Wootton. I mean, a cop got killed, it was the least she could do. We've lost two-thirds of our full time force."

Luna took another look toward the coffin. A tear welled in her eye.

"I'm sorry, Luna," Diana said. "I know you loved him."

"I never loved him," she said. "But he was a good man in his own way. Well, he had some good qualities."

They had a moment of silence. Suddenly Luna had a look of terror in her eyes. "Di, do you remember what he said? That I should start to worry if he was killed, because he was the closest thing I had to a boyfriend?"

"I remember," Diana replied. "Are you worried?"

Luna didn't have to say anything. Her whole body shook with fear.

"Are you all right?" Di asked. "Do you think it's Marlow?"

Luna pulled it together. "He was acting weird, real emotional. I think he had a crush on me and he might have seen Nico and me do it."

She didn't go into more detail. She wanted to save her brain the trouble of painting the picture.

"I know how that is," Di said. She shook her head.

"He's like 'Dr. Marlow and Mr. Jeremy,' and I don't think he can really control his Mr. Jeremy side."

There was an invisible dividing line between the church and state—state being the rest of Crater County. Marlow waited just on the outside of the church's property line, right next to Stephanie. Somehow, the invisible line prevented them from crossing over onto the relatively holy ground.

Marlow's hand still hurt from the second cross tattoo. He had to force himself not to scratch it. He had crossed the point of no return. He knew it. But Luna had given him no choice. She had chosen Nico over him. Now Nico was gone. Good freaking riddance.

"Do you have anything you want to say?" Stephanie asked, turning the camera to him.

"It wouldn't be appropriate for me to comment at a time like this," he replied.

She turned the camera off. "Off the record?"

Marlow couldn't help himself, knew he didn't want to use the word "freak" either when it came to Nico. "I'm sure glad that motherfucker is dead."

He smiled at Stephanie. She didn't write it down. She knew that if she let that statement go, an even better one would come her way. She saw Diana and Luna come toward her. She had given her word to Diana, so she packed up her equipment and headed home.

Luna and Diana had almost made it to Diana's yellow Lexus when Marlow intercepted them. "You haven't taken my calls all week," he said to Diana. He couldn't look over at Luna.

"We've had a lot on our minds," Diana said.

"I'm filing a motion to dismiss, due to the unavailability of your key witness." He tilted his head back toward the church.

Luna stared at him. At that moment, whatever good there was in Marlow was long gone. Just the way he angled his head, about 30 degrees, reeked of contempt. That angle said, "Not only did I kill someone in your life, I dismembered him, and then burnt him to a crisp, and *finally* left him to die in a dark corner of a truck stop."

Or maybe a 30-degree angle just meant his neck was tired.

"I hate to be an asshole on a day like this," he said, "but I have a duty to be a zealous advocate for my asshole client."

Luna looked back at the church and over at Nico's grave, then down at his freshly bandaged hand. "By the way, where were you the night Nico got killed?"

"I was home."

"I don't even have to look under your hand to know what's there." Luna said.

"This had nothing to do with Nico," he said. "Just something attorney-client privileged."

Luna gave Diana a nudge.

"Would you mind coming in for questioning with the special agent when he gets in town tomorrow?" Diana asked him.

Marlow definitely hesitated.

"Or are you invoking the 'ain't saying shit' clause?" Luna piped in.

"I'll be there," he said. "And I won't be invoking anything but the truth."

Special Agent Wootton was a by-the-book NYPD cop-turned-FBI agent, who had recently retired to Santa Fe. He pretended to be a hippie cowboy, a Willie Nelson wannabe with his scraggly red beard. It didn't work. Wootton really wanted to wear a red tie instead of a bolo, and the few strands of ponytail should have never been allowed to escape from the crew cut.

Luna and Diana watched through the two-way mirror. Marlow glanced at them a few times, as if he could see right through the mirror.

Marlow had printed receipts from the ATM, which indicated the time he got some cash, a receipt for his gas, even his receipt for the tattoo from Shark.

He's almost too well prepared, Luna thought.

Wootton was thorough, but in the end, there was nothing.

After an hour or so, Wootton called it a day and said Marlow was free to go. "But stay where we can find you."

"Where would I go?"

Marlow looked right at the two-way mirror and made eye contact with Diana. "Our motion hearing is still on for tomorrow, right? Just pound once if you can hear me."

Diana looked over at Luna and pounded once.

After Marlow was gone, Wootton came over to join them.

"Well?" Luna asked.

"I don't know," he said in his drawl, which almost but not quite eliminated every trace of his native Long Island accent. "If he's as good a lawyer as he is a criminal, you gals are in a heap of trouble."

The motion hearing was done by phone in the cramped temporary judge's chambers at the justice center. Benally was supposedly in the midst of another hearing down in Las Cruces. Luckily, the media had gone home for the week.

Benally's case in Las Cruces had just been vacated. He had taken his cell phone with him and at that very moment he teed up on the ninth hole of the golf course at the Las Cruces Country Club. He told the rest of his foursome, two lawyers and another judge, to give him some distance to take the call.

Judge Benally stared at the beautiful granite pipes of the aptly named Organ Mountains and tried to pretend that he was in Palm Springs. As his clerk set up the call, he desperately wanted to stay in this sunny moment forever.

"Not bad for a half-breed from Sheep Springs," he said to himself as he scanned his present surroundings and then looked back at the clubhouse. "Not bad at all."

He thought briefly about his father who'd owned a trading post back on the Rez. His father's one good idea had been selling mineral water from the local spring, with the seemingly unfortunate name of "Sheep Springs Mineral Water." Once young Benally came up with the funky Sheep Springs Label with its sheep standing in the springs, the bottles caught on with the hipsters back east. His dad had made a small fortune, which had helped finance his campaign for judge.

Benally chugged a bottle of the water and offered a silent toast to his father.

"Okay, Judge," said the clerk over the cell. "We've got everyone here."

Benally headed for the shade of one of the golf course's scraggly palm trees and leaned against it. He tapped his nine-iron against the palm tree. "I call this hearing to order."

In the cramped judge's chambers, there were no palm trees, of course. "Your Honor, the late Nico Walters was their lead investigator," Marlow began. He launched into the latest case law about dead cops and their testimonies.

Despite all the emotions wiggling in her heart, Luna quickly went through the case law that would allow Nico's police reports in as hearsay exceptions. When she heard someone yell "Fore!" in the background, she knew that she would have to hurry it up.

Then she thought briefly about Nico. No, she hadn't loved him, but he had done a lot for her, even if it had only been to get in her pants. She owed him a lot more than she had ever let on.

"Your Honor, even if you do not allow Nico's testimony in, we do not need him. We have Shark's testimony of Jeremy's confession and we have the truckers who will testify of the statement, the medical people.

"We do not need Nico to make this case." Luna looked over at Marlow. "I do not need Nico."

Judge Benally took another look around the country club. Given the choice between spending a week on the golf course in Las Cruces (with a few evening forays down to Juarez) or a week dodging the Crater wind, hiding out in a smelly converted racquetball court, the choice was obvious.

One of the golfing judges motioned to Benally. Time to move on to the next tee. Yet there was something in Luna's voice. She had started to sound like a real lawyer. Maybe it was just curiosity, but Benally wanted to see her in action. The golf course and Las Cruces, much less anything south of the border, weren't going anywhere.

"I won't dismiss," he said. "And I will allow another officer to briefly run down the testimony of the late Officer Walters."

He took one more look at the Organ Mountains. "We'll move my regular Thursday docket over to Monday and start up the whole trial again."

He hung up and walked over to the green and hit the ball.
Shank!

CASE IN CHIEF

Stephanie Park Live now was the queen of Murder County, USA. Other reporters now followed her lead, and the lazy ones just paid her station for the footage. Unfortunately, in the weeks that had followed the Sarah Sanchez part of the case, she hadn't made it to the next level. She had sent her tapes into L.A. and Dallas, and had not heard a word.

"Where the hell is this crater anyway?" one of her friends in L.A. had asked. "Why don't you do a remote from the bottom, just as a set-up?"

Stephanie had actually made a few calls around, until someone politely explained that the county's namesake was indeed just a state of mind.

She had already staked up the best position outside the courtroom when the parties arrived, thanks to Diana's word to the bailiff. The other reporters, grumbling, had to set up behind her.

As the parties arrived, everyone looked too intense and no one wanted to give a statement to her or anyone else. That was all right to Stephanie; sometimes a "no comment" given from a stressed face was far better television than a boring talking head going on about the evidence and what not. Stephanie had learned one thing out here in the Crater, and that was patience.

She had realized from the start that this case wasn't really about the evidence, it was about Marlow. She just wished that Luna would finally grow up and make a game of it. No one, especially none of the powers that be in New York or L.A., liked a mismatch.

· · · · ·

Before they could restart the trial, Benally had to go through his regular docket. His first case was an Ed "Gollum" Gollis, accused of a criminal trespass at the Crater elementary school. There had been no sexual nature to the trespass—Gollum had just hung out with his friend who was the coach and talked about late night movies. After five years of this, the coach had finally grown tired of Gollum and had asked him to leave.

Gollum, as he was affectionately known around town, had been a brilliant astrophysicist until his auto accident on the freeway. He had somehow never left Crater and, like an unlucky ghost, he wandered around town aimlessly, haunting his victims with wisdom about movies and quantum physics.

"Let's make this go away," said Marlow. "Just give me the usual deferred sentence." He had already filled out the form himself to speed the process.

Luna didn't play that game anymore. "Nothing's deferred anymore. You've got to plead him straight up and let God sort it out. Unless you want to take it to trial."

Even Marlow didn't want to go to trial on a trespass case, especially when the defendant was arrested in mid-trespass. Marlow couldn't fight the laws of time and space after all. A straight-up plea it was going to have to be.

Court came to order. Judge Benally looked suspiciously tan for a man who had just finished a long trial. Marlow had Lewis plead straight up. For the first time, Luna didn't feel intimidated by Marlow as she asked for jail time rather than a deferred sentence. She gave a speech about how the residents of Crater needed to feel safe in their homes, and in their bedrooms.

She stared right at Marlow. "Mr. Gollis may have no criminal record, Your Honor, but he is a walking time bomb. Your Honor, I ask for a week in jail."

Marlow wasn't into this case. He was still in his Jeremy mode and had a million things on his mind. "Your Honor, my client has no criminal record. I ask for probation."

That was it. What else was there to say?

His Honor was in a bad mood. He already regretted cutting his

Las Cruces trip short for the likes of this. "Ms. Cruz, I tend to agree with you. Gollum, I hope you brought a toothbrush."

After a few more quick cases, the Jeremy Jones hearing began in earnest. Luna didn't know whether it was good for Shatrock to read Nico's testimony and Nico's impressions of the case. My God, this was the dumbest cop in the world, she thought as he stumbled with every word with more than five letters or two syllables.

She noticed that Van Leit was outside of the courtroom. He was talking with the press. One station had even hired him as an expert.

She gave him a dirty look. She hated dirty cops. Van Leit could sense that, and looked back toward Shatrock. She grew more and more impatient with Shatrock, and she could quickly see that the Judge and jury were losing interest as well.

"Your Honor, may I have permission to lead this witness?"

"Please!" He smiled.

A few of the jurors laughed—laughed *at* her, not with her.

She practically read the statements and had Shatrock say "yes." It wasn't particularly effective, but at least Nico's words had made it into the permanent record. A part of Nico lived on. Not a very big part, but it was something.

On cross, Marlow was as brutal as expected. "Let's begin with your questioning of the witnesses," he said.

Shatrock was confused. "I didn't question any witnesses. Nico did it."

"Next, let's move to your finding of the body."

"I didn't find the body. Nico did."

"Finally let's talk about your medical evaluations. Where did you get your medical training?"

"Umm . . . what training?"

That was it.

Marlow approached the bench. "Your Honor, I must renew my motion to dismiss."

Luna stood her ground. "Your Honor, he's just being used as a conduit to get Officer Walters' testimony in."

"A very poor conduit," Benally said. "Still, I'll deny Mr.

Marlow's motion. But the state had better pick up the pace. No offense to your sweet little town, but until you get a golf course in this god forsaken burg there are places I'd rather be."

In the afternoon, Luna and Diana went through the medical experts. The jury perked up for the gory photographs and charts showing how Thayer Brown had been drugged, dismembered, then burnt while he was somewhat comatose before being left for dead in a dark corner of the Crosswinds.

Marlow said the same thing to every expert. "Could you please point to the name Jeremy Jones in your report?"

And, in each case, they failed. Jeremy's name was conspicuously absent.

That night, Stephanie Park Live said that it was "an uneventful day" in her report that was sent out to several different affiliates all over the country. Ironically, the powers that be at her home station in Albuquerque didn't even put her on at ten because of a breaking bank robbery.

Diana excused herself for the next morning since Yoko Wagatsuma was in town. She damn sure wanted to make sure that Yoko did not make the connection between herself and the bathroom. Luna reported to Benally that Diana was ill and couldn't make it. He didn't seem to mind. The courtroom was cramped enough as it was.

The phone testimony went as well as could be expected. Each witness testified that Jeremy clearly said, "I'm going to kill you both."

Luna would ask them to repeat, and then Marlow would object, "Asked and answered."

Luna looked over at the jurors. Hearing disembodied voices over a speakerphone was not affecting them emotionally. Crater's remote location led to terrible radio reception. This was just one more bad radio show to the jurors. They had already changed the channel in their minds.

• • • • •

After a brief recess, Luna called Yoko to the stand. Yoko was forty-something, and neither a geisha nor a sumo wrestler. She was just a slightly overweight woman who'd met a military man who'd brought her back to America, then took over his trucking business when he died.

Before Luna began questioning Yoko, she looked back at Diana's empty chair several times. Goddamn, she hoped that she wasn't protecting a murderer, best friend or not.

She looked over at the defense table. They looked like twins over there with their bleached blond hair and matching suits. Marlow had boxes of evidence ready to go to impeach Yoko. He had so much material he had moved it over to Jeremy's side of the table as he frantically wrote down notes of what he was he would ask.

Did he know about Diana? With all that information, he must have something on Yoko. Maybe even something about Diana as well. Does he have Diana's bank records? If he does, she would have to put it all on the line to save her friend.

"I'm not going to let you get any of that in," she said to him.

Marlow shrugged and went back to frantically writing down his questions.

"Do you mind?" Jeremy asked. He gave her an evil smile. "By the way, sorry about your boyfriend."

She couldn't bear to look at him and scurried away. She now had a bad feeling in the pit of her stomach.

Benally called court to order. Yoko took the stand. After a few preliminaries, Luna had her set the scene about the bathroom and the two people in there. It might have been dark, but she had good hearing and she vividly described the heavy breathing.

"And what do you think they were doing in there?"

"They were having some kind of sex," she said. "Or maybe they had just finished. . . ."

All the jurors woke up when they heard the word "sex," especially the Illustrated Woman.

"And how do you think a reasonable person would react if he caught the great love of his life having sex with another?"

She steeled herself for Marlow's objection. Nothing.

Yoko answered the question. "He would be very mad."

"Mad enough to kill?"

She waited for another objection from Marlow. Still nothing.

"Yes. He'd be mad enough to kill."

"Are you sure?"

"Very much sure."

Luna moved on to the scariest part of the questioning. Yoko was vague about the third person that came in.

"It was dark, I couldn't see her that well . . . I don't know what she did."

"Thank you," Luna said. It was time to limit the entire mention of the third person to that one question. At that very moment, that "third person" was probably sitting in her hot tub taking a handful of Valiums.

Diana, you owe me one, she thought. She could almost hear her stomach grumbling out loud from the stress. The Illustrated Woman shot her a dirty look. "My stomach really *is* that loud," she thought. "I really *am* that stressed."

Luna clutched the podium for support, and then continued. "So you then ran to the other bathroom down the east hallway?"

She had just asked an objectionable leading question, but Marlow again didn't object.

"Yes. It was around the other side."

"But you did come back around, a few minutes later, right?"

Again leading, again no objection.

"Yes."

"And what did you see?"

She looked over at Marlow. He was genuinely nervous right now, far more nervous than Jeremy. Almost as nervous as she was right now. Good, let him sweat. She found just the slightest bit of a mean streak in herself—like she used to feel in high school when she knew she was the fastest girl in the entire field before a race. Whatever happened to that girl?

Yoko looked over at the defense table. She was scared of what sat over there.

Luna looked back at Yoko. "You're safe here, ma'am." Several of the jurors nodded with empathy.

"We believe you," they said with their eyes.

"Please tell us what you saw when you got back to from the other bathroom."

Yoko gathered herself. "This crazy guy, he was beating up this one man in front of a crying woman, shouting, 'I'm going to kill you both,' over and over again."

There was a gasp from the jurors. This hit home. They now turned their attention to the Counsel table. For the first time, they could see the reality of three murdered bodies lying there in right in front of Marlow and Jeremy. They could see the blood dripping out of those damn tattooed crosses.

"Are you sure?"

"Very much sure," Yoko replied. In her high-pitched, slightly accented voice, you could hear the terror. "He kept saying, 'I'm going to kill you both,' over and over again."

She could see the sweat on Marlow's face. Jeremy was as cool as a cucumber. He stared at some of the files in front of him.

She had a quick panic attack. Maybe those were credit card receipts from the Crosswinds, or worse, pictures of Diana. She forced herself not to ponder those files and focused her attention back at the jurors. She owned the jurors right now. It was time to go in for her own kill. If she could just get Yoko to make a positive ID of Jeremy right now, the case was hers. Diana would be safe.

"Could you identify that man?" Luna asked. "The man who said 'I'm going to kill you both,' could you please identify him for the Court?"

"It's that man right there."

Yoko pointed a finger toward the counsel table.

Unfortunately she pointed right at Marlow.

To make matters worse, she added, "I'm very much sure of it."

• • • • •

Judge Benally did not even wait for Marlow's motion. He excused the jury immediately. "Do you have something to say to me, Counsel?"

"Your Honor, I ask that you dismiss the case," Marlow said. "They have nothing linking my client to the crime."

Short and sweet. He was so confident he almost didn't bother to get into character.

Diana will kill me if I lose this case before lunch, Luna thought. This newfound competitive spirit within her definitely felt good. She thought about how much time she'd gained on the biking part of the Olympic trials. Forget about the ending in the stadium. Remember making it up that hill and passing woman after woman to get into the lead.

"Your Honor," she said. "We have one more witness to go. Shark Bradbury. Shark Bradbury will offer in direct testimony a confession by Mr. Jones to all three murders. Not only that, he will show the meaning of the three crosses tattooed on Jeremy Jones' right hand."

"Your Honor," Marlow said. "Admitting such testimony would be very prejudicial and would have little probative value, if any."

Luna thought how Boo Boo had tried to pass her on the first hill, and she wouldn't let her have the lead. She'd been back in high school cross country, at least in that moment.

"You can't catch me, bitch," she had said to Boo Boo during the race. She had been right for at least an hour. "You can't catch me, bitch."

"Did you just say something, Counsel?" Benally asked.

Oh My God, had she just said that out loud? She shrugged and Benally let it go.

Without coming up for air, she launched into her speech. "Your Honor, every day the defendant mocks us with those three crosses tattooed on his hand. And every day defense Counsel flashes those two of his own. In light of two murders that have taken place, two people who were very close to me, I find those crosses to be in very bad taste."

She took a deep breath. "Your Honor, Shark Bradbury did all

those tattoos on Mr. Jones. Mr. Jones said something to him about what they meant. Your Honor, Mr. Jones confessed. And you know what? Shark Bradbury also did the tattoos on Mr. Marlow."

Judge Benally now stared at Marlow's hand.

"Your Honor," Luna continued, "I am extremely curious as to what Mr. Marlow had to say to him as well. Perhaps there will be some explanation as to why he is showing such total disregard to opposing Counsel with such an offensive display. Your Honor, this man received a tattoo of a cross after the murder of my mother, and then received a second cross tattoo after the murder of my lover!"

Marlow was taken aback by the word "lover." Benally had Marlow bring up his hand and place it on his table. "I had never noticed them before and, based on what Counsel has just told me, I am indeed inclined to hold you in contempt, Mr. Marlow."

"Your Honor, it's my way of getting into my cases," he said. "Like in the Yazzie case, I had a ponytail. And Your Honor, you yourself have a tattoo on your hand, the yin-yang symbol. That stands in part for darkness and light, so Your Honor must have had some experience with both the darkness and the light."

What a strange thing to say. Benally thought briefly about when he had gotten his own tattoo, right after his father had died in an accident on Route 66. His father had been on the way back from bank after the cashing their first big check for the mineral water. The yin-yang symbol had been the perfect way to express both of his emotions.

"I'll let it go, this time," Benally said. "But I do want to hear Mr. Bradbury's testimony. However, I will hear it outside the presence of the jury. Mr. Marlow, you may *voir dire* the witness at that time."

Benally took a recess for lunch.

As Luna got up to leave, Marlow took her by the arm. "You know when you said, 'You can't catch me, bitch?'"

Luna blushed. "Yeah?"

"You're finally starting to sound like a real lawyer."

• • • • •

Back at Crater Ranch, Luna was surprised that Diana was not angry. Maybe the four Valiums and a few of the fourteen days of therapy had finally kicked in. "At least I'm not being disbarred for failure to disclose," she said. "And at least the case hasn't been totally dismissed."

"We're hanging on by a thread, Di," Luna said.

"Well, we will probably lose this one," Diana. "We'll have to deal with it. I did learn the 'serenity prayer' during my shortened stay at the Rancho Relaxo. But we can still win the third."

"That's the toughest one."

"We'll find a way," Diana said.

Diana got up. "I wanted to tell you something. I know that you had your doubts about me, maybe you thought I killed Thayer or something."

"Come on, Di, I never thought that."

"Well I didn't want to tell you, because I wanted to see if you'd still go out and fight for the case. Well you did."

"It looks like I lost it for us."

"Well, we haven't lost it yet. And no, I did not kill Thayer Brown or Felicia. Do you think I'd risk breaking these nails? I got them done in Santa Fe."

Luna looked at the nails. The work on them was exquisite. "My tax dollars at work."

PROBATIVE VALUE VS. PREJUDICIAL EFFECT

After lunch, Diana took Shark's direct examination. Luna watched from the Counsel table. They had told Shark to wear a jacket. Shark had other ideas. He decided to go with a leather vest and a sleeveless T-shirt. Shark's left shoulder alone was enough to frighten Luna. He had his namesake, a great white shark with a cartoon caption reading, "Get your Mark from the Shark."

Just like in the movie "Jaws," the great white headed straight toward a naked woman. Was it Felicia?

Shark looked over at the defense table and shrugged, as if to say, "They made me do this, but don't worry too much. . . ."

Diana went through the preliminaries, including Shark's previous convictions, slowly and deliberately. Shark's hearing magically improved in the courtroom's cramped acoustics. He answered the best that he could. His eyes were on Luna. He played with his left shoulder a bit, even pinched the naked girl.

He smiled as he noticed Luna squirm.

"So what did Mr. Jones say to you, when he got that third tattoo?" Diana asked.

Marlow rose up. "Your Honor, I'd like to *voir dire* this witness before we go any further. I believe his prejudicial value far outweighs anything probative he might say. I also have very serious concerns about this witness's credibility."

"Very well."

Marlow got up and walked to Shark. "First off, I have to disclose that you have done some work on me."

"Yeah. You still haven't paid me yet," Shark said with a smirk.

Diana made a half-hearted objection.

Judge Benally laughed. "This is Crater. I can't think of how many times someone standing before me had just filled up my gas tank or sold me a sandwich. Counsel, you may proceed."

"You tattoo a lot of people, don't you?"

"A couple a day."

"Anyone have a Special Forces tattoo that wasn't really in the military?"

"I don't know."

"You don't check their military records, do you?"

Shark shrugged. "Yeah, right."

"When someone has 'Francine' tattooed on their arm, you don't call Francine, to make sure that she's truly in love with your client?"

Shark shrugged again.

Marlow then made Jeremy take off his jacket, then his shirt, to reveal his upper body. Jeremy may have lost some of his muscle, but once he flexed there was still an appreciative gasp from the Illustrated Woman, and from a few of the men.

"You did this tattoo here, the Crater High logo?"

"Yeah."

"You know that Jeremy dropped out of Crater High School, didn't you? The tattoo listed a class graduation date."

"Yeah but—"

"So since Jeremy did not in fact graduate from Crater High, that would be a lie?"

"I don't remember the date I gave it to him. Maybe he was still in school."

"So you don't remember, or you didn't check?"

"Whatever."

"Here we have a tattoo that says Pat Pong 1 with a picture of a lovely lady. Pat Pong 1 is, shall we say, an entertainment district in Okinawa, isn't it?"

"Bangkok," Shark laughed with a guilty smile, indicating personal experience. Everybody knew about Pat Pong 1, all right.

"My mistake. I said Okinawa, Jeremy was actually stationed there and never in fact made it to Bangkok. So that would be another lie."

Shark looked confused. He had been the one to tell Jeremy about Pat Pong 1. "I guess so."

"You did tattoos for me, these two crosses, right?"

"Not exactly my best work."

"And I am neither a killer, nor a Christian, as far as you know?"

"As far as I know."

All eyes were now on his right hand and on the cross tattoos. Luna was shocked. Oh my God, he's using this against them.

Marlow did not look at Shark. He now looked directly at Luna. "So if I were to tell you hypothetically that I killed two people and got crosses as a way to 'get in touch with my feelings for the dead,' that would that strike you as ridiculous, wouldn't it?"

Luna felt Marlow's stare burn a hole right through her. Marlow kept staring at her. Shark was confused.

"You're a lawyer not a killer, so I guess it would be ridiculous."

Don't be so sure he isn't a killer, Luna wanted to say. Don't be so sure!

Diana didn't say anything, of course. She knew she had just been out-played. You could see her reciting the serenity prayer under her breath.

Don't give up, Di, Luna wanted to shout. But Di already had given up and stayed silent.

"Your Honor, I've been very patient." Marlow had walked up to the bench. "I think that we can strike all the testimony of this witness. His prejudicial effect outweighs any probative value, and must be stricken under the Rules of Evidence."

Benally did not hesitate, did not even look at Diana. "So ordered. The witness is excused."

Shark got up. He didn't know whether to be happy or sad.

Diana and Luna then looked down at their table. They had no more witnesses on Thayer's case. Diana ran through the serenity prayer again.

The Judge then looked at Marlow. "Mr. Marlow, do you have any motions on this case?"

"Your Honor, I move for a dismissal on the two remaining counts of murder."

"Mr. Marlow, you disappoint me. We still have one more case to go."

They all looked at him, not quite sure what he meant. "I'll meet you halfway. I will give a directed verdict on Count 2, but we still have the remaining testimony on Count 3. I still want to see if the state can put on some kind of case. Court is adjourned until Monday."

The court cleared out. Marlow didn't even look at her. Smoky dragged Jeremy out. Marlow walked beside them.

Outside the Justice Center, the media must have come out of the woodwork. It was as if there had been a roadblock on I-40 and every news van headed somewhere had been diverted down into the crater. The throng surrounded Smoky, Jeremy and Marlow by the transport car. All three basked in the attention. "Thank you," Jeremy said to Marlow, under his breath. "This is fucking great! Fucking great! Fucking great!"

Marlow didn't reply. He had hoped that Benally would dismiss all the cases and he could move on with his life, put Jeremy far behind him.

"Are you pleased with the result?" Stephanie Park Live asked Marlow.

"Of course," he said. "But this isn't over, not by a long shot."

Marlow let Smoky and Jeremy walk away. He took one last look at Jeremy's face as Smoky pushed him into the dusty SUV. Jeremy looked fatigued, as if his one-minute of flexing had taken a lot out of him. Jeremy was a rock star, all right, but definitely one on the way down, as if his Neverland ranch had shrunk into the back of the SUV.

After the crush of media left for the interstate, an attractive woman in a tight black shirt and leather pants came over. Marlow couldn't help but think that some spies had come up with a computer generated fantasy woman designed to target his profile. She looked like a slightly sluttier version of Luna. The woman touched his arm slightly, said she was from some big Hollywood agency and wanted to option the "Three Crosses Killer" story for a TV movie.

Marlow thought for a moment as the woman tightened her grip. Everything was finally falling into place, but it was too early. Way too early.

"Not until I know how it ends," he said, shooing the woman away.

Luna was surprised. She didn't feel the same hurt that she had felt after the last one. Boo Boo had caught her right at the changeover to the last leg of the triathlon and that's when she had panicked and the race was essentially over.

That wasn't going to happen on the final leg here. She probably wasn't going to win, just like before. But she sure as hell wasn't going to walk into the stadium.

This race was still on and far from over. Maybe she needed to get a cross or two of her own.

IN THE DISTRICT COURT
14th JUDICIAL DISTRICT
COUNTY OF CRATER

STATE OF NEW MEXICO, PLAINTIFF

vs.

JEREMY JONES DEFENDANT

COUNT III

FOR THE MURDER OF FELICIA SANCHEZ,
A NATURAL PERSON

CHANGE OF VENUE

Luna did not go for a swim or even a long bike ride the next morning. She reluctantly took her mother's old car and drove over to Hell's Hills. With the windows open, she was almost okay.

At first, Luna felt like she was cheating but after a few wind sprints up the advanced trail, she knew she'd get a complete workout. She started slowly until the Yazzie wreck and then ran full speed the last hundred yards to the summit. She now easily made it all the way to the top as if it were a flat, yellow brick road.

She remembered to bring enough water with her, Sheep Springs Mineral Water, of course, even though the logo looked like the sheep were peeing in the water. Who knows? Maybe that was the extra ingredient that made her go faster. Luna kept a few bottles at the trailhead as a reward.

While heading home, she pulled off the road and stopped by Felicia's wooden cross. Coming from a mixed marriage, Luna had never been particularly religious, but she felt like praying for the first time in awhile. She didn't really know what to say to the wooden cross, so she just had a moment of silence. Both God and Felicia would know what she had meant after she finished with a soft amen.

When she arrived home at the satellite, she looked at her extremely cramped space. She looked around at the athletic bras, bike shorts and running shoes littering the room. She had forty pairs of roommates in a few square feet. She put down her keys. Moments later, she could not find them in all the piles of rubble. She threw down more piles, then freaked when a pile moved by itself.

Was there a cockroach or a rat under there? Luna didn't want to know.

I'm a real lawyer, damn it! This is not how real lawyers live!

She searched the satellite for an hour until she finally found what she needed—Nico's hammer.

With Nico's hammer, she pulled out the nails, then pried open the boards that covered the doors and windows of the Mothership. It was much easier than she thought—either Nico had failed to do a good job hammering in the nails or she was getting stronger. Probably a little of both.

Inside, the Mothership had not changed. Nothing had moved a millimeter since Nico had boarded everything up. Just way too much dust. She went into the closet and broke out the cleaning supplies.

After a few more minutes of cleaning, then hours of hesitation, she finally made it into her mom's room. Nothing had changed, and her mom had always been the clean one in the family. Nico had called in a State Police clean-up team, once the evidence had been secured. Ruth's room just needed a good dusting and a few quick spurts of freshening spray. She went with the purple "Mountain Berry" scent. The room was once again fit for human habitation.

My mom is still here, she thought. I don't want to offend her.

She hadn't prayed for months, and now twice in one day. "Mom, I'm going to move in here. Please let me know if it's all right."

She looked around as if waiting for a mirror to crack or a picture to fall over. Nothing.

She put her own pillow on her mom's bed.

"I'm going to make you proud of me," she said. "I'm going to be a real lawyer."

Marlow had returned to Window Rock, to Jonathan Manygoats and his blessing ways. Manygoats had a small stucco building that he used as a waiting room while his ceremonial center and sweat lodge were in the back. Apparently Manygoats was out back finishing up some kind of detoxification ceremony for another client that had to be done by this morning. The waiting room could have been a doctor's office except for the small trinkets on the wall. Marlow browsed through an old issue of *People* magazine about the twenty sexiest people in the world. One woman, a promising young Brazilian singer, looked exactly like Luna.

Marlow was not alone in the waiting room. A Navajo with a crew cut sat reading *Time*. The man had a photo ID badge indicating that he was a federal probation officer. The probation officer impatiently waited for his client.

"My clients usually don't respond to the forced AA regimen," the probation officer said by way of explanation. "By using traditional medicine, we're able to treat the whole criminal and not just the crime. I've had amazing success."

"I know what you mean," Marlow said. "I guess that's why I'm here."

"What are you in for?" The probation officer asked. "DWI?"

"Attempted murder," said Marlow.

The probation officer stared at him.

"It's for a murder I haven't attempted yet," Marlow said.

The probation officer nodded, taking Marlow's statement at face value. He tilted his head to point toward the medicine man's ceremonial grounds out back. "He's usually good with those."

After what seemed like forever Manygoats emerged, wearing his ceremonial clothes. On the way out, Manygoats signed the papers for the young criminal who handed them to his probation officer.

"Can I help you?" he asked Marlow, strangely. "Do I know you?"

"It's me, Marlow. Do all us palefaces look the same?"

Manygoats laughed. "I almost didn't recognize you, Marlow. That case must really be getting to you."

"I know. I know. I know." Marlow caught himself. When did he start saying things three times like that?

Ever the opportunist, Manygoats touched him on the arm. "I can help you with your client, if you want me to talk to him."

Marlow laughed. "I don't see my client as being a believer in traditional medicine," he said. "I have a spirit that I can't seem to get rid of, something like that." Marlow didn't really know what to say, but that sounded appropriate.

"I can see you tomorrow," Manygoats said. "I have to take care of a lot of paperwork for the insurance on some other cases."

Luna slept well in her mother's bed. There had been no bad dreams or anything. She often threw off the blankets when she tossed and turned at the satellite, yet she was still tucked in when she awoke just before dawn.

"Thank you, Mom," Luna said.

The next day Luna had Wootton come down from Santa Fe to open up Felicia's house. It had been boarded up, of course, and no one had entered it. The few house-hunters left in the county certainly didn't want to disturb Felicia's ghost. The home was adobe and looked remarkably like the satellite, but Felicia's Mothership had been a mile away down the road.

"Was she killed inside the house?" Wootton asked.

"No one knows," Luna replied. "Jeremy might have grabbed her inside and dragged her out. There were no signs of a struggle, other than the old one from the night her mother was killed."

Luna pointed to an old bloodstain against the wall. Wootton looked it over. "Not a happy couple."

"Not anymore."

"What exactly are you looking for?" he asked. "Didn't a forensic team go through here already?"

"I'm not looking for anything umm . . . forensic."

Wootton shook his head. He'd run into enough New Age type stuff since he moved to Santa Fe. They went up to Felicia's bedroom. There was a pile of her old papers and diaries, most from high school. Her last high school diary, the one from the evidence box, had been returned. It was in a different box, and still had a yellow evidence tag on it. Apparently Diana had returned it here to avoid totally cluttering up the office.

"Here's something that *isn't* evidence." Wootton didn't even have to look at the dates on the diary to guess its age. "Why is that even tagged?"

"I don't think you understand. That's exactly what I was looking for."

She started reading the diary as Wootton looked around the place a few more times. She couldn't really get into it while he hovered over her.

"I don't see anything that they didn't get already," he said, taking the hint. "Do you mind if I head on home?"

She nodded. She thought he would never leave.

It was cold and windy out in the ceremonial area behind the modern structure. Marlow forced himself to sit still as the ceremony went on and on. Manygoats danced and chanted. Marlow drifted in and out of consciousness. He didn't know if he felt anything. Certainly nothing had changed within him.

Why am I even doing this? Because something's definitely wrong with me, he thought, and it's not the type of thing you can just go and down a few Prozacs and make it disappear.

Finally, after what seemed like a million more chants, Manygoats came back to him, shaking his head. He didn't want to say anything for a moment. Marlow stared at him. Manygoats was perhaps a bit too slick, but he had been such an effective expert witness because he was so honest and came across as someone who really knew his stuff and make it make sense for the Anglos.

"Is something wrong?" Marlow asked him.

"I'm sorry," Manygoats replied. "But whatever you've got doesn't want to go away."

Marlow put his clothes back on and started to reach for his wallet.

Manygoats frowned. He was genuinely sad that he had failed. "Keep your money. I don't want to see you around here for a while, okay? Not until this whole thing is settled. Some things you can only remove by yourself."

Once Wootton was gone, Luna put on some of Felicia's music. The woman had liked country—the Dixie Chicks, Shania Twain—female singers, mainly. Luna hated country music, but soon found herself humming along with the songs. It helped get her into the mood. Felicia was the sort of woman featured in country songs—the heartbroken bad girl who got done wrong by her man.

She then went through Felicia's closet and put on some of Felicia's clothes—a little black cocktail dress that had fringes in all the wrong places, and shoes that her sorority sisters would have called "fuck-me pumps." The girl really had small town tramp style, something out of a "Traveling Salesman and the Farmer's Daughter" joke. Luna was nonetheless surprised at how well the clothes fit her, especially after she found a red push-up bra.

Luna looked in the mirror. Maybe Felicia wasn't so bad after all. Luna felt really good in the clothes. *"I'm just a girl who can't say no,"* she hummed from the musical from high school. Was that from *Oklahoma*?

"You didn't deserve to die, Felicia," she said to the mirror. "I'm sorry for everything I ever said about you."

She stumbled a bit in the pumps and decided she favored New Balance running shoes after all. She took them off. "Let's not go overboard here."

Still in Felicia's black dress, Luna read through the diary as she lay on Felicia's bed. She hit the high school years quickly and soon came to descriptions of a woman named "D."

"I kinda like D," Felicia had written in her girlish hand. "But it's starting to get like all weird. I think she loves me, loves me that way. As if!" Felicia wrote about some of their experimentations. Felicia had cut it short, and never let Diana get past an innocent kiss.

Luna imagined herself as Felicia and looked about on her bed. Felicia and Diana had just been two lonely girls playing around. It had been a game to Felicia, even if it had meant something more to Diana.

There was a brief passage about Diana's friend—"a bony little bitch who thinks she's all that!" It took a second for Luna to realize that the "bony little bitch" was herself.

She scanned all the portions of the diary and was disappointed to realize that was her only mention. She had rated only a single sentence in Felicia's life. Then again, she had said only a few short sentences about Felicia, and most of those involved the word "tramp."

After a few more pages about Diana, Felicia then wrote about Jeremy for the first time. Felicia must have learned a new word in school, charisma, because over and over she had written, "Jeremy has charisma." Jeremy was also the world's greatest lover. Luna blushed.

Luna tried to imagine Jeremy and Felicia making love as she read the passages. "We wanted to go where no one would know us," she had put in.

It took her a minute to realize that Felicia had lost her virginity in that same ladies' bathroom in the Crosswinds. She could suddenly imagine Jeremy seeing her and Thayer Brown there all those years later, and what it would do to him.

Shit, now I'm thinking like Jeremy.

Luna looked at the bed. Although the bed had been moved from her mother's house, this had been the same bed where Felicia and Jeremy had made love on many occasions. She felt a shiver run down her back, yet couldn't help but feel strangely excited. She couldn't imagine sex with Jeremy, though. It made her gag.

Still, she wanted to get into character, like Marlow always did. This was legal research, she kept telling herself. In the next few pages, she read how Felicia's relationship with Jeremy changed for the worse. Jeremy had begun failing school, doing drugs and drinking. Luna knew what was coming. Felicia then wrote of how Jeremy never beat her, but constantly threatened her with dire consequences if she ever left him.

"He's like a volcano," she had written.

And there it was—on page 333. Thirteen years ago, this month, Jeremy had said to her, "I'm going to kill you, bitch, someday."

"I believe him," Felicia had written in the next line.

She read it again. "I'm going to kill you, bitch, someday."

"Stay away from him!" she yelled at Felicia between the pages. "Don't take him back!"

Then she found another entry on the next page. "More than anything else in the world, I hope and pray that he can really change."

Luna surprised herself by crying. "You really were an optimist, weren't you, Felicia? You really tried to see the best in people."

"I'm just a girl who can't say no," she sang again.

Felicia's last entry in the diary was "Jeremy went off to San Diego today. I finally feel safe for me and the baby."

Luna sighed. That baby would never come. Neither would safety.

She went back to page 333 and read the line over and over again. Why did you take him back so many years later, Felicia? Why did you take him back?

Luna looked through the other boxes, at clippings and various other memorabilia of the rest of Felicia's short life. The baby would be stillborn, Felicia would run around for a while, and then settle into a somewhat respectable life. She'd get a job as a secretary at the church and run a day care center with her mom, until people in the town stopped having kids. Not a great life, but an honest one.

One picture showed Sarah and Felicia surrounded by a gaggle of children all holding up a sign saying "Merry Christmas."

Felicia held one little girl on her lap, and looked at the little girl as if it was her stillborn one all grown up. The day care center had closed after Sarah and Felicia had died.

Felicia also had a small dusty bible that had been autographed and given to her by the priest. For a short period, Felicia had actually been religious. Felicia started to come into focus for Luna. Perhaps she really hadn't been a tramp, she just went around trusting people she shouldn't have trusted. That's fine with children at a Christmas party, but not when you dated someone like Jeremy.

By looking around the room, Luna filled in the gaps in Felicia's life. Each picture told a story. Jeremy comes back from the Marines and lives in town for a couple of years. No pictures of Jeremy. That meant no contact. Apparently, Felicia didn't take him back right away. Good for you, Luna thought.

Still, Felicia wasn't a total angel. There was a picture of her and another man. It took a second to recognize him with the hair, but she knew that smile. It was Nico, all right.

Shit. The two of them had gone skiing up in Taos, and then posed standing in front of the ancient adobe blocks and vigas of the Taos Pueblo.

"Well, Felicia, I guess you and I had more in common than I thought," Luna said to the photograph. She tried to pretend to herself that Felicia was a Christian at that point, and certainly wouldn't have done anything with Nico.

She didn't entirely succeed.

She couldn't help but do what her sorority sisters had called "rogering." She'd slept with Nico, Nico had presumably slept with Felicia, and Felicia had slept with Jeremy. All those links in the chain flashed through her head.

Then came the letters from Jeremy from about five years ago. He must have been writing from various locations within the New Mexico Department of Corrections. He loved her and wanted to get back together again.

"I'm a changed man," he had said. Since he was locked up at the time, Felicia must have felt safe enough to write him back.

There were no copies of the letters she had sent back to him, although she could see the imprint of the words "I love him so much," on the back of the diary, as if Felicia had written a letter in bed, and used the diary for support.

Luna traced the indentations with her finger.

Jeremy was actually a pretty decent writer. No one had ever questioned his intelligence. He was a romantic, a poet, and there was no doubt at all in her mind that Jeremy had honestly loved Felicia.

She traced Felicia's indentations on the back of the diary again. No one had ever written love letters like that to her.

The first picture she saw was Jeremy getting out of Santa Fe North after his eighteen months, Felicia was there at the door to drive him home. They smiled in front of the closed gates.

"Damn it!" Luna said as she looked at the picture. "You stupid bitch. Don't take him back!"

There were some happy photos of the two of them together. For one brief moment, Luna could see true happiness on both of their faces. They really were in love; you could see it in their eyes.

Then a bunch of photos of Jeremy from exotic locales taken from the top of his truck. Jeremy really had turned his life around to be worthy of Felicia. But he traveled a lot, and he was still a very jealous man.

Then there was a picture of Felicia and Thayer.

It grew late. She nodded off between the photos.

Her dreams quickly turned to Marlow. She imagined him taking her in his arms. Soon he was deep inside her.

God she wanted him! God, she loved him!

Each thrust took her into a magical place, but then the dreams turned darker. She couldn't see anything anymore. A big male hand put a rag over her mouth and nose. She knew that smell from a DA continuing legal education class about poisons—it was chloroform. She tried to struggle, but she didn't have the strength to resist.

As he eyes began to close, she glimpsed moonlight through her window. She saw the face of the man who had put the cloth over her face. It was Jeremy, not Marlow. Or were they the same person? It was hard to tell in her dream. The face seemed to shift from one to the other and back again.

Luna could no longer open her eyes. She felt the man tighten his grip around her neck. She didn't fight it anymore. Maybe she could see the white light or maybe it was just the full moon. She felt herself fly up to the moon.

Yet somehow she was still half alive as she made it out to the desert. Then she felt herself float and she could see her body below her as the man laid her face down onto the sand. The sand was eerie yellow in the moonlight. She kept floating over that same spot in the desert, even after the body was taken away and the sun rose. Some people from the church put up a wooden cross where her body had lain.

Luna finally floated away, up toward the moon as those red roses were laid before the cross right at dawn. Her last memory looking down as she floated upward was seeing those three red roses blow away in the gusty Crater wind.

Marlow's mind was in a daze as he got back in the Saturn outside Manygoats clinic. He wasn't sure which direction he headed in once he got back on the interstate or how long he drove. He could have been in Flagstaff, in Amarillo, Albuquerque, Santa Fe or Las Cruces. He might have made it all the way to Phoenix, Tucson or even all the way to L.A. when he pulled off the freeway and spotted a bookstore down the street.

He wasn't sure if the bookstore was a Barnes and Nobles, a Borders, a Hastings or even some small independent. Marlow just knew that he needed to buy something, anything just to read or look at to get his mind off this. But blocking his way was a man dressed in a black shirt and a black jacket, looking vaguely like Keanu Reeves in the "Matrix" movies.

"Like a good story?" the man asked too loudly.

"Not really." Marlow replied. It was late, but the man was apparently hawking some kind of book, a novel. He looked like he'd been there all day. Marlow scanned the store, the man would know whatever magazine he was buying.

The man seemed to know too much, as if he could see right through him. Marlow gave the man a defensive wave, backed out and drove home.

He finally made it home right around dawn. He wondered how his own story would end. He still had some time to read, but all he had left were ancient copies of "Sports Illustrated." Damn, he should have bought that book!

The next morning Luna woke up in Felicia's bed. She took off the clothes and felt relieved to be back in her familiar bike shorts, athletic bra and CU sweatshirt. She looked through Felicia's jewelry cabinet until she found a small silver cross necklace. She put it on gingerly, almost as if she expected it to burn at her touch.

"This is going to be my tattoo, Felicia." The silver felt strangely warm, but that strangeness was comfortable somehow. The cross nestled comfortably against her neck as if it had been there all her life.

Luna then jogged the mile or so over to the Crosswinds. She still felt the taboo as she made it into the parking lot, for a moment she feared that some guardian monster, like the three headed dog of

Greek myth, would emerge out of the sludge of the gigantic oil tanks of the refinery behind. Undaunted she forced herself through it and went inside. She went all the way back to the famed ladies' room. This was it?

Other than a coin-operated condom machine and a coin operated shower for the few female truckers, there was nothing about the ladies room that could explain all that had taken place here. Hell, she herself had taken her panties off at the prom in this very room.

She forced herself to see it as Felicia would see it, a place of memories and passion. A clean place where the rest of her life had been so dirty. Luna put a coin in the shower and let it run.

Felicia had used this shower. She just knew it. She wiped her hands in the warm waters. There was a slight acidic smell, but that smell was strangely comforting. It reminded her of the waters from Crater Lake.

Outside, there was a small gift shop that sold flowers. She bought three red roses. First, she walked slowly behind the truck stop to the corner. There was still some discoloration on the ground.

Heidi Hawk, the clerk, saw her in the corner. Heidi looked at her with rage as if Luna had peed on the grave. "Go away, that's private!"

Luna turned and showed Heidi the roses. "I'm family," she said.

Heidi didn't smile, just emptied the trash into the dumpster, then walked quickly away. God, she couldn't wait to get the hell out of Crater and go home to Gallup where people were sane!

Luna dropped the first rose on the discolored earth. "Thayer, I didn't know you. I just know that you didn't deserve to die."

She took the second rose. "Nico, I miss you."

The Crater winds cooperated with her as she jogged. She had extra speed to make it all the way out to Felicia's wooden cross. She touched the rose to the silver cross that lay around her neck, then touched it to the wooden cross, almost as if the rose carried a message from one to the other.

"Felicia," she said after a moment. "I'm going to do this for you."

She laid the rose down at the base of the cross.

REHEARSAL

Marlow didn't study the files over the weekend; he knew what they had on Felicia's case, and it wasn't much. He quickly went through a checklist then thought briefly about the diary. It was from high school, a high school that didn't even exist any more, so why even bother?

He'd never even read it. Jeremy had probably threatened Felicia a few times. But then again, back when he was in high school, he himself had threatened everyone who had wronged him with a swift and horrible death. They didn't believe him, of course, even though he was quite serious.

His only actual teenage rebellion had been flooding the first floor library bathroom with paper towels stuffed in a toilet. He hadn't even been good at being an alienated teenaged loser.

Marlow thought of the diary again. Oh, he'd make a motion when the time came, not that it mattered either way. All the other memorabilia wasn't real evidence anyway. Real evidence was blood and there wasn't much of that linking any crime to Jeremy.

Instead he rented Jeremy's favorite movies or the ones that he could find in the three racks of the convenience store—the town's only collection of films. He thought of Sarah of course, but didn't worry that everything was rated R.

"Take that!" he said as he walked out with a pile of films. Mostly they were war movies and a few psycho killer ones. It was strange watching these movies from the psycho-killer's perspective, but he quickly got used to it.

While watching *The Shining,* he couldn't help but cheer for Jack Nicholson to take out that whiny Shelly Duvall. "All work and no play makes Jack a dull boy," he said to the screen over and over again.

When he went into the bathroom, he glanced at the Shrine of rejection letters. God, he hated the Shrine. He looked at Alan Iverson's picture on the basketball card. Iverson smirked back at him.

What had Iverson said in his Georgetown admission essay? Today, the congregation of the Shrine, Iverson especially, mocked him more than ever. "There were many fine candidates but we are unable to offer you a position." That was the best thing someone could say about the life of Sam Marlow, that he was one of many fine candidates? Is that what his epitaph would be? Sam Marlow, one of many fine candidates?

All work and no play makes Jack a dull boy all right. It was time to burn the letters and that damn card, so he went outside and started a little bonfire in the stone barbecue.

"Good bye, Marlow," he said after the last of the letters and that card were little more than ash floating away in a swirling Crater wind. "Have fun with those other fine candidates."

Diana and Luna prepped Shatrock one more time in Luna's cramped office. Shatrock was in his brush-popper shirt, big belt and hat. If it wasn't for the beeper, with his Silver Star and handlebar mustache he could pass for the long arm of the law back in pioneer days.

Diana took Shatrock through the discovery of the body until he now almost sounded like a real cop. They had to admit that Shatrock was a likeable guy with his down-home drawl. Unfortunately, it was clear that as a farm boy he was indeed far more comfortable with animals than people. Being locked in a room with two smart women intimidated him even more. Yet Diana gave him enough encouragement that he finally warmed up to the task.

"You know, I did a play in high school once," he said.

"I'm sure you were very good," Diana lied. "Here at Crater High? What play was it?"

"It was called *Fiddler on the Roof.* I was Tevye."

Luna laughed about the famed Crater High production, ten years before their time.

Then Shatrock started singing, *"If I was a rich man."*

Damn, he wasn't that bad.

Luna then took up the diary, and put it on the table. It now had several Post-it notes for the relevant passages.

"That's not getting in," said Diana. "That's like a hundred years old."

"Let's just have him read it, okay?" Luna replied. "Maybe we can get it in as a pattern of behavior under Rule . . . ," she hurried to the statutes until she found the appropriate cite, "Rule 404."

Diana was dubious, but reluctantly allowed Shatrock to read. Shatrock must have become nostalgic for his thespian days, since he attempted to do a high school girl's voice. To Luna, it sounded like the screeching of fake fingernails down a black board.

"Just do it in your normal voice, okay?" she said

When he did it in his normal voice, he still sounded like a bad actor trying to reach a little too far in an audition. They practiced a few more questions.

"What did you think?" He asked anxiously. "Did I get the part?"

"Don't call us," Luna said, ushering him quickly out the door. "We'll call you."

Shatrock hummed, *"Matchmaker, matchmaker, make me a match,"* as he left. He really did have an amazing voice.

Alone, the two friends stared at each other, then stared at the three small piles of papers that constituted their evidence for the final case. Even under the best of circumstances, and if they were two experienced prosecutors rather than two baby lawyers, this would be an uphill battle.

"Do you think Jeremy will come after us when he gets out?" Diana asked. She'd already mentally prepared herself for Benally to say the words "not" and "guilty."

Luna at least had a smidgen of hope of winning the case and avoiding that situation. "Seriously?" she asked.

"Seriously," Diana said. "I mean, we did try to put him to death on three separate occasions. Assuming that we lose, which is a good bet, and he's released, wouldn't he be kinda pissed at me and pissed at you?"

"I guess so."

"Shit. . . ."

They said nothing for another minute or so. "What else do we have?" Diana asked.

They looked over all the files in all three piles of evidence.

"Aren't we forgetting something?" Luna asked her.

"What?"

"We've still got that Katy Baca on the witness list who heard Jeremy say that he was going to kill them at the 66 Tears."

"You're right." Diana was not impressed. "So?"

"We've got the bloodstains at Felicia's house."

"That was struck when Van Leit's evidence was thrown out," Diana said. "Wasn't it?"

"No, it wasn't. Just all evidence after he left Felicia's house and went to Sarah's. So it wasn't any good at Sarah's trial. Well now it would be relevant since this is *Felicia's* trial."

They both laughed at the absurdity of that comment. That would be a fun argument to make at closing argument. We want you to consider this blood found at one house, even thought this very same drop of blood was thrown out when it was planted at a different house.

They stared at each other for another minute. "He really is getting out. *Deal* with it," Diana said at last. Dealing with the prospect of an acquitted Jeremy did not make either of them particularly happy.

"We can get the prior history of domestic violence in through Shatrock, I suppose," Luna said just to break the silence.

"We've got a 911 operator," Diana said helpfully. "Felicia did say one time that she was scared he was going to kill her, right?"

"That's still not enough." Luna said. "I mean we have all this evidence from a million other people testifying about Jeremy wanting to kill Felicia. And so far we haven't had any luck."

"What else do we have?" Diana said. "I mean, the two of us can always move to another county and join the witness, I mean, the lawyer protection program, and get new identities to hide from Jeremy."

Luna thought for a long moment. She finally liked her identity. She didn't want to change it now. "We need Felicia."

Diana gave her a look. "Ummm . . . Luna my love, I think you're forgetting something here about Felicia."

"We've got the diary."

"I told you it's not getting in and Shatrock will be the one reading it. He's a regular Meryl Streep when it comes to voices."

Luna said nothing. "We'll cross that bridge when we come to it."

"Your call," Diana said.

Luna looked over at Diana and came to a realization. She was the sophomore now, and Diana was the freshman.

"Now if we could just get Jeremy to come out and confess. . . ." Diana said stupidly.

"We'll cross that bridge when we come to it."

PATTERN OF BEHAVIOR

Luna spent another night in Felicia's house. Normally, she'd run in almost any kind of weather, but it was too windy even for her to run outside. There were dust devils everywhere. The house shook in the wind. She hoped that the winds would take the entire house up and fly it to Oz. Reluctantly she decided to stay inside. Felicia had a little solo weight machine, so Luna forced herself to do weights over and over again as she listened to a Dixie Chicks CD.

"You can't catch me, bitch," she said to her reflection on the vanity mirror. Since the wind sprints, she finally looked like an "almost Olympian" again. She slept soundly after the workout. She tried to banish all thoughts of Felicia's somewhat colorful past but did not entirely succeed. She had that same Marlow dream, making love to him. Then someone strangled her and left her out in the desert to die.

She still couldn't see the man's face.

Marlow did not sleep at all. This case would probably end tomorrow, one way or another. What would happen next? He expected to win tomorrow, and then Jeremy would be free. Could he ever go back to being a simple country lawyer pleading speeding tickets to deferred sentences after all that he had seen and done?

He looked down at the two crosses. Without expensive and painful laser surgery, they were here to stay. Manygoats himself had told him that some kind of spirit was still inside him, the kind that didn't go away. A few years ago, he never would have believed that sort of thing, but he couldn't even get Yazzie completely out of his system, and it had now been well over a year since Yazzie had been executed. Jeremy was not going to leave him quietly either.

And Luna, the lovely Luna. She'd finally become the woman that he wanted, more than he had ever imagined. His love at second sight had finally been justified. But it was too late. He was too far gone. She would never have him now, not with the crosses.

If I can't have her, no one can. That's what Jeremy would have said and Jeremy had now become a part of him—his id and his superego at the same time. Most of his ego had just burnt away in that barbecue. He no longer knew where Jeremy ended and he began.

When he woke up that morning, he put on the red tie that he had bought with Luna.

Stephanie Park Live stood in front of the justice center when morning broke. Unfortunately, her cameraman was still in Albuquerque nursing a hangover. She was now a solo act as she set up the equipment. Behind her, scores of late-arriving vans had decided that Murder County, USA was the place to be.

Stephanie laughed and couldn't resist telling somebody from CNN about going over to catch the sunset from the Crater walls. The man had already setup in the exact place where the first rays of the sun would blind the camera.

Fuck him, Stephanie thought to herself. She then thought of her new friends Diana and Luna. "We were Crater County when Crater County wasn't cool."

Stephanie had finally heard from a Denver station. It wasn't L.A., but it wasn't Albuquerque either. "Send us another tape," they had said. "Send us something juicy."

She had covered a few more gang-related shootings in Santa Fe, but there were gang-related shootings everywhere. She knew that State v. Jeremy Jones was going to be her juice, her ticket out of Albuquerque. She filmed Judge Benally as he walked to court. He nearly bumped into her, his eyes half-asleep. So much for juice.

· · · · ·

Benally didn't even bother to apologize to Stephanie Park Live when he nearly bumped her. All the cameras and reporters shouting questions made his head hurt. He had driven through the night from Mexican border. He'd seen a New Mexico State Aggies game against the UNM Lobos down at the Pan Am in Las Cruces. The game had been delayed from its usual pre-Christmas date because of a bomb threat. With the exception of a handful of East Coast exiles, all the judges in New Mexico were either Lobos or Aggies.

Benally was a Lobo, undergrad and law. He'd won the bet so he'd taken a bunch of his colleagues over the border to Juarez, and they'd tested various tequilas. A non-drinker, he'd been the designated driver, (and unfortunately the designated man with the wallet). Somehow, the potent Mexican alcohol and the even more potent tobacco had passed into his system by osmosis.

As designated driver, he had to drop all his designated drinkers off at each of their hotels, all over El Paso and Las Cruces. He was a good listener, so every judge told him a tale of woe. Some of them had even worse scandals than the criminals they sentenced. Finally, after he'd dropped the last of them off, he headed straight for Crater, up I-25 and then over onto I-40.

His head hurt and that put him in a far worse mood than usual. He played with his tattoo. Judge Yin was definitely taking a sick day; it was Judge Yang's day to preside.

Pulling into Crater made his head hurt even more. Breathing that dusty air blocked the flow of cleansing oxygen into the brain. He'd left Sheep Springs and gone to law school to avoid places like Crater for the rest of his career.

This trial would end today, one way or another.

Diana was also in a foul mood. On the one hand, she was glad that Luna finally asserted herself. Unfortunately, power was a zero sum game after all, and Luna's newfound power came at her expense. Still, she couldn't stay mad at Luna. Luna my love. Her little freshman friend had finally blossomed, finally become a full-fledged member of the cool girls' clique. She was proud of her little Luna, damn it!

Her nerves still bothered her. She wished she could go back to Tucson and spend the next fourteen days talking about her old issues rather than a whole new twenty-eight days for talking about her new ones. She'd eaten at the Rustler by herself last night, just soup and salad, and she had heard rumblings.

"What would Felicia think if her killer walked?" She swore that she heard something like that over at the salad bar.

"It would definitely be Diana's fault," someone else said.

"Maybe they could get a real DA out here," someone else said, purposely loud enough for her to hear. "A real DA."

"I've got a cousin in Albuquerque. He's a real lawyer."

No, she wasn't a real DA, much less a real lawyer. Never had been, and didn't know if she could ever be one by herself. She didn't have to do it alone. Maybe with Luna's help, maybe she could become a real lawyer. Not just for herself. She owed Felicia that much.

Her left foot shook again. No, she definitely couldn't do this alone.

Smoky drove Jeremy over to the Justice Center, as if he were his limo driver and Jeremy were the celebrity. Jeremy looked over at the rising sun. Crater actually looked beautiful in the early sunlight. All the grayness now had a pink glow to it. He knew that when the sun rose tomorrow he would be a free man.

One way or another.

"This is it," he said.

They both smiled when they drove through the gauntlet of media vans. "Looks like we finally done made the big time," Jeremy said, overjoyed.

Smoky said nothing, just puffed away.

When they arrived, Stephanie noticed that Jeremy limped just a bit. As the cameras all turned toward him, he somehow managed to get a spring back into his step.

Smoky walked him past Stephanie. Jeremy made him stop, and shifted positions so Stephanie could get a better shot, then made Smoky rotate him around for the throng of other media. "Make sure you all get my good side," he said.

He then looked directly at the camera. "Good Morning, Crater County!" He imitated Robin Williams as he said that. "I want to give a shout-out to Cellblock 1 over at the Discount Prison! You guys rock!"

Judge Benally called the court to order at eight A.M. sharp. When he started early, he generally could stay early all day. He had to do a real quick docket call. Gollum had re-offended. Indecent exposure this time. Benally didn't bother listening to arguments after the plea. He just ordered an in-patient psychological evaluation over at the Las Vegas Mental Hospital.

"A transport from the state hospital arrives in a few hours," Benally snarled. "If any of you try my patience today, you will be joining Gollum for a psych consult. Remember, it's a Friday, and you could be spending the weekend up there with the sex offenders."

Benally noticed that Van Leit was in the back of the courtroom. "Sir, please get out of my courtroom." Van Leit scurried out. He had some kind of envelope for Luna, but hadn't found a chance it to get it to her.

After a few preliminary motions, Luna called the first witness, the 911 operator, a petite forty-something Anglo woman named Monica Martin. After few more preliminaries, Martin testified about several of the calls that Felicia had made. There was only one tape available, but on it, you could clearly hear Felicia say that she thought Jeremy was going to kill her.

The sound quality was poor, and the Crater radio fatigue set into the jurors' box. Hearing a scratchy voice from beyond the grave was just like hearing some stupid DJ from Albuquerque fade in and out. The jurors just weren't that into it.

Luna tried an old trick. "You just heard Felicia say that she was afraid that Jeremy was going to kill her, did you not?"

"Yes," Martin said before Marlow could object on the grounds that it was leading.

Marlow was about to make a motion to strike, but it was too

late. Luna had just let the skunk out. He noticed that the jurors had long since stopped looking at Martin. Every eye was on Luna. She was the one on stage, not the witness. The jurors might not listen to the 911 tapes (the scratchy voices did sound like a distant station in the car radio), but Luna had now become their trusted companion for the ride. The one who said, "Turn it up, I love this song."

And if Luna loved something, the jurors figured it had to be good.

Marlow hit Martin hard during cross-examination. This tape took place a few weeks before the incident, Felicia had never pressed charges, Martin hadn't been there and thus had no personal knowledge, and so on and so forth.

Martin agreed with all the statements, didn't argue. Just said yes or no when appropriate.

Luna got up for re-direct. "Ms. Martin, Mr. Marlow just stated that you had no personal knowledge. I bet you have quite a bit of personal knowledge. In your twenty years as a 911 operator, has someone called in a domestic violence call and then been murdered?"

"Yes."

For re-cross, Marlow asked the opposite question. "Has anyone *not* been murdered after making a call?"

"Yes."

Marlow looked over at the jurors, expecting them to revel in his brilliance by asking that question, but the point seemed too little too late. Their eyes were still on Luna. The jurors liked her. They were afraid of him.

Diana called the next witness, the waitress, Katy Baca, a Latina in her fifties who had worked at the 66 Stars since it had been a stopping point for the westward migration of the Great Depression. Or at least it just seemed that way. She always had a smile and a warm hello to nearly all who came by. Baca gave a quick run-down of some statements that Jeremy had made about "killing" over at the 66 Stars.

"He said he would kill Felicia," Baca testified.

Baca then made a positive identification. Thank God.

Diana sat down. Hopefully, that was good enough for her to keep her job for at least another hour. She still feared that somewhere in the gallery was this mysterious "Somebody's cousin from Albuquerque," who was poised to take over her job if she failed.

Marlow didn't like Baca much. He'd forgotten to tip her once at the 66 Stars and, ever since then, she wouldn't say a word to him other than to chide him for leaving his coat behind. On the few nights he had ventured back there, she'd plop down his beer without a word, all the while chatting up the lost trucker from Oklahoma like they were kin.

Marlow put his anger into his cross-examination. He pointed out quite correctly that in her statement Jeremy had threatened Felicia's mother, Sarah, rather than Felicia herself.

"Well, I think he meant both of them," Baca answered.

"So you've had a chance to talk with the prosecutors and they've helped you with your answer?"

"Yes."

"By the way, you are aware that the charges against Jeremy for killing Sarah Sanchez were dismissed, aren't you?"

"Yes."

Marlow sat down. He could probably never go back to the 66 Stars. Baca gave him a look as if she would tamper with his beer if he ever did. It had taken an extra witness, but he felt that the skunk was definitely gone and the courtroom had been fumigated.

Diana frowned. She noticed that one of the male jurors was staring at her boobs; he'd been doing it the entire time. Slightly embarrassed, she buttoned an extra button on the blouse.

She looked around. There were a couple of people she didn't know back in the gallery. A couple of people could be the mysterious cousin, but they were probably just out-of-town reporters. She looked back at Stephanie Park Live, saw this short, attractive woman write something down into a notebook with a delicate scrawl. The woman looked like that totally cool war correspondent at CNN. Diana smiled at her. Stephanie Park Live smiled back.

At first, Diana thought that Stephanie was just smiling by way of ingratiating herself, but Stephanie let the smile linger for just a second too long.

"I still got it," Diana thought to herself

Diana and Luna then split the scientists to end the morning. None of their facts were in dispute. Each testified about how scientific evidence showed that Felicia had been drugged, strangled, then left for dead, all in the span of a few hours.

Then there was that weird fact about some kind of sexual intercourse around the time of death.

"Around the time of death?" Marlow asked each scientist. "Before or after?"

No one could give him a definitive answer. He stressed the point that it seemed ridiculous that someone would have consensual sex with someone right before they were killed.

The jurors now came back over to his side. They seemed to dislike each successive scientist more and more. Marlow then hit hard on the one fact that was in dispute over Felicia's death—who had actually killed her? As before, he had each scientist admit that there was nothing linking Jeremy to anything.

With the last one, a medical examiner named Goldfarb with coke bottle glasses, Marlow decided to test the man's eyesight. "I want you to read each of the letters I am holding up."

Marlow flashed letters and the man recited. "I see an r, an e, a, s, o, n, a, b, l, e, d, o, u, b, and t."

"What's that spell?"

Goldfarb might have been a brilliant scientist, but he wasn't much of a speller. He actually had to write it down. "Reasonable doubt," he said at last.

"Motion to strike," Luna yelled.

"Granted," Benally said. He couldn't help but laugh at the effectiveness of the stunt. He didn't always like Marlow, but the man had done his job. He nodded at Marlow. Good move. Marlow nodded back.

By their faces, Benally could tell that the jurors had split down gender lines over Marlow's last stunt. The men liked it, the women thought it was way overdone. It didn't matter. This case wasn't going to the jury anyway.

Judge Benally looked over at Luna. He felt sorry for her. Maybe by next trial she'd totally hit her stride. She would be one of the great ones. She was just overmatched today.

He looked down at his watch after Marlow sat down. "Lunch break. I want everyone back here by twelve-forty-five!"

They all ate lunch at the Rustler, but no one had any appetite. Diana and Luna sat at one table, Marlow at the other. Benally had missed breakfast, so he ordered the Big Bad Rustler, but he held off on the chile on account of his rumbling stomach.

They had nothing to say to each other at a time like this. Luna was so tense she almost ordered a drink. Then she decided to have some Sheep Springs Mineral Water instead.

They all got back to court early in anticipation of the Benally. She looked over at Marlow and Jeremy as they sat by the table. Marlow did not meet her gaze, almost as if she was beneath his notice. He stared only at the clock.

Jeremy, on the other hand, could not take his eyes off of her. He stared at her, mentally undressing her with his eyes, but it seemed more like a real hunger than something sexual. The man didn't look right today.

She thought back to the first time she'd seen the two of them together, back in the police interview room. Jeremy had been the sun, and Marlow had been the moon. Now, the roles were reversed. Jeremy looked like Marlow had drained a bit of life out of him. He was paler, not just from incarceration, but like he'd been bitten by a vampire or something. Marlow was that vampire.

As if he could read her thoughts, Jeremy flashed his teeth at her as though he wanted to get his fluid levels back up to where they'd been before Marlow had drained him dry. She flashed hers right back at him. Two can play at that game.

• • • • •

Benally called court to order at twelve-forty-four. On pace, on pace, on pace.

Luna called Shatrock to the stand as the jurors were still shuffling to their seats. He actually wore a tie, and took his hat off for the first time in his life. She took him through the crime scene and had him show a few pictures of Felicia's dead body. Luna shivered when she saw the picture of Felicia face down in the dirt. She thought of her dream. She hoped her flower was still there next to the wooden cross.

Luna next approached Benally. Marlow followed. "Your Honor, we'd like to introduce Felicia's diary into evidence," she said. "It was on the list of evidence and has already been provided to Counsel for inspection."

Marlow had expected this and was ready. "Your Honor, that diary is thirteen years old and describes the relationship back when Jeremy and Felicia were in high school. A lot has changed since then. The diary's prejudicial effect far outweighs any probative value."

Luna did not flinch. "Your Honor, we're asking that it be admitted to show pattern. We've already established that the defendant had a pattern of violent behavior toward the victim. This would be admissible under Rule 404 and would indeed be probative. Counsel has shown that he is very effective at cross-examination. He could point out the age of the diary at that time."

She took a breath and stared at Marlow. "Unless Counsel doesn't feel up to it."

That came as a direct challenge to Marlow. "I'll stipulate to its admission, Your Honor."

"I don't know." The Judge pondered for a second. It was only one-thirty. This was the state's final witness and would delay the inevitable for about an hour. Assuming no defense testimony, they could still get to Marlow's directed verdict arguments by the end of the afternoon, and he'd be heading home on I-40 by five-oh-five.

He looked into Luna's eyes again. She had come such a long

way since he had first seen her six months ago. He didn't want to base a decision just on those eyes, but in them he saw a passion for justice. He'd had that passion once.

What had caused him to lose it? Golf, of course. Tennis had certainly been a willing accomplice.

Maybe he just wanted to hear her voice a little more before getting on I-40. He just wanted to know what happened to Felicia. Then, after a decent interval, he could direct a verdict for the defense and still make it home to catch his favorite TV show.

"I'll allow it," he said. "But please be brief. We'll take a ten minute recess."

Luna went to the ladies' bathroom. She washed her hands over and over again. She felt like everyone was in the bathroom with her—not just Felicia, and her mother but also Nico, Thayer, and even Sarah Sanchez. Luna looked like she was in some kind of trance when Diana joined her a moment later.

"I hope I'm not interrupting something," Diana said with a smile. "I seem to do that a lot in bathrooms."

Marlow waited in the courtroom with Jeremy. Jeremy looked nervous. He kept glancing back at the army of cameras.

"Well, you're finally compelling," Marlow said.

Jeremy forced a smile. Marlow couldn't read that smile—was it happiness, fatigue, resignation or triumph?

The smile quickly faded.

"Are you all right?" Marlow asked.

"Stage fright."

"Do you want some water or something?"

Jeremy looked at him strangely. "Water is the last thing I need right now."

"Seriously Jeremy, you look like shit."

"I'm fine," Jeremy said. "Fine, fine, fine. Everything's going exactly the way it's supposed to go."

• • • • •

When court came to order, nine minutes later, Luna planned to have Shatrock establish authenticity and chain of custody, that sort of thing. But Marlow stipulated again to speed things along. He wanted to get this over with, like everyone else.

She then had Shatrock read a passage or two. The man couldn't make out words in the best of circumstances and getting through a paragraph in Felicia's girlish hand was torture for all concerned.

"Your Honor," Luna said, "perhaps it would be best if I read the passages to the witness, to lead him as it may. . . ."

She had a smile, a guilty smile, as if she'd just set a trap.

Jeremy was the only person in the court who caught that smile. He elbowed Marlow, as if to get him to object. "She's up to something."

Marlow was about to, but then he too wanted to hear what Luna had to say. What harm could it do?

"If there's no objection and if it will expedite things. . . ." Benally said.

"It will, Your Honor."

As Luna spoke, a miracle happened. She read Felicia's words of fear and horror and it was as if Felicia had returned in person to tell her tale of woe. The jurors weren't just listening to the radio anymore. Felicia was there, right before their eyes. They all looked at the shimmering silver cross dangling around Luna's neck. A ray of sunlight from one of the new windows caught it just right. Marlow couldn't help but remember how Luna had looked like an angel out in the desert the first time he saw her.

"He said he was going to kill me," Luna said in Felicia's voice. "He said he was going to kill me one day," she said again. Then almost as an afterthought, "That's what the passage says, doesn't it officer, Shatrock?"

"Yes. That's what it said."

She read passage after passage, had Shatrock agree with each line. Somehow she managed to get an hour's worth of Felicia into the record. Even Jeremy was transfixed. He, too, saw Felicia come back to life and he nearly gagged when he saw the silver cross. He knew that cross. He had given it to her himself!

She read the words "Jeremy went off to San Diego today. I finally feel safe for me and the baby." She then sat down and didn't even wait to ask Shatrock if those were the words. She touched the necklace, ran her finger down to the cross, then said, "Pass the witness."

All of the jurors, male and female, had tears coming on. The Illustrated Woman even asked for a tissue from the bailiff.

Jeremy had not cried since he got his last tattoo, but suddenly he felt the waves of emotion pass through him—love, loss, and then anger all over again. He tried to control himself.

Marlow didn't know what to do. You can't cross-examine a ghost. He stared at Shatrock. The man had barely said anything, and he couldn't really put Luna on the stand. She had in fact read the lines verbatim. He couldn't ask her "Are you sure?"

She was sure.

He looked over at Jeremy. It was getting worse.

"I'm going to kill that bitch," he said, "all over again." His words were a little too loud to be considered "under his breath." Jeremy was now a caged tiger who was late for his five o'clock feeding.

"I'm going to kill that bitch," he said again.

One of the jurors heard him. So did Judge Benally.

"Your Honor, I'd like to take a brief recess," Marlow said.

Benally felt a twinge. I-40 at five-oh-five was now out of the question. "That might be best," he agreed.

When court resumed, Marlow asked Shatrock a few questions about the age of the diary. Marlow was able to confuse the deputy a bit, but the damage was already done.

When he tried to keep pressing the same points over and over again, Luna stood up. "Every time he asks the same question, the diary does indeed get a little older, Your Honor."

"If there's nothing further," Benally said.

Marlow had nothing further. He sat down.

Jeremy kept shaking. He had pulled himself together in the bathroom, but now he was back to falling apart.

Luna gave one glance at Jeremy then focused her attention on Shatrock. She walked over to him for re-direct. "Your Honor, I have only one question. Officer, you've heard testimony about the pattern of abuse that has dated back for more than a decade. You yourself have responded to domestic violence calls at the Sanchez residence, and also have experience through the late Officer Nico. Based on your opinion as a law enforcement officer, is there any doubt, any doubt whatsoever in your mind, any doubt that Jeremy Jones killed Felicia Sanchez?"

"Objection!" Marlow yelled. "Deputy Shatrock is a lay witness. He can't offer an opinion on an ultimate issue!"

"I don't think we really need to hear the officer's opinion," she said before the judge could rule. "I'll withdraw the question."

As she sat down, she felt like she had killed a skunk right in front of Marlow, then beheaded it and threw the head and tail into the jury box. This was a stink that wasn't going away any time soon. That is if the case ever went to the jury. To Luna, the judge still looked as if he had already headed out to the highway.

She felt a tinge of fear, but only a tinge. "Your Honor, the State rests."

Benally excused the jury and then asked for any motions. He turned to Marlow, giving him his cue.

Marlow nodded. "Your Honor, I move for a directed verdict. The state has failed to meet their burden to prove a prima facie case linking my client to the murder of Felicia Sanchez and I move that the court direct a verdict for the defense."

Marlow went on for a few more moments then looked at Judge Benally. No need to try the man's patience, quit while you're ahead. He talked about burdens a few more time then sat down.

Luna was a woman possessed when she took the podium.

"Your Honor, the burden has indeed been on the state and we have met that burden." She ran down each of Marlow's points. "No Your Honor, we have no DNA, but we have the word of the victim and the word of witnesses of Jeremy's pattern of abuse and his statements. Your Honor, please let the jurors decide this case on the merits. For Felicia!"

It was a cheap ploy. Benally hesitated for a second. This could all be over with the bang of a gavel.

Some light from Felicia's silver cross reflected into his eyes. Oh what the hell, he thought. "I will deny the defense motion for a directed verdict," he said after a moment. "I feel that the state has met its burden and indeed has presented sufficient evidence that could be considered by a jury."

He paused. "Just barely! In closing argument, I expect the State to rely on evidence and not emotion."

Marlow was disappointed, but he knew, knew beyond a reasonable doubt that he would still kill her in closing argument. "Evidence and not emotion," Benally had said. Marlow laughed for a second, under his breath. He usually played the emotion card and the state almost always had the evidence. Luna now played his usual game.

"Does the defense have any witnesses?" Benally asked.

Marlow looked over at Jeremy. Jeremy looked purple with this newfound madness. Even in the best of circumstances, he would not put Jeremy on, especially since he had no idea what Jeremy would say. And these certainly were not the best of circumstances.

"No, Your Honor," Marlow said. "We have no witnesses. The defense rests."

"I'm giving you both an hour to prepare your closing arguments." Benally looked down at his watch, noting that it was almost time for dinner. He asked the clerk to bring in frozen pizzas from the convenience store across the street. "No one leaves," he said. "Until we are done, done, done."

CLOSING ARGUMENTS

The most boring part of a trial is when the judge reads the jury instructions, then cautions the jurors that what is said in a closing argument is not argument. Judge Benally was beyond tired by this part of the day and the frozen pizza and Code Red Mountain Dew did little to wake him up. He nearly left out a jury instruction or two, before both sides protested.

"They get it," he said sternly. "The instructions are right there in front of them."

The jurors nodded. They got it, all right.

It took some heavy lifting and balancing, but Stephanie Park Live set up her cameras to focus on the podium. Diana did the State's first closing argument. She was solid and listed every instance when Jeremy had said he wanted to kill Felicia. That was pretty much it. She had a checklist and ran down every point, then put a check next to it. She then hit the elements of murder in the first degree-murder, natural person, malice aforethought, blah, blah, blah. . . .

It wasn't pretty, but it was solid. Stephanie had stopped taping after the first few seconds, although she did give Diana a smile and a thumbs-up.

Diana looked over at Luna. Luna would have to carry them with the rebuttal. Diana scanned the gallery. Still no sign of the mysterious cousin, or anyone else out for her job. She smiled at Stephanie.

Marlow thought about waiving his closing argument. Diana had been fairly mundane in her close, and he was way ahead on points. He had heard that some baby lawyer had waived closing argument in a murder trial down in Aguilar to great success, but this was Crater County. After the first Yazzie trial, people expected a show from him and he did not want to disappoint them. He looked over at Jeremy. Jeremy definitely wanted him to say something.

He stood up and took a dramatic pause, mentally counting to ten, which was the number of cameras behind the windows that were focused on him. This was the big time.

"I said from the beginning that I am Jeremy Jones. I still am." He glared over at Luna. "I said at the beginning that we are not on trial here, the State is. They still are. She still is.

"They have to prove this case beyond a reasonable doubt. What is a reasonable doubt?"

He read the definition of "reasonable doubt" right out of the jury instructions. It was something about a doubt causing you to hesitate in the graver affairs of life, and so forth. He took a pause and remembered what one of the adjunct instructors had taught in Trial Advocacy 101. He took another look at the piece of paper then ripped it into shreds.

He then walked over to the jurors. "All it takes is one reasonable doubt and you have to acquit my client. First reasonable doubt: no scientist had any DNA evidence on the day of the murder linking Jeremy to the crime. None."

He put a shred right down in front of one juror. It barely stayed put on the slippery wooden rail separating the jury box from the rest of the court.

"Second, the State has offered a diary from thirteen years ago, saying that Felicia feared that Jeremy would kill her. Thirteen years ago! Who hasn't hit a bad patch in a relationship and given voice to your deepest fears?" He put another shred down next to the first one.

That came out a little harsher than he had intended. The jurors stiffened. He'd lost them a little. "People don't always understand where you're coming from and sometimes get the wrong idea. They sometimes jump to wrong conclusions. That's what I meant to say."

He looked over at Luna as he said that. Good pick-up, Luna thought to herself.

All in all, he had twelve scraps of paper, one for each juror and, with every scrap, he felt the jurors return to him.

"And remember, I have provided twelve scraps, each a reasonable doubt. All you need is one. Remember, each one of you is Jeremy Jones. Each one of us is on trial. Don't let them convict us!"

He counted the ten cameras again, nodded to each one then sat down. He was good and he knew it, and so did they.

Jeremy roused himself somehow, shook Marlow's hands as if they were a wrestling tag team. There already was a tag team from the old days called Murder Incorporated, right? But after he took back his hand, Jeremy was back in his weird daze, as if the very air in the room had him in some kind of a chokehold. . . .

Time for the final round. Luna stood up. She couldn't help but think of the start of the Olympic trials when those other women had intimidated her. She smiled for a second. With the poor ventilation, the smell was almost the same. She was still the skinny girl from Crater, but this was her home turf.

She picked up the first scrap of paper from the wooden rail and put it in her pocket. "Mr. Marlow is mistaken. There was DNA evidence found. The blood on the wall found by Officer Van Leit at Felicia Sanchez's house on the day that her mother was killed. That was indeed admitted into evidence."

Marlow frowned, and searched his brain. She was right. But so what?

"Secondly, Mr. Marlow asks, 'Who hasn't been in a relationship where there weren't emotions that led to violence?' Even when she was a high school student, Felicia feared for her life from this man here. We dishonor her memory by discounting her fear."

She then lit a match and burned the scrap of paper in her hand.

"Objection!" Marlow shouted. "She's turning the courtroom into a circus."

"Your Honor," Luna replied calmly. "This is closing argument. I am allowed some leeway."

"I said before that I expect you to rely on evidence and not emotion. You are walking a very thin line, Counselor, but I will allow it.

And Mr. Marlow, the elephants started marching in the moment you began your opening statements."

Luna returned to the rail. She then countered each of Marlow's arguments one by one. Each time, she answered a point; she took a shred of paper and crumpled it back into her pocket. The jurors noticed that each time she crumpled up a piece of paper, Jeremy winced, as if she had some kind of a voodoo spell on him. Each piece of paper was like another needle.

She then walked in front of Marlow and Jeremy again. Jeremy's face now looked red. There was definitely something wrong with him, but she didn't care. She had to push on.

Benally kept his hand on his gavel; any moment he could stop this trial.

"I didn't really know Felicia," said Luna. "Then I read her diaries and she came alive to me. She is alive to me right now. Mr. Marlow states that all of you are Jeremy Jones. Well, I am not. And you are not. We are not killers."

She picked up the diary. "We are all Felicia. We are all the innocent victims of a ruthless abuser and killer. . . ."

She stopped for a second. "I am Felicia, I am Felicia! Do not let this man get away with my murder!"

Benally banged the gavel. "That's it, Counselor. You're done."

She stood there for a moment. No one was sure whether she was done or not. No one wanted to move.

Jeremy gave a quick glance back at the armies of cameras. All the red light were on, like one big giant sunset. Jeremy lifted both of his hands over his head, as if surrendering. He waited until he heard Stephanie Park Live say, "I've got to get a close-up on his hands."

He heard an audible gasp from those behind him in the gallery. He then slowly lowered both of his hands at the same time and turned them so the knuckles faced right toward Luna. He did not move one other muscle or change his expression.

Luna couldn't help but see the three crosses on Jeremy's right hand. She then glanced at Jeremy's left hand. That's when she noticed that he had two more tattooed crosses already there. She noticed that Jeremy had drawn a little arrow in pen, an arrow point-ing to the empty space for the third cross.

In an instant, it came to her. Jeremy had been responsible for the other killings. He had people on the outside, maybe even Marlow, who did his dirty work for him. This whole thing had been a set-up just to get to this very moment.

"Am I the third cross?" Luna asked him.

As if to answer, Jeremy suddenly leaped across the table and quickly had his hands around her neck. Marlow tried to grab him, but Jeremy kicked him so savagely that he knocked the wind out of him.

Or maybe that's what Jeremy wants me to think. Luna's brain came up with that strange thought.

That was her last thought as she began to lose consciousness. She began to float.

Felicia, I'm coming to join you.

Shatrock must have gone out for a breather. There was no one there to save her.

Gunshot!

Jeremy's hands relaxed around her neck.

"Finish the job," Jeremy said to someone in the audience, but she couldn't tell whom he had said it to. For a moment, she thought it was already too late.

After a few more moments, Marlow lifted Jeremy off of her. She could breathe again. But who had shot Jeremy?

She looked up. Judge Benally held his gun up. He really did have one under his robe all along. "I told you we would finish this trial tonight."

The bailiff rushed over to Jeremy, briefly examined him, then looked up. "He's dead, Your Honor."

Benally looked over at Diana. "Madam District Attorney, I think we have clearly established that I was acting in the defense of another, and that person was facing immediate and grave bodily harm. I believe I used appropriate force under the circumstances."

Diana said nothing for a moment. She looked over at Luna, as if Luna were the boss. Luna nodded.

"Your Honor," Diana said. "I can assure you that you were acting appropriately under the circumstance. I don't think our office intends to file any charges against you."

"Good," he said, banging a gavel. "Court is adjourned. I guess we have already completed the sentencing phase."

Marlow looked at Jeremy's dead body as Smoky dragged it away. He had half expected Jeremy to melt, and that the spell would be over. The wicked witch is dead!

Jeremy was still very solid, and the spell continued unabated. All ten cameras now focused on Jeremy's body. For a brief moment, Marlow swore that Jeremy winked at him, then winked at the ten cameras beaming his passing to the millions across the world. There was no doubt about one thing. Jeremy was smiling.

"Maybe I'm supposed to be the wicked witch now," Marlow said to himself.

SENTENCING PHASE

The next afternoon, Luna cooked with Diana in the kitchen of the Mothership. Luna had taken one of her mother's recipes and had all the ingredients sent down special from Santa Fe. She had broken into her mother's wine cellar. They sipped on something red, from nearby Los Alamos.

"You have to admit that you've never had wine from Los Alamos before," Luna said to a skeptical Diana. "That's pretty atomic, I mean, exotic."

"I just hope it's not radioactive." Diana's fear soon turned to awe as she tasted the soup course with a spoon. "You're getting good. We had something like this at Coyote Café."

"You paid for that meal," Luna said. "Well the taxpayers did. I'm paying for this one."

"I'm paying back all the money," Diana said with a smile. "It was a couple of grand. I'm probably keeping these, however." She pointed towards her breasts.

Diana opened up the window. Instead of a Lexus, there was now a used pick-up truck. "I always wanted to drive a pick-up. It goes with my new life-style."

"What do you mean?"

"I'm now going to be an assistant district attorney and I have to get used to my lower standard of living. I'm going to resign."

"Who will they get to replace you?"

Diana laughed. "I don't see a big line forming to take over the job. It's yours if you want it."

They said nothing more for a while, slurping some of the soup as Luna put something delicious into the oven—something with *chipotle*.

"Well at least we don't have to worry about Jeremy coming after us."

"I don't think it's totally over," Luna said. "Jeremy had help on the outside."

Diana frowned. "You still think its Marlow, don't you?"

Luna said nothing for a moment then said, "I'll get some more wine."

"From someplace without a nuclear waste dump next to the vineyard, okay?"

There was no delay in shoving Jeremy into the ground. He didn't get a church funeral. The Discount Prison had a small graveyard within the fences and Jeremy would rest there until the end of the world. His one satisfaction would have been that Stephanie Park Live filmed from on top of one of the guard towers. The other cameras settled for long shots from out in the parking lot.

Stephanie was perhaps the only happy one there. There were a few inmates, a few guards and Marlow. No one was emotional one way or another.

The warden read a brief speech that was prescribed by law for this occasion. He asked if anyone had anything to say.

Marlow was about to say something and then thought better of it. Somehow, he felt like Jeremy wasn't really gone.

As the inmate gravediggers lowered Jeremy into the sandy earth, he thought to himself, there's one more thing I have to do and this will all be over. He looked down at the two crosses on his hand. No, the spell wasn't broken. Like Manygoats had said, some curses you need to lift yourself.

Luna and Diana had a delicious meal and talked until eleven. They sipped the bottle from Los Alamos, then moved onto the bottle from Argentina, then one from Slovakia, or Slovenia—it was hard to read the label by that time. They only had a few sips from each, but it definitely had an effect. Her mom really did have excellent taste in wine, or excellent taste in friends who had given the bottles to her as gifts.

"To my mother," Luna said.

"To your mother," Diana responded.

"To Felicia," Luna said.

"To Felicia."

Diana wanted to drive, but Luna wouldn't have it. She called Shatrock over to give Diana a lift home. Luna definitely was the grown-up now.

After Shatrock dragged Diana off, it was almost eleven-fifteen and time to go to sleep. Luna felt a little wobbly on her feet. Maybe she wasn't so grown up after all.

She got in her mother's bed. The room spun around her. She was not a drinker, and the alcohol had definitely got to her. She drifted into that same dream again. She always liked the first part when she made love to Marlow.

She thought she heard her window creak open, but that was just part of her dream, right? She heard footprints on her mother's carpet. She slowly came awake, but she was still a little buzzed. No, someone was definitely in the house. Her mother had not believed in guns. Until Judge Benally's actions, neither did she.

More footsteps.

"Marlow?" she called.

She tried to sound tough as she looked at her empty hand. "I know it's you. I've got a gun."

She walked through the house. The window was definitely open, but the house was empty. Someone had probably come in, then gone out. A local kid. She shut the window.

She went back into her room. She noticed that there was a bloodstain on the dresser.

Shit.

She looked around the room. Still nothing. "I know you're in here, Marlow!"

No answer.

Maybe it was someone else. Van Leit knew she didn't want him back as sheriff. "Van Leit?"

Nothing. She waited another forty minutes, and called out a few more times. No sound at all. Even the wind didn't move a muscle. It was just before midnight when she convinced herself that there was nothing in the house. It was just the Crater wind.

Luna looked again at the drop of blood on the dresser, then looked at her hand. She'd been bleeding. She must have cut herself on one of the splinters on the window. The blood must have been hers. She looked around one last time. She was alone now. Safe. She went back to bed. She was very, very tired. Luna drifted back into sleep almost immediately, back into the same dream.

As before, she felt a man's hands around her neck. She felt the life drift out of her. Then she opened her eyes. A man in a ski mask really was strangling her! And there was no one around to shoot him.

Jeremy had tried to strangle her and she hadn't liked the feeling then. She certainly didn't like the feeling now. She broke free of the man's grasp and kicked him hard and, with every ounce of her strength, pushed him off of her.

She punched him in the face. All the swimming in the muck of Crater Lake had given her a pretty good left jab. She then used her one week of martial arts training and gave the guy a good kick in the balls. All those wind sprints made her kick a lethal weapon. The man was definitely down for the count.

She punched him in the head, for good measure. He was definitely out now too. He was still breathing. She saw some facial hairs rise and fall. Beard. Marlow didn't have a beard, did he? Van Leit had only a mustache. She pulled off the hood. It was Smoky. Jeremy's guard.

Why hadn't she seen the obvious? Smoky was Jeremy's best friend, before, when he was on the outside. What had someone once said? Jeremy and Smoky were like a bride and groom, but the groom wore the handcuffs?

She looked at him. She didn't even know if he could speak. She was a prosecutor—time to prosecute.

"You have one chance to live!" she yelled at him. "Tell me what the fuck is going on!"

Nothing.

She lifted her fist. "You have the right to remain silent—"

Smoky wilted. Luna sure didn't hit like a girl. "Jeremy paid me," he said. He had a deep voice with a slight Spanish accent. "Nothing personal. Jeremy already paid me ten grand to do you if he couldn't pull it off."

"Why?"

Smoky shrugged. "I just needed the money. We don't make shit."

Luna figured that, but Smoky's motivation was unimportant. "I meant Jeremy. Why would he try to kill me?"

"He got all crazy after Felicia cheated on him. He felt like a total nobody and he always thought that he was this big deal."

Smoky found it funny somehow. "He wanted to live forever as the Three Crosses Killer *and* the Three Crosses Copycat. It was compelling. That's what he kept saying—he wanted to be compelling, whatever the hell that meant."

Luna didn't lower her fist. She could be compelling too.

"You were the third cross," Smoky said, nervous. "Just like Felicia. We was going to do Diana, but she didn't have no family or nothing . . . and you kinda look like Felicia."

Luna suddenly remembered back in court, when Jeremy stared at her mother, as if he had seen her before. Her mother looked like Sarah Sanchez.

"Did you kill my mother?" Luna cocked the fist again. If all cross-examinations could be this fun.

"No. Someone else. Jeremy had a lot of money from some drug deal and he was passing it out like candy."

"Marlow? Was Marlow in on it?"

Long pause.

"You won't go death penalty?" he asked. From the look in her eyes, he knew that there was no way he could avoid jail time. "Let me go somewhere out of state?"

"I'll put in a word to the DA," she said. She sure as hell wouldn't make any promises. Time to stick the pressure on him. "Or I can put you in with the general population right now. You'll stay there over the weekend. They'd love to get their hands on a guard for a weekend. Well?"

Smoky thought for a second. He was a dead man no matter what, and he knew it. But the prospect of the inmates turning on him without Jeremy to protect him, that was scary shit.

"Nah," he said. "It wasn't Marlow."

Long pause. "Shark is going to get him tonight," he said. "Make it look like he got you. The whole murder/suicide sort of thing. He's doing it right now."

She tied him up and tried to call Shatrock to tell him to get his ass over to Shark's Tattoos. There was no answer. Only in Crater would the one cop on duty turn off his pager. She thought about calling Monica Martin over at 911, but then she realized that Monica could only call Shatrock. The closest cop she could think of was Wootton, but he was a few hours away in Santa Fe. She called Wootton, anyway, told him to send state troopers from the district office one county over.

"Just sit tight," he told her.

"Sure," she said. "I'll sit tight."

Luna looked at her watch. It was twelve midnight now. Shark was always late, right? She knew Marlow's home phone. She dialed it. No answer. He must have already left. She realized that she didn't know his cell phone. She guessed she didn't know him that well after all.

I should probably just let Marlow die, she thought to herself. But she thought about it. Why had Felicia taken Jeremy back after all those years? She had always thought it was battered wife syndrome, but then she read the letters. She knew that for all his evil, Jeremy had genuinely loved Felicia. Loved her more than any other man ever had, or could. That's why she had taken him back.

Luna remembered something that Felicia had written in her diary. "More than anything else in the world, I hope and pray that he can really change."

She had to take that prayer to heart as she looked down at Felicia's silver cross. She took Smoky's gun, then put on some sweats and got into her mother's car. It was too cold out and, since she barely drove the damn thing, she shouldn't have been surprised that it didn't start. The light was still on in the garage. She could see her bike.

She couldn't help but laugh. "I'll always hate cars." Luna was glad to throw open the car door and slam it behind her.

"This is your chance," she said to her bike. "Don't let me down this time."

Luna locked the safety of the gun. She didn't want it go off while she rode now, did she?

Marlow had wondered why Shark could only see him this late as he drove down the dirt road. How could the man be so busy? Shark always set him up for appointments at weird off hours and yet Shark never seemed to have any customers other than Jeremy, and that business had dried up. Shark certainly wasn't going to get rich tattooing crosses on lawyers. The man did have that new Harley—the money must have come from somewhere.

This was just something he had to do. What had Jeremy said, "to get in touch with his feelings?"

This was his way of getting in touch with his feelings.

Jeremy was pure evil, of course, but Jeremy was a human being and now that he was gone, Marlow wanted to honor the little humanity that had been there.

That was what it had all been about. The crosses were there as a reminder. Everyone in the world saw his clients as animals, but he had succeeded—for the most part—by finding the one good thing, the little piece of humanity about them. That's why when he said, "I am Jeremy Jones," he was telling the truth.

Ironically, he felt that once he got the last cross, he could finally start to become Marlow all over again. Whoever the hell that was. Then there was the whole Luna question. She was definitely out of his league now, both as a lawyer and as a woman.

He passed the unearthly glow of the refinery behind the Crosswinds, then hit the dirt turn-off to Shark's. He soon passed Felicia's wooden cross, then pulled his car into Shark's parking lot. He'd always thought it was strange that the cross was so close to

Shark's, but never thought about it too much. He saw the mural and the sea creature inviting him to "Get your mark from the Shark."

His hand tingled with the anticipation of the pain. "This will be the last mark I ever get," he said to his poor hand. "Don't worry."

Luna pedaled in the moonlight. Crater County really did look like the surface of the moon, especially on nights like tonight. She even felt a lower and somehow stronger gravity. She could see a light pull into Shark's driveway. She would be too late. She had just now made it to Felicia's wooden cross. Right as she passed the cross, she felt the Crater wind push her even harder.

"Thank you, Felicia," she said, and pedaled harder with the wind at her back.

Marlow sat in the chair. He saw the little plastic alien with the caption that read, "At Shark's, no one can hear you scream."

He was now more than a little uncomfortable. Shark had gone to the other room, and he was starting to squirm. "Could we hurry this up?" he yelled to Shark.

"Give me a minute."

Shark had a bit of a dilemma. If he used a knife, there was always a chance that Marlow would bleed. A stray bit of blood that he couldn't explain might linger when the cops inevitably came around. The same went for bullets. When he'd shot Ruth, he'd worried about the three drops of blood left on the pillow, but as an artist, he thought it seemed like a nice touch.

Murder was just another work of art. Jeremy had given him a couple of grand all together, which had sat there in the safe since the day Jeremy came to get the three crosses tattoo. That money was more than enough for a down payment on that shiny new Harley. He'd lost his old one the first time he'd been sent away to prison. Damn, that was a nice bike! But this one more than made up for it.

Shark was disappointed that he'd let Smoky do Luna, since she was smaller. Now Luna was a fine piece of ass. If he ever got his hands on her. . . .

Marlow was just a bonus. It hadn't been that hard to set up the killings around the times that Marlow got his tattoos. Jeremy wanted to set everything up perfectly. Jeremy was soft on Marlow, but the agreement was that if it looked like Marlow had failed, Shark had to finish the job. Shark had given his word, and he was a man of his word.

He was also still an artist who appreciated symmetry. Murder-suicide. Luna and Marlow. He would dump Marlow and Luna in the Yazzie wreck. The perfect ending. Now that was art worth twenty-thou.

"Just a second," he called out again to Marlow. "I've got just the thing."

What the hell, he'd go with a knife after all. There was always disinfectant to get the stains out. And who was going to investigate this place, Shatrock?

He headed toward Marlow, the knife under his sleeve.

Shark's door had been held shut with wire, ever since the raid. It was Shark's way of saying that if you're stupid enough to come in here, you'll get what you deserve. Luna hesitated for a second, then undid the wire just as Shark headed for Marlow. "Hold it right there."

The most important words of her life, yet Shark didn't pay attention. Or perhaps he couldn't hear her. Being a prosecutor wouldn't be enough now.

What does she say now? "Ummm . . . District Attorney's Office, you're under arrest."

Shark laughed in her face, it didn't matter whether he heard her or not. "Yeah, little girl, you're really going to shoot me."

He kept heading toward Marlow, but he couldn't help but glance back at Luna and make sure she was too scared too fire.

At that moment, Marlow kicked him hard. The kick distracted him for only a second, but Marlow somehow got the knife out of his hands. It fell on the floor.

Shark outweighed them both put together. He pushed Marlow against the wall and knocked him out cold.

Shark now turned toward Luna. Luna looked behind her. There was someone else who was going to do this, right?

Out of the corner, she quickly read the sign behind the monster. She was alone, all right. She would have to do this. She saw his tattoo of the shark, about to eat the girl.

"Just put down the gun," Shark said. "This won't hurt a bit."

He kept coming closer. She pointed the gun right at him and pulled the trigger.

Nothing. The safety was still on. By the time she could get it off, he had it from her in that iron grip of hers.

At that moment, Marlow became Jeremy. Every ounce of weakness that had once defined Marlow was now buried deep within him. Even his brown eyes changed to Jeremy's wiry blue. He was Jeremy's rage, his passion, even his strength prior to the years of drugs. Marlow had been waiting for this moment his entire life. Marlow launched himself like a human missile at the vast target that was Shark. Direct hit!

Shark was dazed for a second and his knees buckled. Luna kicked him hard, right in the balls. Nothing. Shark was still too damn strong and the tattooed demons on his chest must have acted like some kind of guardian devils.

Marlow punched him a hard right to the gut. That would have knocked out an ordinary man, but Shark was no ordinary man.

Shark still fiddled with the gun. Both Marlow and Luna jumped on top of him. The three of them struggled right there for a few moments. Shark was easily stronger than Luna and Marlow put together, and he quickly gained leverage. He was now about to fire right at Luna's heart.

Luna pushed his gigantic hand with all of her might, tried to push the gun away from her.

Bang!

APPEAL

Diana resigned as DA the next week, and adjusted to her new life as a simple assistant county prosecutor. In her most persuasive argument ever, she managed to convince Stephanie Park Live to give up her dreams of stardom and move in with her at Crater Ranch. Stephanie now ran a legal news website since the Internet had finally made it to Crater. Diana helped her with her legal connections and the two made a great team, personally and professionally. There was some grumbling from some of the more conservative locals, but Diana was the last of the Craters, so she did get some respect. Once Judge Benally was bumped up to the Supreme Court, there was talk of appointing her to a judgeship.

Marlow took a couple of months to get Jeremy totally out of his system. His hair grew out brown and he started wearing his glasses again. No ponytail this time. He liked to think he was almost back to being the funny guy that Luna had met for lunch every Thursday. He took more cases out of town.

Once she took the DA job, Luna quickly slipped into a new routine. The first week she went on a few obligatory shopping sprees, but quickly decided to avoid becoming the old Diana.

She was often called in by the Attorney General's office to become one of the special prosecutors. When there was a lull in crime in Crater, which was quite often, she prosecuted big cases all over the state. But somehow, whenever she made it back and saw that "Welcome Home to Crater" sign, she felt relief. "There's no place like home."

After a few months, enough time had passed and she and

Marlow were back on speaking terms again. She thought about taking it to another level a few times, but she just couldn't. The crosses were just too much for her. He'd started wearing a band-aid again when he sensed her concern, but that still wasn't enough.

Despite the barrier between them, they still went out to eat every Saturday and Sunday. Always at the Crosswinds. They played their little games with every car and truckload that stopped in. Made up stories about all who came in.

One day, those two UCLA students, Remy and Jeannie stopped by the Crossroads on their way back home from school. It wasn't that great of a coincidence—there really wasn't anywhere else for a hundred miles in each direction. They had to stop somewhere.

They recognized Marlow as he sat with Luna. He smiled at them. "I got a better offer."

They shook their heads and quickly got back on the road.

Luna laughed when she heard the story. "So I'm a better offer?" After a couple of months of this, she was finally ready to accept that Jeremy was indeed dead, or at least in remission, and that Marlow was Marlow again.

She then took a big step. She'd slacked off for a few weeks as the demands of her practice increased. The Olympics were coming up again, and it was time to start training again. She needed a training partner to get her motivated. Marlow had kept at his workouts since his Jeremy days. Maybe they could make a trial run, so to speak, at training together.

One Saturday afternoon, they went out for their bike ride together. Their goal for the afternoon was the top of the "advanced course." She looked at him. Time had definitely passed, but then that's what Felicia had said about Jeremy.

They made it to the top, and then looked out over the entire county. It was an amazingly clear day and they could see past the furthest ridges of the valley, off to the mountains beyond for the first time ever. If there had ever been an actual Crater, they could now see over the walls.

She sighed. There's no place like home. She glanced at him again. He sure was cute, and there was no doubt in her mind that he cared about her more than life itself. He gave her his bottle of water. She closed her eyes and leaned forward to kiss him.

They kissed. No one was around, except for the ghosts of the car down below. The ghosts didn't seem to mind. Maybe they could take this further. Both of their electronic pagers rang simultaneously. Hers was a call from the felony division in Albuquerque; his was from the public defender's department.

They scanned the screens. There had been a school shooting over in Albuquerque. A high school kid had taken out three people. They looked at each other for a moment then she started pedaling back toward her house. He tried, but it was impossible for him to keep up.

How the hell did she get in such good shape?

THE END